A Matter

of Marriage

ANN COLLINS

Compass Point Press

This book is a work of fiction. The characters, incidents, and dialogue have come from the author's imagination. Any resemblance to actual events or persons, living or dead, is coincidental.

For permissions and information, email Compass Point Press at *contact@compasspointpress.com* or go to *www.compasspointpress.com*.

ISBN: 978-0-9636558-2-0 (paperback)
ISBN: 978-0-9636558-1-3 (e-book)

Cover design by Ann Collins.
Body of woman photo © Oleksandr Shevchenko - Dreamstime.com
Woman's head © coloroftime - istockphoto
Other photos © Ann Collins
Tall ship *Californian,* Maritime Museum of San Diego

*This book is dedicated to all the people
who have cared for and kept alive historic sites
across the United States, including the Hotel del
Coronado in San Diego, California.*

Acknowledgments

Writing fiction is not an easy or solitary process for me. Alex and Julia's story has been a long time coming, and many people have helped me along the way with my historical research and storytelling. They know who they are, and I am grateful to all of them. Special thanks go to Janet Wellington and Cheryl Howe for their insights.

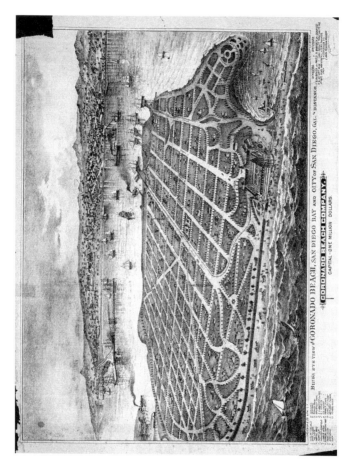

Historic American Buildings Survey Sketch by E. S. Moore, Crocker and Company, Lithographers 1888 LITHOGRAPH OF CORONADO. Repository: Library of Congress Prints and Photographs Division Washington, D.C. 20540 USA http://hdl.loc.gov/loc.pnp/pp.print

Prologue

San Diego, California
November 1897

Julia Fairbanks swallowed hard and buried her hands in the folds of her black mourning skirt. What wasn't Mr. Byrnes telling her?

The lawyer sat across from her, behind his expansive oak desk. As he continued avoiding her gaze, a sheen of perspiration broke out over his balding head. He nudged his spectacles higher on his ruddy nose.

Julia's heart thudded. As her father's only living child and heir, she had expected the reading of his will to be nothing more than a formality, something to endure while she coped with her grief. But this meeting was not going as expected.

"What are you keeping from me, Mr. Byrnes?"

He patted his folded handkerchief against his head. Outside the office window, a wagon clattered by on the San Diego street.

ANN COLLINS

"Nothing, Miss Fairbanks. I suspect you already know your father updated his will last year, after the death of your stepmother."

Julia drew a quivery breath and tried not to think about her stepmother's passing. Harriet had suffered for months, wasting away. After she passed, an emptiness had spread through Julia, almost as vast as the desolation she had felt when she lost her mother years earlier. Now, her father was gone, too.

"No," she managed to say. "I did not know." She also didn't know why her father would have changed his will. Or what the changes would have been.

"Oh, well, not that it matters, I suppose." He shuffled through several loose papers. "Let me just say again how sorry I am for the loss of your father. I know it must have been a shock, his heart suddenly giving out like that."

"Yes, it was," she whispered. He had seemed so robust. One minute he was demanding she leave hotel matters to him, and the next, he had dropped to the lobby floor, never to move again.

Julia blinked at the scalding tears in her eyes. Would her father still be alive if she hadn't been so determined to help him run the hotel?

Mr. Byrnes cleared his throat. "Uh, why don't I just get to it. The final wishes of Lloyd Alwin Fairbanks are as follows." He started reading, outlining what would happen to the four-hundred-room Hotel Grand Victoria—her home.

She tried to listen, but her mind drifted back in time to her happiest memories. As a fifteen-year-old girl, Julia had watched the resort hotel grow from a sandy patch of scrub-covered land on Coronado Island to a fairy-tale castle of red-roofed turrets and towers.

The interior had been her mother's domain. Lillian Fairbanks' tasteful touch was everywhere, from the framed hunting pictures in the Men's Smoking Room to the silk draperies in the Ladies' Billiard Room. Julia always felt pride in the final choices because she had helped make them. She and her mother had spent countless cherished hours together as they looked over sample fabrics and wallpapers.

"We will be sharing our home with the world, sweetheart," her mother had said, "and we want it to look its best." Two years later, having become pregnant against doctor's orders, her mother had died the day after giving birth. She had never stopped trying to give her husband what he wanted most—a son. She had disappointed him again, though, her final effort having produced another girl. Lloyd Fairbanks had shown no interest in his newest child, and little regret when she passed.

As the lawyer droned on, Julia struggled to subdue a sob. Despite having lost her entire family, she told herself she wasn't truly alone. She still had the Hotel Grand Victoria.

"Did you hear me, Miss Fairbanks?"

She glanced up to find Mr. Byrnes finally looking her in the eye. "I'm sorry. What were you saying?"

He pursed his lips and laid the papers on the blotter. "I will speak as plainly as I can. Despite your being his only surviving family, your father placed a condition on your inheritance. In order to obtain legal ownership of the Hotel Grand Victoria, you must marry within

3

the next six months. Five months and twenty-eight days, to be precise."

She stared at him. A highly inappropriate and unexpected laugh bubbled up her throat. She tamped it down. "Excuse me?"

He sniffed. "I believe I was clear. You must wed in order to inherit the hotel."

His serious manner and words penetrated her disbelief. "Mr. Byrnes, there is obviously a mistake. I have no wish to marry. My father knew that." As a girl, she had dreamed of marriage, dreamed of being loved and having a family, but after witnessing the heart-wrenching, harsh realities of childbearing, losing her mother first and then her baby sister, Julia had grown up. She had also realized how much power the husband wielded in the marriage relationship. She preferred to hold the reins of her own life.

"Yes, he did know," Mr. Byrnes said. "Hence, the stipulation. Due to his wives' failure to provide him with a male heir, he has bequeathed that duty to you. There is no mistake."

"But—" She jumped up from the cowhide chair. "No! This is wrong. How could he do this?" And yet, Julia knew it was just like him. Even dead, Lloyd Fairbanks was brandishing his power like a king lording it over his subjects. He intended to use her, just as he had used her mother and stepmother in his quest for a male heir who would one day rule the Hotel Grand Victoria in his place.

Mr. Byrnes tucked his head into his shoulders, having the grace to look abashed. He said nothing though.

"What happens if I don't comply with the stipulation?"

"The hotel will be sold at auction. The proceeds will pay off the mortgage, and the remaining money will be placed in a trust fund for any male offspring you may eventually produce."

She whirled away from the desk. A hollowness opened inside her, painful enough that Julia gasped for air. To Lloyd Fairbanks, she was a means to an end. Nothing more. As hard as she had tried to earn her father's approval, she had never been good enough for him. He hadn't wanted a daughter, even one who had learned everything she could about running a world-class hotel. What a fool she'd been! As big a fool as her mother had been to keep trying to give him a son.

"Miss Fairbanks, please calm yourself and sit down."

"I don't want to sit." She could not let her father's final maneuver pin her in place. Why had she never let herself see the truth that had always been in front of her?

She sighed, knowing the answer. He was her father, and she loved him no matter what.

"I know this is difficult for you," Mr. Byrnes said. "To be honest, I don't approve of your father's methods, but he was my client and I had to do as he wished. If you don't marry within the specified period, you will be left penniless and homeless."

And the Hotel Grand Victoria would be left to the whims of a new owner, someone who cared more for profits than the constant care the enormous wooden structure needed. And what about the employees?

ANN COLLINS

Many of them had shown her father nothing but
loyalty since the hotel's opening nine years ago. A
new owner might dismiss them, bringing in different
staff. Julia had to stop this, but how?

She paced in front of the window, ignoring the
buggies and people passing outside. No one cared
more for the Hotel Grand Victoria than she, but her
father had dismissed her feelings until now, when they
suited his purposes. She imagined him laughing,
utterly pleased with himself for having the last word,
manipulating her from his grave in order to get a
grandson. Her shoulders sagged with her disappointment in her father. He knew she could never bear to
leave the hotel. He also knew that her greatest fear was
to lose a child.

Julia felt herself caught up in a breaking wave, the
ocean's power tumbling her in the foam and depriving
her of air. She desperately needed to find the sandy
bottom and spring to the surface, saving herself. "I'll
contest the will."

Mr. Byrnes sighed as she kept pacing. "I am sorry.
At your father's explicit request, I made sure there
were no loopholes. Any attempt to circumvent his will
would only be a waste of precious time. Miss
Fairbanks, you need to begin your search for a
husband immediately."

A husband she didn't love and who didn't love her.
A man who would have charge of her and the Hotel
Grand Victoria. He would have the right to
consummate their marriage.

Julia shuddered. Marriage meant pregnancy and all
its inherent risks. Coming to a stop, she stared at her

6

reflection in the window. Under the brim of her black hat, a lock of her ash-blond hair had come loose. She let it be, looking beyond herself to the scene outside. A young woman pushing a baby carriage strolled by. Tiny feet peeked out, batting aside a blanket. The woman smiled and stopped. Leaning down, she tucked the blanket back into place.

Julia felt her stomach twist as her buried dream of having a child of her own rose from deep inside her, but then she remembered the pain of losing Lily, her baby sister. Her fears crowded back in, along with thoughts of her father's scheme.

As the woman and baby continued along the street, an idea struck Julia, a possible way out of her predicament.

She pushed the stray lock of hair behind her ear and stepped back from the window. "Mr. Byrnes, did my father's will say anything about the marriage being consummated?"

"Not specifically, just that you must marry within the next six months."

"So nothing about me producing an heir?"

"Well, no."

Her father had not been as smart as he thought. He assumed that once she married, the children would come. But what if she married a man who conveniently abandoned her after the ceremony? She would have satisfied the will's stipulation, and the Hotel Grand Victoria would be hers. No one could ever take it from her, and she would never have to worry about losing a child because she would never have one.

Mr. Byrnes picked up his fountain pen. "Miss Fairbanks, I know this is a lot to take in, but there are several other matters that need our attention. First and foremost, a manager must be hired to take your father's place."

"That won't be necessary, Mr. Byrnes. I will be taking over as manager."

His jaw dropped. "But women don't operate businesses the size of the Hotel Grand Victoria."

She fought an urge to roll her eyes. Mr. Byrnes was no different than every other man who believed women incapable of doing more than keeping house. Well, her house just happened to be a lot larger than the average home. "Then I shall be the first. I love the Hotel Grand Victoria, and I will care for it with everything that is in me."

Mr. Byrnes removed his spectacles and rubbed his fingers against his temples. "This is not what your father had in mind when he made you his beneficiary."

"I am sure it wasn't. Is there any stipulation prohibiting me from being manager?"

"No. There is, however, a matter of marriage to settle."

"Rest assured, Mr. Byrnes, before the seventh of next May, my name will no longer be Fairbanks." She ignored the dissenting voice in her heart that urged her to think hard about what she would be giving up. If she followed through on her plan, she would never be able to marry for love.

Chapter One

Coronado Island, San Diego County
May 5, 1898

As the sun descended in the western sky, it dappled San Diego's harbor with a bright glow. Alex MacLean picked up his battered leather traveling bag and hurried away from the ferry terminal.

He was glad to leave behind the awkward stares of his fellow passengers. He hated feeling like an object on display. Even after three and a half years, he still hadn't gotten used to the looks he received—some of pity, some of revulsion, and some of curiosity.

He probably never would.

Alex headed for the Hotel Grand Victoria, his destination. Inside the pocket of his faded blue work shirt was the job advertisement he had torn from a Los Angeles newspaper.

Down to his last few dollars, he needed this job, but he hadn't come all this way just for the work. Alex wanted to see the hotel. The sepia picture postcard he'd come across up north had whet his interest. Besides, there had been nothing and no one to keep him in Los Angeles.

He wished there had been someone. Anyone.

Fifteen minutes later, Alex turned into a wide carriage drive and whistled softly. Cone-shaped towers covered with red shingles topped a white gingerbread-style castle adorned with balconies, verandas, and decorative railings.

He could almost imagine himself entering a storybook instead of a hotel. The architecture was exquisite, Queen Anne style at its best. Though such whimsical detail had never matched his aesthetic, he admired the workmanship and felt the strangest sense of belonging, as if he was supposed to be here. He shook off the odd feeling and wondered who had designed the structure. Undoubtedly he would have recognized the name.

Shoes crunching against a drive laid with broken shells, Alex continued his appreciative perusal. He wandered past a manicured lawn, meticulously pruned shrubbery, bright-colored flowers, fancy metal hitching posts, and a gurgling, splashing fountain.

Near the hotel's front entrance, he stopped to admire the façade and its myriad paned windows, some of them of stained glass. On a balcony above the entrance, someone shifted terracotta flowerpots inside a box that brimmed with red geraniums. To the far right, behind one of the windows, a little boy pressed his palms against the glass, looked out, and grinned.

Alex froze, his gaze fixed on the boy. Memories surged forward, pummeling him with the image of his four-year-old son the last time Alex had seen him.

Danny had also been standing at a window, but he had not been smiling like this boy. Between smoke-filled breaths and deep coughs, his only child had been crying out for help. "Daddy! Daddy!" His little hands beat at the unyielding glass on the third floor of their home.

"Sir?" a female voice called out. "Are you all right?"

The voice broke into Alex's agonizing reverie and released him. Sick at heart, his stomach in knots, he still stared at the window. It was empty now, the boy gone. He had disappeared as Danny had, though not forever, not like Danny.

"Sir?"

Alex gave his head a shake and forced all thoughts of his son back into the dark cave inside his soul.

Shading his eyes, he could make out three women standing on the hotel's front veranda. One started toward him down the short staircase. When she emerged from beneath the portico into the waning sunlight, he felt as if the earth's rotation had come to a halt and knocked him off balance.

She was Aphrodite's twin. A loosely pinned knot of ash-blond hair crowned a flawless face set with eyes as blue and brilliant as the California sky. Alex tried to study her dispassionately, like a sculptor examining a statue, but this was no statue and he was no sculptor.

Running a hand over the back of his head and dark, untrimmed hair, purposely keeping the undamaged side of his face to her, he found enough air to whistle under his breath. She was even more beautiful than his deceased wife, who had been a beauty in her own right. And yet, this woman showed concern for him, acting nothing like Elizabeth, who had expected the world to bow at her feet.

Alex's heart gave an odd lurch as the woman closed on him, moving with a natural grace. He imagined long, lean legs beneath the light gray skirt that swayed with each of her steps. A matching, lace-trimmed jacket accentuated the smooth curve of her neck and angled in to a slender waist. Lord Almighty, he hadn't bargained on ever feeling this way again.

"Is something wrong?" she asked him from ten feet away. At first, he welcomed her approach, but then he feared her inevitable reaction to his face. She kept coming. "You looked rather lost."

"I'm fine," he managed to say, "but thanks." With a resigned sigh, he decided he might as well scare her off now and be done with it. When she stopped a few steps away, he slowly turned and faced her straight on, revealing the ridged scar that vertically sliced his right cheek in half.

Her eyelids fluttered briefly, but to his surprise, she did not flinch or gasp or exhibit any sign of an imminent fainting spell.

The sense of belonging Alex had felt upon seeing the hotel suddenly returned. He tried to dismiss the ludicrous feeling. Since losing everything, he belonged nowhere. And that wasn't likely to change.

When the young woman held his gaze instead of looking away, his admiration for her grew. He would have liked to study her longer, but a blur of airborne movement distracted him. He glanced up to see a geranium-filled flowerpot flying straight at the woman's head.

Alex dropped his bag and hurled himself at her.

Her eyes opened wide, but she was clearly too shocked to avoid him or scream.

He grabbed her and held tight as they hit the ground, rolling together over the drive's broken shells. With his body and his arms, he protected her from the sharp edges as best he could, gritting his teeth at the piercing jabs. He rolled her away, pressing her face to the hollow between his chin and shoulder as the flowerpot crashed to the ground. Petals, pottery shards, stems, and dirt pelted the drive. Their motion came to an abrupt halt when his back slammed into a hitching post. His breath burst from his lungs.

He let the woman go, lay back, and struggled for air.

She scooted away from him on her backside. Fear, shock, and confusion lit her blue eyes. Her creamy face flushed pink. She looked beautiful. And unhurt.

"What … on earth … did you think you were doing?" she demanded. Her voice shook.

Trying to gulp down air, he waved his hand toward the shattered pot. Someone with a strong and accurate throwing arm had aimed that pot directly at her.

The woman's gaze darted between him and the debris of broken terracotta and geranium remnants spread over the area where she had been standing. Her face paled. "Oh. Oh, my." She swallowed visibly. "You … protected me."

He nodded. As a trickle of air entered his lungs, she peered at him with a look of honest amazement on her

13

face, as if no one had ever watched out for her before. How could such a woman not have a father or brother or husband to protect her? He must be wrong.

"Thank you," she said. "I'm indebted to you."

He shook his head. While trying to draw more air, he surveyed where the flowerpot had come from. No one stood on the balcony. A vacant spot showed where the geranium had once sat with the other pots in the flower box.

"You're hurt!" She scrambled back to him on her hands and knees. "I'll get the doctor. He'll know what to do."

As she started to get up, Alex grasped her wrist and grunted what he hoped sounded like "No." Someone had tried to hurt her, and he didn't want her running off by herself.

"Sir, you need help. I can see you're in pain. Going for the doctor is the least I can do after ..." She glanced up at the balcony. A tremor moved through her body, strong enough that Alex felt it under his fingers. She looked next at the debris scattered nearby. "And I must tell someone to check that the remaining flowerpots are secured."

He didn't release her, and he didn't have enough air to explain that the pot did not just fall off the balcony, as she apparently presumed. Finally, the muscles in his torso started to relax. He inhaled a breath sweetened with the scent of orange blossoms—her scent. She smelled so good he made the mistake of breathing more deeply. His ribs shrieked a protest.

Alex locked his teeth and stifled a groan of pain and frustration. He could not afford to be injured, not when he needed a job and place to stay. But who would hire a carpenter who couldn't saw lumber or swing a hammer?

She unsuccessfully tried to tug her wrist free of his grasp. Color returned to her face. "Sir, I am grateful for what you did for me, but I must insist you release me immediately."

He inhaled more carefully. "Do you promise ... not to run off?"

"If my staying here will put you at ease, then I can certainly send someone else for the doctor."

"I don't need a doctor." He let her go, eased himself into a sitting position, and breathed as normally as he could considering his aching ribs and the woman's nearness. His body well remembered the feel of her pressed against him only moments before. Her very proximity was enough to raise his heart rate. He'd forgotten how that felt.

"Of course you need a doctor," she said. "You must be looked after."

Her genuine concern for his well-being took him aback. It had been a long time since anyone cared about Alexander MacLean. His late wife had given a good impression of caring when they'd been courting, but it changed soon after their wedding. He had discovered that beneath her beauty and sophistication lay a powerful streak of self-indulgence. What Elizabeth wanted, Elizabeth got.

"Let me help you," the woman said as he tried to stand up.

"There's no need." Alex wanted to show her he would be fine on his own, but getting up proved more difficult than he expected.

She crouched, shoved aside several locks of hair that had escaped during their tumble, and positioned herself under his right arm. On his left side appeared a spry old man wearing wire-rimmed spectacles and a bellboy's navy blue uniform. Gold braid decorated each shoulder and cuff. He grasped Alex's left arm and, with the woman's assistance, gently hauled him to his feet.

"Thanks," he grunted, wishing he hadn't needed their help.

"Theo," she said, "I'm going to take this gentleman to the doctor's office. Will you see that the geranium pot is cleaned up and the others are not in danger of falling?"

At her uncommon air of authority, Alex tilted his head. Who was she to give orders to a bellboy?

"Yes, Miss Fairbanks," Theo answered, "but are you sure you don't need a hand with him?"

Now steady on his feet, and having noted her name, Alex stepped out of their hold. "I'm fine now. It's you, Miss Fairbanks, that I'm worried about."

"Me?" she said. "I appreciate your concern, but our roll across the drive did not harm me. I'm just a little dusty." She batted at her clothing, raising a cloud of dust. Someone laughed from the veranda, and she looked up. "Oh dear, we've attracted a crowd."

Alex followed her gaze and cringed.

Guests stood at the veranda railing like patrons in an opera-house box. The women wore dresses of silk and satin, their hair done up in what Alex assumed were the latest styles. He hadn't kept track. The men sported fedoras or derbies, high collars, and tailored frock suits, a far cry from his patched brown pants and old work shirt. It was unlikely he knew any of them, or, if he did, that they would recognize him now. Few people had seen him after Danny's and Elizabeth's deaths.

"Miss Fairbanks, we need to talk. Let's go inside." He hated all this attention, and she needed to know the flowerpot had been intentionally thrown at her.

She turned to the bellboy. "Theo, please take— I'm sorry, what is your name, sir?"

"MacLean. Alex MacLean."

"Please take Mr. MacLean's traveling bag inside the lobby. He and I will be meeting with Dr. Dolan." She cast Alex a look that dared him to challenge her.

He scowled, first at her, then at the bag that had somehow ended up beside the older man. "I can carry my own bag. And if I decide to see your physician, I'll find him myself."

"Mr. MacLean," the bellboy said, adjusting spectacles crowned by wiry white eyebrows, "please allow an old man to offer you a bit of advice. Just do as she says. It'll be easier in the long run. Miss Fairbanks is the owner and manager of the Hotel Grand Victoria, and she has your best interests at heart."

Alex nearly moaned aloud. Great. Just great. He rubbed his fingertips over the stubble on his jaw. She was the one who would decide whether to hire him or not.

"Theo is a wise man, Mr. MacLean. He knows I won't be able to rest until I'm sure you have not been seriously injured. The Hotel Grand Victoria has a resident physician and is well-known for the service it offers to its guests."

He knew all about the solicitous courtesies of a first-class hotel, but that had been another life. "I am not a guest," he said as the bellboy disappeared inside with his bag.

"You're quibbling, Mr. MacLean. Once you've registered, you will be. Now, please, come with me."

Alex gave in. Irritating his future employer would be foolish. And Miss Fairbanks would find out soon enough why he was here. Once they were inside, he would splinter the illusion she held of being safe on the grounds of her hotel. "You're the boss. Which way?"

"Follow me." She started toward a pathway along the exterior of a huge round room lined with tall, double-hung windows. "The doctor's home and office are in a cottage on the other side of the Grand Ballroom."

Alex tried to keep an eye out for another assault. However, his attention kept veering to Miss Fairbanks and the innate elegance of her body's movements. He admired the bold purpose in her walk. She belonged here and she knew it. He envied her that. He belonged nowhere, and his life had no purpose. Surviving day-to-day wasn't nearly enough for him, and it hadn't been for a good while now.

Four months ago in Oregon, he thought he'd found his sense of purpose again. Emma Turner had treated him like a man instead of a monster. She hadn't stirred him the way Miss Fairbanks was doing, but Emma had eased his loneliness with conversation and shared with him her dream of having a family. Alex had realized then that, without family, without a wife and children to love and provide for, he was nothing but a piece of flotsam drifting aimlessly on the current. Wanting to remarry and settle down again, he had asked Emma to be his wife.

Horrified by his proposal, she had unloaded her true feelings for him. What did she want with a poor, appallingly scarred carpenter who kept his past to himself? She'd only engaged him in conversation out of pity, and in hopes of attracting the new preacher's interest.

Alex had immediately taken to the road again, continuing his empty existence until today, when a woman unlike any other needed his protection. Needed him. For a moment, his life had purpose again, and it felt good.

If only that feeling could last.

* * *

Julia stifled a residual shiver from her narrow escape and glanced back at the tall, broad-shouldered man who had risked his own safety for hers. If Alex MacLean hadn't thrown himself at her, conveying her away from that flowerpot … well, she would no longer have to worry about the looming deadline her father had set for her.

Finding the right man had taken some doing and three false starts that wasted four of the precious six months specified in her father's will. Those men had seemed like good prospects, but once each of them set eyes on her and found out who she was, they became like salivating dogs. They had wanted more than she was willing to offer, much more. She had settled on her fourth choice, Phillip Williamson, an old friend who would not take advantage of her. He was due to arrive today after a long journey from Pennsylvania. She expected him at any moment, had been waiting for him on the veranda when Mr. MacLean arrived.

Tomorrow, she and Phillip would speak their vows, meeting the deadline with one day to spare. She prayed nothing would go wrong. For the last few weeks, every time she crossed another day off her calendar, Julia wished she had traveled to Phillip, but she hadn't wanted to leave the hotel in someone else's hands. Ignoring her roiling stomach, she told herself Phillip would be here as planned, then leave, also as planned. Her life would be just as she wanted it, except that she would never again feel what she had felt a few minutes ago in Alex MacLean's powerful embrace.

Initially, when Mr. MacLean had grabbed her, crushing her to him, she had been overcome by her shock at his conduct. Now that she'd had time to think about his actions, though, Julia realized she had felt a gentleness in the way he held her. He had not hurt her, nor let her be hurt. Mr. MacLean had taken the brunt of their fall, carrying her weight as if it were nothing.

She marveled at his strength, agility, and reflexes. He had selflessly protected her, leaving her with a lasting warmth that was unfamiliar and all too enticing. She felt it still as she remembered him pressing her face to his soft shirt and hard chest. The scent of wood shavings and fresh-cut lumber had filled her senses, taking her back to the hotel's creation and construction, momentarily soothing her.

She aimed another look at him, wondering about him and where he was from.

He gave his shirt a shake and brushed at the carriage-drive dust on each sleeve. "Is there something wrong with what I'm wearing, Miss Fairbanks?"

"No!" She abruptly faced front, her cheeks heating. "Of course not. I'm sorry. I didn't mean to stare."

"Everyone stares," he said, his voice deepening with what sounded like despair and resignation. "It's human nature."

Julia wanted to disappear into the shrubs bordering the path. She had spoken without thinking and put a foot in it. Of course he would think of his scar. No wonder he had wanted to go inside when he saw the guests watching them from the veranda. The poor man. His poor face.

Seeing his scar had taken her by surprise, but she had controlled her reaction, as well as her sympathy for him. He did not strike her as a man who wanted anyone's pity. But now he had been physically hurt on her account.

He deserved better from her.

She slowed her steps, letting Mr. MacLean come up beside her. "Is your back paining you?"

"I'll live."

"I'm glad." She slanted a look at the handsome side of his face. He did not meet her gaze. A days' growth of beard darkened an appealingly strong jaw framed by sun-lightened brown hair. Longer than customary, his hair fell across a high forehead, which she had always believed marked a man of character. His eyes were a rich brown with golden flecks.

Having spent her life in two hotels, she had seen many good-looking men, but this man was different. To her, what set Mr. MacLean apart was the way he had been admiring her hotel when she first noticed him from the veranda, as if the Hotel Grand Victoria were more than just a building to sleep in and eat in. His appreciation had made her smile, but then his demeanor had changed. He had stared up at the building for so long she'd grown worried. Now, Julia could not forget how alone he had appeared. On reflection, he had seemed almost devastated by something only he was seeing.

"A penny for your thoughts," Mr. MacLean said, his eyes very much on her.

Caught looking at him and thinking about him again, Julia felt her face heat for the second time in a matter of moments. "I ... was just thinking about your arrival," she said, wanting to be truthful without giving away all of her thoughts. "You seemed to like the look of the Hotel Grand Victoria."

"I do like it." He continued watching her, as if he were speaking about more than the hotel.

She felt impossibly warmer and suppressed an urge to fan her cheeks. Memories of his arms wrapped tightly around her, and her face pressed to his chest, filled her mind and made her long for what she would never have—a marriage based on mutual attraction and love.

Julia gave her head a shake. This had to stop. In less than twenty-four hours, she would be a married woman who needed to uphold her spotless reputation. With a ring on her finger, she would become the legal owner and caretaker of the Hotel Grand Victoria. That was what she wanted, and she mustn't let anything—or anyone—distract her from the course she had set.

As they approached the two-story, beachside cottage, Julia wracked her brain for something to fill the potent silence. "Dr. Dolan has lived here with his wife and daughter for five years. Having a physician on the premises is a great comfort to the hotel's guests, many of whom come to Coronado for their health. The ocean air is very beneficial."

"I can imagine." Though he didn't smile, his eyes seemed to shine with what she suspected was amusement at her expense, as if he knew how he was affecting her.

Julia ground her teeth. Her reaction to him was really beginning to annoy her. She considered leaving Mr. MacLean on the doctor's doorstep and returning to her duties. But how could she? He had likely saved her life. In addition, he was a guest, and she always treated her guests with the utmost respect and hospitality. Besides, if she didn't take him to the doctor herself, he might not go at all, and she could not bear it if he neglected an injury incurred on her behalf.

Stepping up to the door, she knocked harder and louder than necessary.

Mary Dolan opened the door. "Julia!" The older woman smiled. Dabs of flour speckled her round face and red apron. She smelled of cinnamon and nutmeg. When she looked at Alex, her smile faltered at the sight of his scar, but then her smile widened into one of delight and welcome. She grasped his hand and pumped it vigorously, oblivious to the pain thinning his lips. "Mr. Williamson, it's wonderful to finally meet you. We've been so looking forward to meeting Julia's young man."

His eyebrows rose, and he glanced over at her.

Julia cringed. She opened her mouth to correct Mary's mistaken notion, but her friend barely paused for breath as she released Mr. MacLean.

"My dear girl, you have chosen yourself a … a strapping fellow. A little dusty around the edges, perhaps"—her gaze avoided his face and traveled over the dirt and bits of shell that still clung to his clothing—"but very strapping. Kate will be jealous. Just this morning she was asking after you. We both want to know every last detail about your wedding arrangements."

She winced at her friend's eagerness to be involved in a wedding that was nothing more than a business arrangement—not that the Dolans were aware of that fact. Ashamed of what her father's will was forcing her to do, and half afraid the Dolans would try to talk her out of her plan, she had not confided the truth to them. They knew nothing about the rapidly approaching deadline imposed on her, only that she was marrying a man she had known as a girl back in Philadelphia and that his business affairs there precluded his arriving any earlier. Keeping her secret from the Dolans had placed a heavy weight on her heart, but it couldn't be helped, not if she wanted to secure the hotel's future.

"Mrs. Dolan," Alex said, rubbing his now-floured

hands on his pants, "as much as I enjoy receiving compliments from attractive women such as yourself, you have me confused with someone else. My name isn't Williamson. It's MacLean, and I've only just met Miss Fairbanks."

Mary blushed as colorfully as her apron. "Oh, dear me. I just assumed. You see—"

"Mary," she broke in, "Mr. MacLean is a guest. Phillip has not arrived yet, though I expect him very soon. I brought Mr. MacLean here because he is in need of the doctor's services."

"Oh, my goodness. Please come in. I do go on sometimes." She rubbed her hands self-consciously on her apron and stepped back. "I hope it's nothing serious."

"Only a few bruises," he said, motioning Julia to precede him into the cottage. "They'll keep." As Mary closed the door, he added, "Miss Fairbanks, my congratulations on your upcoming nuptials. When is the happy event to take place?"

Happy event? Ha!

"Tomorrow evening," Mary answered for her, eyes sparkling. "A privileged few of the hotel staff have been taken into Julia's confidence, and they are as eager as I to set eyes on her beau. If I had my way, she would invite everyone to the ceremony and arrange a huge reception in the Grand Ballroom, but she insists on a small and quiet affair."

"Mary, Phillip and I agreed to keep the occasion private." For more reasons than Mary Dolan could ever guess.

Mary pushed out her bottom lip. "But it just doesn't

seem right. You're the owner of the Hotel Grand Victoria now. When your father married your stepmother—God rest her soul—he put on the biggest party Coronado had ever seen."

"Yes, he did." Julia wished she could forget. Just thinking about it made her blood boil. He had married less than a year after her mother's death. The party cost a small fortune and celebrated nothing but his latest attempt to father a son—his latest failed attempt. Harriet Lincoln Fairbanks had tried her best, but she conceived only once and miscarried halfway through her pregnancy. Her devastation had brought back Julia's memories of her mother pining for the babies she lost, as well as Julia's own devastation when she found her two-month-old sister cold and lifeless in her cradle.

"Mary," she said, slamming the door on her painful memories, "as you well know, I am nothing like my father. I do not wish to marry with any fanfare." A civil ceremony in San Diego would have suited her and this sham of a marriage, but she had to make some concessions to her position.

She slid a glance at Alex, who stood patiently beside her, watching and listening with more interest than she expected—or wanted—from a perfect stranger. His brows were drawn together, as if something puzzled him. Julia wished she knew what he was thinking, then decided she'd rather not, because she probably wouldn't like it.

Mary clucked her tongue and sighed. "Very well. Whatever the bride wants, she shall have. It's no wonder you're looking tired. Losing sleep is to be expected. Wedding day jitters are perfectly normal you know. All will be well after tomorrow. Just tell me what time Kate and I should come over to help you dress."

"Oh, uh, honestly, that won't be necessary." If she let Mary and her eighteen-year-old daughter help, they would flit around her apartment, eagerly discussing love and children. The Dolans wanted the Friday evening ceremony to be beautiful and romantic and perfect, her once-upon-a-time dream wedding. "I bought a ready-made dress at Marston's over in San Diego, and it's a very simple design. There are some buttons in the back, but I should be able to manage on my own."

Mary's face fell, and the twinkle in her eyes dulled. "Oh, I see." She fluttered a hand in front of her. "There I go again, keeping Mr. MacLean from the doctor. Please, this way."

As Mary ushered them along the hallway, past the empty white bench occasionally filled with waiting patients, tears clawed at Julia's eyes. She hated hurting her friend, hated everything her father's final decree was making her do. She had not been sleeping well. If only her wedding had come and gone, she could get on with her life.

Mary knocked at the office door, then pushed it open. The smell of soap drifted into the hallway. "Harold dear, you have a patient. A Mr. MacLean. Julia has brought him."

"Come in, come in," Dr. Dolan said, his white shirtsleeves rolled above thick forearms. Stepping away from his cluttered roll-top desk, he waved them inside.

They entered the combination office and examining area. Mr. MacLean followed so closely behind her that a tingling sensation climbed Julia's spine, taking her mind off her trials. His male strength seemed to tower over her, encompass and warm her. It also set her nerves on edge and confused her. She quickened her steps, opening the distance between them to where she could breathe more easily. She tried to dismiss his curious effect on her.

The doctor greeted them and ambled over to Mary. They were a matched pair, like bookends or salt-and-pepper shakers. He brushed his thumb over a spot of flour on her cheek. "My dear, I can see that I am going to be eating something delicious later today."

The twinkle returned to her eyes. "Oh! My pie crust! I must get back to it before it dries out." She gave her husband a loving smile. "And, yes, it will be delicious."

Julia turned away from them and the fond and familiar touches they shared every day, the type of loving touches she envied and would never know. She stared out the paned window overlooking the beach and ocean. Gulls wheeled and screeched above the surf, carefree, as the sun dropped toward the horizon. Pressing her fingertips against the cool pane of glass, she touched the tangibility of the Hotel Grand Victoria and accepted her choice. Keeping her face to the window, she quickly brushed away an unbidden, traitorous tear sliding down her cheek.

When the door clicked shut, Julia turned to find Mary gone and Dr. Dolan shaking hands with Mr.

MacLean.

"That's a nasty scar you've got there," he said, reaching toward it, index finger extended.

Mr. MacLean reared back, shying like a thoroughbred and grimacing at his own sudden movement. He pressed a hand to his ribs.

"I'm not going to hurt you, young man. My interest is purely clinical." The doctor didn't touch him, but he leaned in close, squinting his eyes. "Looks to me like you didn't get medical attention as soon as you should have. What happened?"

Mr. MacLean moved his head this way and that, clearly uncomfortable at having someone peering at him so closely. "You have a good eye, Doc."

"And you were lucky not to have lost an eye." Dr. Dolan straightened and waited for him to tell his story.

Julia waited as well, though she was torn between a desire to know what had happened to him and a need to protect him from talking about an incident that obviously distressed him. She did not want to cause him more pain than he was already feeling.

He said nothing.

Dr. Dolan pursed his lips, waited a moment longer, then said, "Perhaps it's a story for another day. Mr. MacLean, what has brought you to my office late this afternoon?"

Julia let out a quiet sigh of relief.

"I fell against one of the hitching posts." He pointed to a lower section of his back. "I expect I've got a couple of bruised ribs."

"He did not fall," she said. "Mr. MacLean is being modest. He struck a hitching post in the act of protecting me from a flowerpot that accidentally fell off one of the balconies above the hotel's entrance."

Her protector turned a very direct gaze on her. "There was nothing accidental about that geranium pot. Someone threw it at you when you walked out from under the portico."

If he didn't look so serious, she might have laughed at such a notion. "Mr. MacLean, I don't mean to seem discourteous or ungrateful, but do you normally wear spectacles?"

His shoulders seemed to grow bigger. "My vision is perfect."

"If there is any doubt," Dr. Dolan said, "I have an eye chart Mr. MacLean can look at."

He scowled down at him.

"Or not." The doctor stepped to the far side of his examining table.

Mr. MacLean slanted his scowl at her next. "Who wants to hurt you, Miss Fairbanks?"

"No one!"

"Someone does. Someone with a strong arm and deadly aim."

She swallowed hard. He couldn't be right, could he? "I ... will admit that some of the hotel staff resisted my taking charge after my father's death, but that was six months ago. Now they're accustomed to having me as their manager." Well, some of them were. Even after all this time, there were still a few holdouts. "I cannot believe anyone would want to physically hurt me. A child playing on the balcony could have knocked the pot over."

"That flowerpot had an angled trajectory. A little

earlier, I saw someone moving around on that balcony, but I couldn't see who. The geraniums were too thick."

Dr. Dolan pulled at one of his graying eyebrows. "Julia, maybe you ought to listen to the man."

"No, I cannot believe it," she said, unwilling to accept that someone could hate her enough to try to injure her. Searching for a reason not to trust Mr. MacLean's statement, she remembered her concern for him when he'd seemed lost in the sight of something only he could see. "Perhaps you were confused. Forgive me for saying this, but, moments before, you had been staring up at the hotel like a fortune teller in a trance."

Air hissed through Alex's teeth. "I was not in a trance. I was ..." A haunted look came over his face, a look of soul-shattering sadness. He turned toward the window.

Julia's heart beat harder. She recognized that deep well of sadness. She had seen that same look in her bedroom mirror when she lost her mother and then Lily. Had Mr. MacLean also lost someone close to him?

She took a step toward him. "I'm sorry, Mr. MacLean. I did not intend to cause you pain. That's the last thing I would have wanted."

"I'm fine. Forget about it."

"Is there anything I can do to help you?"

"No." He turned back but avoided her gaze. "No one can. Worry about yourself, Miss Fairbanks. I'm not confused about what I saw or how far away the flowerpot landed from that balcony. You're the one in danger."

She frowned. He truly believed her life was at risk. If he was right, then she had been living in a fantasy world, naively believing everything was going well, that her guests and employees cared about her as much as she cared about them.

Julia chewed on her thumbnail, hoping he was wrong. She had enough to worry about without adding "beware of assassins" to her list. Not watching out for herself would be foolish, though. She would take care. In addition, she would make certain Mr. MacLean was all right. She owed him, and she would do whatever she could to help him, whether he wanted her help or not.

Chapter Two

Dr. Dolan patted the cushioned examining table. "Have a seat, Mr. MacLean, and I'll take a look at you."

Julia arranged her skirts and settled herself on a nearby chair to wait upon the doctor's verdict.

"Julia," Dr. Dolan said, propping his fists on his hips, "last week your presence was appropriate when you brought in that six-year-old boy with the scraped elbow, but I imagine Mr. MacLean would appreciate some privacy."

"Oh!" Glancing over at the man hitching himself onto the table, she started to get up. "Of course. I'm sorry."

"She can stay if she wants." To her surprise, he began unfastening his shirt. Evidently Mr. MacLean's discomfiture with his face did not extend to the rest of his body. He did not look at her.

"As you wish," the doctor muttered when she dropped back onto her chair.

Alex's fingers deftly moved from one button to the

next, and the impropriety of her being there flew out of her head. She couldn't seem to look away from him. With her attention riveted on his body, she forgot about his scar. The widening V of his exposed flesh and chest hair fascinated her, making her heart race even faster than the first time Edison's electric lighting system was switched on in the hotel. She didn't understand how the incandescent lights worked, but their illumination had taken her breath away, just as Alex MacLean was doing to her now.

Julia decided she should leave the office after all. Her reaction to this man was making her think and feel things outside her realm of experience. She needed to maintain control of herself and her situation. However, before she could get up, he tugged his shirttail free of his pants and shrugged off his shirt.

Her pulse rose, and she let her gaze wander over his impressive physique. Not even the bathing costumes her male guests wore into the ocean exposed this much flesh. Alex exhibited a tanned and muscular figure. From this angle, he showed no signs of injury, only the harnessed strength she had felt while in his arms.

Imagining herself back in those arms, Julia felt breathless, as if she had climbed to the hotel's fifth floor without using the elevator.

A knock at the door made her jump.

Dr. Dolan answered it, and Theo stuck his head inside.

"Miss Fairbanks, forgive the intrusion, but I wanted to report that the geranium debris has been cleaned up, and I've checked the other pots on that balcony." He stepped inside and gently closed the door. "It's the strangest thing, though." He pulled on one of his wiry, white eyebrows.

"What is?" she asked, afraid she already knew the answer.

"Number one, no one is registered to that room. Number two, that pot should not have fallen. Even if it had, it wouldn't have landed where it did."

She laced her fingers tightly together in her lap and met Alex MacLean's knowing gaze. She could not dismiss his claim anymore. She trusted Theo. Since his first day of work when the hotel opened, he had been reliable and observant.

"I can hardly bear to say this, Miss Fairbanks," Theo said, "but I think someone picked it up and threw it."

She nodded, the movement jerky. "At me."

"You know?"

"Mr. MacLean shares your opinion."

Her protector shifted on the examining table and spoke. "Theo, have you told anyone else what you found?"

"No, sir, I came straight here."

"Then don't. I think it's best we not alert whoever was on that balcony that we know what he did."

Julia nodded. "And I'd rather not frighten the guests." She did not foresee any danger to them since she had been the apparent target. "Did you notice anything else, Theo?"

"The door was unlocked."

"So anyone could have gotten in there," Alex said.

"Yes, sir."

"Call me Alex." He rubbed the side of his ribs. "As

a bellboy, you have access to the entire hotel and everyone in it. How would you feel about keeping your eyes and ears open for anyone acting suspiciously or speaking against Miss Fairbanks?"

"Of course I'll do that." He faced her. "I don't want anything to happen to you."

"Thank you," she whispered, her throat tight. His loyalty and concern touched her deeply.

"I'll be going then." Theo reached for the doorknob. "I'll report anything I find out."

When the door clicked shut behind him, Julia found Alex and the doctor watching her, as if they expected her to start crying or collapse in a heap of nerves on the floor.

"Doctor," she said, "please go on with your examination. I need a few moments to think." Except that she didn't know what to think. She didn't want to believe that someone wanted to hurt her.

"Very well." The doctor walked around behind Alex and leaned in to examine his back and side. "Hmm." He probed the area with his fingers.

His patient sucked in a breath. "You found the spot, Doc."

"It wasn't difficult. A good-sized bruise is already coming up." He pressed several more places. "The shells from the drive have left their mark as well, but fortunately they did not break the skin."

"Miss Fairbanks," Alex said, his muscles taut and voice rough, "while the doctor inflicts more pain on me, tell me about any enemies you might have. It's a sure bet some of your male employees aren't happy about working under a female."

She straightened in the chair. From outside the open window came the rhythmic ping of rackets hitting a tennis ball across the net, the joyful squeals of children playing in the sand, and the sound of waves washing the beach. Julia hated the thought of danger lurking in the idyllic setting of her home.

"No one has been outwardly menacing or threatening." She kept her eyes fixed on Alex's face so his chest would not distract her. "If someone was that unhappy about working for me, he could have left at any time since I took over."

"Not everyone has the luxury of leaving a good job," he said, then glared over his shoulder at the doctor when another tender spot was probed. "Has anyone been especially rude to you?"

"Take a deep breath," Dr. Dolan ordered.

Alex inhaled slowly and deeply, wincing.

Julia winced, too. He was in pain because of her.

"Only one person comes to mind," she said. "Mr. Chalmers works the registration desk, and he has made no secret of his feelings for me. He dislikes new ideas, unless they are his own. Getting him to implement my ideas is a constant battle. I think he enjoys undermining me, but I keep hoping he'll come around."

"You ought to get rid of him," Dr. Dolan said, moving around Alex's side. "He thinks he's better and smarter than you. Not to mention the rest of us. I know he covets your position as manager."

"I can be tough with him if necessary, but it would be a shame to lose him. He's fast, efficient, and adept at using the telephone. He knows how everything works, and he's been here long enough to become acquainted with the returning and long-term guests. He knows their idiosyncrasies—the little things they want and expect during their stay."

At the doctor's prompting, Alex raised his arm. "Your Mr. Chalmers sounds like a prime suspect," he said. "Anyone else?"

"What about that fellow who tried so hard to buy the hotel a couple of months back?" Dr. Dolan asked.

"Tyler Wolff." A well-spoken, self-made man only a year or two older than her twenty-five years. She believed she must have seen his picture in the newspaper, because Mr. Wolff had looked familiar to her when they met the first time he tried to purchase her home. "He wasn't the only man who tried to buy the hotel after my father's death, but he was the most insistent. I was more insistent, however. I rejected all offers. The Hotel Grand Victoria is not for sale." And it never would be once she and Phillip said their marriage vows. She wished he would hurry up and get here. He had boarded the train in Philadelphia several days ago. "Mr. Wolff has not contacted me in three or four weeks. I assume he gave up and returned to Boston."

"Maybe." Alex rubbed his whiskered jaw, his fingers rasping over the stubble. "It'd be worth checking. He could have hired someone to try and push you out of the picture. What about former suitors who've heard you're about to marry?"

Suitors? She stifled a laugh. Despite the male interest she had received over the years, she never took any of those men or their proposals seriously. They had wanted her for the way she looked, as an adornment to their life. Or they wanted her because of the hotel they assumed would one day pass to her. None of them would have wanted a woman who preferred running that hotel to attending society outings in the finest silk and lace.

"The only ... suitor who has never given up hope of an alliance with me is Coronado's marshal. And he would never hurt me."

"Well, I wouldn't count him out." Creases dented the length of Alex's broad forehead. "For a bride on the eve of her wedding, you don't strike me as being very excited about your imminent nuptials."

"Julia," Dr. Dolan said, pushing a hand through his gray-streaked hair, "I have to admit I've been thinking the same thing. Mary and Kate are more excited about your wedding than you seem to be. It is strange."

She stared at the spotless floor, feeling cornered. Never a proficient liar or actress, she regularly kept things to herself, just as she had done with the reading of her father's will. Only when her vows were said did she intend to tell the Dolans the truth about her sham of a marriage.

"Very strange." Alex must have shifted on the examining table, because it creaked under his weight. "My wife was spinning like a top before our wedding."

She jerked her head up, shocked to feel a stab of ... jealousy? "You're married?" He hadn't seemed married to her. He had arrived alone.

"No." He stared at the eye chart. "My wife is dead."

"Oh. I'm so sorry." She ignored the unseemly wave

of relief moving through her, relief she had no right to feel on the eve of her wedding day. She should be feeling sad for him and the loss he suffered. Alex was young to be a widower, in his early thirties, she guessed. Was his wife's death the reason for the sorrow she had seen in him? Had he loved her the way Julia could only dream of being loved?

Dr. Dolan cleared his throat as the silence lengthened. "My condolences as well." He shuffled around in front of Alex. "I've finished my exam, and the prognosis is good. Your ability to breathe doesn't seem to be too affected, so I think I can safely say you didn't break or crack any ribs. You're a very fit specimen, and I see no need to wrap you up."

"Good. Thanks." He eased off the cushioned table.

Julia stood. "I'm glad you're going to be all right."

"I knew it wasn't serious," he responded.

Dr. Dolan handed Alex his shirt and leaned his head back to meet his patient's eyes. "Serious or not, your bruises will take on some interesting hues, none of them pretty, and the area will be tender for a good while. You'll need to take it easy."

"Mr. MacLean has come to the right place for that. I mentioned to him before that the Hotel Grand Victoria is a favorite place for recuperation."

"That's the truth," the doctor said as Alex slipped on his shirt. "We have all the necessities. Even a barber, if you're looking for a haircut or shave. I go to him myself."

Alex scraped a finger along his jaw. "Are you trying to tell me something, Doc?"

Dr. Dolan raised his hands in mock innocence.

"Me? No. I would never presume to tell a man what to do with his whiskers."

"Sure you would." Alex fastened the last of his shirt buttons. "As for recuperating, I already told Miss Fairbanks I'm not a guest here."

"Only because you haven't registered yet," she said.

"No, because I came in answer to an ad I read in a Los Angeles newspaper."

"An advertisement?"

"The one seeking carpenters. It was in the paper a few days ago." He frowned. "You are hiring, aren't you?"

"Yes! Yes, I am," she said, trying to overcome her confusion. She had assumed from his behavior and manner of speech that he was a well-educated gentleman, not a laborer. Of course she could not deny his roughened hands and the power she'd felt in his arms. He obviously used his body in a physical way. And his clothing was not in the best of shape, but she had learned over the years that you couldn't always judge a person's wealth by the clothes he chose to wear.

Dr. Dolan rolled down his sleeves. "Julia is always looking for carpenters. This place needs an army of them. It's the largest wooden structure west of the Mississippi, and the salt air plays havoc with it. But don't you go sawing wood, lifting heavy boards, or hammering nails just yet, young man. Not with those bruised ribs."

"I haven't been hired, Doc. That's up to Miss Fairbanks."

"So it is," the doctor said, sending her a pointed look.

She squirmed, lifting and lowering one shoulder, then the other. Alex deserved a job, more than a job, after what he'd done for her, but her unanticipated attraction to him and her more-than-in-passing curiosity about him worried her. If she hired him, she feared she might start looking for him everywhere she went in the hotel. She might even seek him out, which she mustn't do as a married woman.

"Are you sure you want to work for a woman, Mr. MacLean?" she asked.

"I don't care who the boss is, as long as I'm paid a fair wage."

Julia liked that he wasn't bothered by her gender. "Do you have any references?"

"Sorry. I haven't stayed anywhere long enough."

She exchanged glances with the doctor. Alex had just given her a reason not to hire him, but he had also been honest with her, and she valued honesty. "I appreciate your candidness. Where have you been?"

"Los Angeles, Colorado Springs, Omaha, to name a few. I've gotten as far north as Canada and as far south as Texas."

"You're a drifter then." Had his wife's death led him to a life on the road?

He shrugged. "That term is as good as any."

She felt an inkling of relief. She could do what was right and hire him, knowing he wouldn't be around long enough to cause her any trouble or embarrassment. But would she have enough time to help him ease the sorrow she'd seen in him? "How long do you intend to stay?"

"I don't know. Probably until I have enough money to move on. Miss Fairbanks, I'm a good carpenter and a hard worker, and I'd be proud to work on a structure as beautifully designed as the Hotel Grand Victoria. I can promise you, no matter how long I stay, you'll get your money's worth."

"I don't doubt it, Mr. MacLean." Though she barely knew him, she believed him, trusted him.

"Do I have a job then?"

"Yes, but you won't start until Dr. Dolan allows it. While you are recuperating, you'll be my guest in the hotel. Once you are fit, you can move to the boarding house up the street or into one of the employee rooms on the top floor of the hotel, should one become available."

"I'll move into the boarding house today."

Dr. Dolan glanced from one to the other and muffled a laugh.

She pursed her lips. "Mr. MacLean, I want you to be my guest. You put yourself at risk for me this afternoon, injuring yourself in the process. I intend to compensate you for that as best I can."

"Hiring me is all the payment I need."

"But it is not enough to satisfy me." She gripped the folds of her skirt. "Mr. MacLean, as you can imagine, I have a great deal on my mind right now. I would really appreciate it if you'd let me do this one small thing for you. If you don't stay here as my guest, I will worry that you're not taking care of yourself."

He raised his hands in surrender. "I wouldn't want you to worry, Miss Fairbanks."

"So you'll stay?"

"Yes."

"Thank you." She smiled at him, feeling a giddy happiness she was afraid to dissect. "I'll show you to the lobby so that you can register."

"Appreciate it." Alex turned to Dr. Dolan and shook his hand. "Thanks, Doc. I'll be seeing you soon, and you'll pronounce me fit to work."

"I'll make that pronouncement when it's time, and no sooner. Perhaps four or five days from now," he said as Julia opened the office door. "But it'll be longer if you do anything to exacerbate your injuries. In the meantime, hot baths should ease some of the stiffness you'll be feeling."

Preceding the men into the hallway, Julia heard a rapping at the cottage's front door. She opened it to Tilden, one of her bellboys. He stood as stiffly as an army officer. His dark hair, shot through with gunmetal gray, was impeccably groomed beneath his uniform's pillbox hat. His personality was as formal and sober as Theo's was lively and cheerful, but in the nine months he had worked at the hotel, he'd shown himself to be a dutiful employee.

"Does someone need the doctor, Tilden?"

"No, ma'am. This telegram came for you." He handed her an envelope. "Mr. Chalmers instructed me to deliver it immediately."

"Thank you."

"What is it, Julia?" Dr. Dolan asked, coming up behind her.

She turned. "A telegram. Hotel business, no doubt, and probably important. Mr. MacLean, would you mind letting Tilden take you to the lobby while I stay behind and read this?"

"Only if you promise to keep an eye out for falling flowerpots."

She understood his meaning perfectly, and she found herself basking in the blanketing warmth of his concern for her. She smiled up at him. "I promise I'll be careful."

"Then I'll be going," he said, a huskiness in his voice that hadn't been there before.

But he didn't go. He stood over her.

She gazed up at him, her heart thumping faster and louder. Alex's current preoccupation seemed very different from his earlier lapses.

"I will look for you later," Julia heard herself say. "I always like to check on my guests."

He tipped his head to her, twice. "Until later then." He finally turned away, reluctance in his movements.

She watched as he motioned Tilden onto the shell path ahead of him. He glanced back once, his gaze dropping to the telegram in her hand. Questions had returned to his eyes.

Dr. Dolan shut the door behind them. "Nice fellow, and good looking if you can see past the scar. Not much for smiling, though."

Now that the doctor mentioned it, Julia realized she had not seen Alex smile. He hadn't laughed either, not even when Dr. Dolan brazenly commented on his need for a barber.

"He sure enjoyed looking at you," he went on, hooking his thumbs in the waistband of his pants. "Too much, now that I think about it. I expect your future husband would not approve. Mr. MacLean should probably move on sooner rather than later."

"You may be right." Though Phillip wouldn't care about Alex's interest in her, she would be a married woman with a reputation to uphold. "Now I had better take a look at this." She waved the envelope and sat on the bench.

"I'll be in my office if you need me." He shuffled down the hallway.

She opened the envelope, extracted the telegram, and started to read.

BROKE LEG IN FALL FROM TRAIN DURING TRANSFER IN DENVER STOP WILL NOT GET TO CALIFORNIA STOP SORRY STOP PHILLIP

Julia gasped. Her hand shook, rustling the flimsy paper. Phillip was injured, badly enough that he couldn't travel. He wasn't coming. He wasn't coming.

This was a disaster. Her concern for him warred with the devastation of what his injury meant—she would lose her home. She'd done everything possible to comply with her father's stipulation. But it wasn't enough. Even if she could board a train this very minute, it would not get her to Denver in time for her to secure a marriage license and meet her father's deadline. She didn't even know where to find Phillip. The poor man, and his poor leg. She felt responsible. If it weren't for her and the money she offered him, he would never have left Philadelphia.

Tears blurred her eyes, and a sob escaped her throat. She was going to lose the Hotel Grand Victoria. Everyone and everything she loved would be at the mercy of new owners.

The telegram slipped through her fingers, fluttering to the floor as she buried her face in her hands.

* * *

Alex fell into step beside the bellboy, his mind still on his hostess and her enchanting smile. For a moment there, he'd lost himself in that smile, in the way Julia Fairbanks made him feel cared for and special. He even forgot the past three and a half years of his life.

But he couldn't forget for long. The losses and injustices he'd suffered had been carved more deeply into his soul than the scar etched into his face.

He pushed his hands into his pockets and thought of Julia again. Hopefully, she really would be careful. Whoever had thrown that flowerpot probably wouldn't try again right away, but there was no telling.

Tilden glanced back him, as if to make sure he hadn't lost his charge.

"I'm still here," Alex said, looking forward to settling in. He might even lie down and sleep for a while to rest his ribs. However, he'd likely end up dreaming about Miss Fairbanks. Not that he would mind dreaming about her—just looking at her made his body react like it hadn't in a long time—but he did not welcome dreams of the impossible. She was his employer. Worse yet, she belonged to another man, their wedding only a day away.

Alex discovered he didn't like thinking about her with another man, especially when he conjured up images of her on her wedding night. He pictured her lying in the center of a wide bed, her glorious, silvery-blond hair cascading over the pillow. Some of it draped her naked breasts, the myriad fine strands strategically veiling ...

Alex shook the arousing image away. Maybe a nap wasn't such a good idea. "Tilden," he said, trying to think about something else, "who was the Hotel Grand Victoria's architect?"

"I wouldn't know, sir. That question hasn't been asked of me in the months that I've been here." He picked up the pace. "I'm sure Miss Fairbanks could enlighten you."

"I'll ask her then." Though it'd be hard to concentrate on architectural details when Julia was doing the describing.

At the hotel's entrance, wheels crunched over the drive as a carriage pulled up bearing two stylishly dressed couples. A wagon piled high with trunks and cases followed. The horse tossed his head, and the harness jingled.

"Will you excuse me, sir?" Tilden said. "I must see to the new arrivals. You'll find the registration desk inside."

"Thank you." Alex left the bellboy and entered the hotel's Rotunda, a large, elegantly appointed lobby with marble tile flooring and tall ormolu sconces. Huge vases of fresh-cut flowers—yellow daffodils, purple iris, and green foliage—decorated ornamental Chinese sideboards. Seating areas included plush, back-to-back red velvet banquettes and a grouping of dark wicker chairs.

Coquettish giggles made Alex look up to a second-floor gallery. Two young women paraded there, both of them smiling down at him—until they saw his face clearly. Their smiles froze, and their fans halted in mid flutter.

He ground his teeth, then remembered Julia's reaction to her first sight of his entire face. She had not been repelled by his injury. She didn't even ask about it, as many people did, giving in to their morbid curiosity. In the doctor's office, Julia barely noticed it once he removed his shirt. He chuckled at the memory, enjoying himself. He could not deny how good it had felt to attract a beautiful woman's attention for the right reasons.

He dismissed the women staring down at him and strode to the registration desk, his step lighter. He shoved aside the distinct feeling that his hostess might have unintentionally claimed a corner of his tortured heart.

The clerk, a sallow, weasel-faced man around his own age, was speaking into the telephone. Alex had seen a few telephones before, but the idea that people could hear each other over a wire still amazed him.

While he waited for the clerk, he ran a hand across the desk's smooth finish and finely carved oak trim. When the clerk finished, he said, "This is a fine piece of workmanship."

"It serves its purpose." The clerk's haughty, disapproving gaze slid over him, landing on his dusty, faded shirt.

Alex again ran his fingers over the woodwork.

"Do you mind?" The clerk huffed out a breath.

"This is not a museum open for public inspection. I suggest you be on your way." He waved his arm toward the front entrance.

Alex felt his eyebrows lift. This had to be the infamous Mr. Chalmers. "You're supposed to be courteous to your guests."

"I don't see a guest." The weasel folded his arms over his torso.

Flexing his fingers, Alex squinted back and agreed with the doctor. Julia needed to get rid of the man. "I'm here to register."

"There's nothing available. Try the boarding house up the street." He turned his back and busied himself at the wall of pigeonholes.

Alex fisted his hands. Dr. Dolan had said he wasn't to exert himself, but teaching this weasel some manners would take no effort at all. However, he didn't think Julia would thank him for it. She needed Chalmers more than she needed him. Besides, he'd only end up drawing attention to himself.

He uncurled his fingers. "Your insolence won't be forgotten, Chalmers."

The weasel's hand paused in the act of stowing a key. He spun around.

Alex gave him a piercing look and strode away.

"Wait! Come back here! How do you know my name?"

Alex kept walking.

Chapter Three

"Julia?" Dr. Dolan dropped down beside her on the bench and squeezed her shoulder. "What's wrong? Talk to me."

She slowly lowered her hands and looked over at him, her face wet with tears of surrender. She'd lost. Phillip was hurt on account of her, and the Hotel Grand Victoria would be auctioned off to the highest bidder—Tyler Wolff or some faceless group of investors—who would take control of her beloved home and do as they pleased with it.

"Julia, you're worrying me. I've never seen you like this."

She had never felt like this, devoid of hope. She pointed at the telegram half hidden by his shoe.

He picked up the paper, read it, and sighed. "What rotten luck. But, Julia, a broken leg isn't the end of the world. His leg will heal. You'll have your wedding eventually."

She shook her head and swiped the backs of her hands across her cheeks. "You don't understand. I need a husband now. I can't wait any longer."

His graying brows came together. "Julia, you're not making sense." He lifted her wrist and held his fingers against her pulse. "You should lie down."

She pulled her wrist away and wrapped her arms around her waist. "I don't need to lie down. I need a husband. Anyone will do. Help me, Dr. Dolan. I can't do this on my own anymore."

His gaze dropped to where her arms covered her stomach. "You're … in trouble?"

"Yes. I should have told you sooner. Both you and Mary. I wanted to, but I thought I could handle everything myself." She laughed what wasn't a laugh at all. "Look how that turned out."

"Uh, maybe I had better get Mary before you go any further."

"Yes, please. Maybe she knows an honorable man willing to marry me within the next two days."

The doctor hopped up as quick as a well-fed rabbit and disappeared into the kitchen. He quickly reappeared with his wife, who clasped and unclasped her hands. Flour still smudged her cheeks. She smelled of apple pie, but not even that could sooth Julia's despondency.

"Oh, my dear girl," she said, sinking onto the bench. "I am so sorry. So very sorry. I never imagined …" She shook her head, apparently unable to finish.

Julia leaned back slightly. "Imagined what? You don't know what's wrong yet."

"Of course we do. We know these things happen, even in the best of families."

"What are you talking about?"

"The baby," Mary answered. "Your baby."

Julia's mouth fell open, and she started to laugh, a high-pitched hysterical sound she had never made before. They thought she was with child? She doubled over, afraid to stop laughing for fear she would start sobbing.

"Harold, do something!" Mary's hands fluttered in the air. "She's gone batty."

"Give her a minute, dear. I fear we may have jumped to a mistaken conclusion."

Julia nodded, her hysteria ending with a hiccup. "I am not going to have a baby, Mary."

"You're not? Well, why else would you need a husband?"

"To save the hotel." She explained her predicament, describing her father's stipulation. "So you see, if I don't marry by Saturday midnight, the hotel will be sold. I'll be forced to leave, and there's no telling what changes a new owner might impose on everyone. Phillip was my last hope, and he has broken his leg during his journey here." She looked toward the door. "I must try to reach him and make sure he's all right."

Mary tapped Julia's arm. "You can telegraph him later. Go on with your story."

"Oh, uh, I was telling you about Phillip. He agreed to marry me in exchange for three thousand dollars. Once our vows were said and the papers signed, he was to return East, to his … man friends."

Dr. Dolan eased himself onto the other end of the bench. "Well, this explains your lack of excitement regarding your wedding."

"Well, I don't understand anything." Mary

knuckled several loose, wispy hairs out of her face. "What do you mean by 'man friends'? He was your childhood sweetheart, wasn't he? Why wouldn't he live here with you?"

"Mary, he wasn't my childhood sweetheart. When Mother, Father, and I lived in Philadelphia, Phillip was an employee in Father's hotel. He was a good friend, and more trustworthy than the three traveling salesmen I initially approached with my proposal. They all wanted … more than I was willing to give, including more money. Phillip agreed to the amount I offered, and since he's not the kind of man who is attracted to women"—Julia paused during Mary's rapid, indrawn breath—"I believed him to be the perfect candidate for a husband I didn't want but was being forced to have."

"Oh, my dear girl. This is truly dreadful. I had thought you were marrying for love. You deserve love, and lots of children as beautiful as yourself." Tears slid down Mary's cheeks, forming trails through the flour. "Your father had no right to interfere with your life this way." She lifted her apron and dabbed at her wet face.

Dr. Dolan got up and paced the floor in front of them. His footsteps echoed through the hallway and up the stairs. "Is there no way to challenge the will?"

"None. I did try, even though Father's lawyer told me I'd be wasting my time. The only way for me to hold on to the hotel is to marry before the deadline."

"Then you must do exactly that."

"Harold!" Mary stared at him open-mouthed.

"We have to be practical, my dear. Julia accepted her situation months ago and knows what must be done. The problem lies in finding the right man, and I believe I know just the one."

"You do?" Julia leaned forward, hope returning. "Who? Someone in San Diego?"

"Yes, I met him recently when I was checking on the health of the inmates at the county jail."

"A guard?" Julia said, knowing the doctor volunteered his services there on a regular basis.

"No, a man who was recently sentenced to hang for murder. He is scheduled to travel to the State Prison at San Quentin next week."

She gasped. "You want me to marry a murderer?"

The doctor shrugged. "Well, he won't make a nuisance of himself at some later date."

"I'd sooner marry Alex MacLean. At least a drifter wouldn't taint the hotel's reputation." Julia could just imagine the scandal if the newspapers discovered the heiress to the Hotel Grand Victoria married a convicted killer sentenced to hang.

Mary smoothed her apron over her lap. "That's not a bad idea."

Julia frowned. "What's not?"

"Your marrying Mr. MacLean."

Julia's heart skipped a beat. She sat back with such force the bench shook. She hadn't truly been serious about him as a potential husband. Besides, though she hardly knew him, she got the distinct impression he wasn't the kind of man who would just sit back and let her do things her way.

"No," she said, "he's not the right man."

"Why not?" Mary asked.

The doctor tapped his chin. "Hmmm. I think Mary

is onto something. Mr. MacLean could be exactly what you're looking for—a husband who will walk away."

His wife nodded.

Dr. Dolan went on. "He's a drifter down on his luck, in need of money, and unmarried."

"He's also polite and well-spoken." Mary brushed at a spot of flour on her apron. "But his poor face."

His face was the least of Julia's worries. Alex's obvious attraction to her was a much bigger problem. If Alex MacLean married her, Julia had a strong suspicion he would want a wedding night.

Imagining herself enfolded in his arms again, shut away in her apartment with him, she shivered, the feeling not entirely unpleasant.

"No," she said, louder than intended. "I can't marry him. Why, he doesn't even have references." If she had known she might be interviewing him for the job of husband, she would have asked him more questions.

Dr. Dolan threw up his hands. "Julia, the man risked his own self to protect you. What better reference can there be?"

The doctor had a point, and yet …

He grasped her hands and hauled her to her feet. "Young lady, you are out of options. Go find Mr. MacLean and make him an offer he can't refuse."

* * *

Julia reluctantly cast her reservations aside and hurried along the front veranda. The doctor was right. She was out of options and had to be practical. To hold on to the hotel, she was going to propose marriage to Alex MacLean.

Inside the hotel's entrance, a high-pitched yap stopped her. A Yorkshire terrier with a tiny pink bow on her head peered beseechingly up at her.

"Hello there."

The dog yapped again.

She picked up the small dog and stroked her silky hair. A velvety tongue licked her hand, and she laughed softly. "You're a friendly little thing. Where's your owner?"

"I was wondering the same thing."

Julia's heart jumped into her throat. She whirled. "Mr. MacLean! You startled me." She hadn't expected to see him this soon. She wasn't ready to see him. She needed time to work out how best to present her proposition.

He shrugged. "I didn't mean to."

When he said nothing more, such as where he'd been, what he'd been doing, or how he happened to be here the very moment she was, she said, "How do you like your room?"

"I don't have one. Your favorite desk clerk claims the hotel is full."

She shut her eyes a moment and blew out a breath. "We are not full, and he had no right to turn you away." She settled the dog against her chest and eyed Mr. Chalmers across the Rotunda. The desk clerk was serving a well-endowed matron dressed all in black. A matching hat pinned over white hair was trimmed with netting that obscured her features. "I really must do something about him."

"I demand to see the manager this instant!" came an imperious, irate voice from the matron.

Julia tried to stay calm, telling herself, *One thing at a time. I can handle whatever comes if I do it one thing at a time.*

The terrier squirmed and whined.

"Young man, if you won't call the manager," the woman said, her voice rising even higher, "I will."

A small group of guests chatting beneath the gallery turned as one, their conversation halted. A man wearing a cutaway walking suit paused while peeking inside the door to the Crown Room, as many visitors did, to admire the large dining room. From inside came the clink of silver and china as waiters set the tables for the rapidly approaching evening meal.

"Where is he?" The matron's foot drummed the marble floor, perilously close to the shiny brass spittoon.

Julia cringed. A guest this displeased would spread her dissatisfaction, ultimately hurting the hotel's reputation and bank account. Her employees depended on her and the success of the hotel to pay their wages. Between mortgage payments, staffing, maintenance, food costs, and the price of a bridegroom, she could not afford to lose any customers.

She pushed the dog at Alex, giving him no choice but to take her. "Please excuse me. I need to sort out a problem."

He handled the dog with ease, and the tiny terrier lay without complaint in the palm of his hand.

Julia strode away, but she glanced back once and would have laughed if she hadn't been so distracted. A man of Alex's size and build holding a miniature dog with a pink bow was an astonishing sight, one she wouldn't soon forget. He looked so … sweet.

Arriving at the registration desk, Julia installed a professional smile on her face and stepped up to the woman, then nearly gagged when the matron's liberal use of lilac water struck her in the face like a gust of wind.

She held her ground and glanced between the woman and desk clerk. "Mr. Chalmers, may I be of help?"

He pressed his lips into a thin line, then gestured toward the matron. "This is Mrs. Hensley, a new arrival. She insists on seeing the manager."

"And so she shall. Mrs. Hensley, I'm Julia Fairbanks, manager of the Hotel Grand Victoria. I'm also the owner." For the next two days anyway. "How can I be of service?"

Mrs. Hensley looked as surprised as if she had bitten into a lemon instead of a cream puff. "A woman? Well, as I live and breathe. How extraordinary!" One hand fluttered near her heart. The diamonds in her ostentatious bracelet flashed.

"I'm pleased to meet you, Mrs. Hensley. Welcome to the Hotel Grand Victoria. What can I do for you?"

Chalmers answered for her. "Mrs. Hensley claims she was promised an ocean-view room."

The woman sniffed. "And that is not what I was given."

"Oh, I am so sorry about the confusion," she said in a sympathetic tone, knowing full well that none of her desk clerks ever promised a particular room unless she approved of it first. Only so many west-facing rooms existed. "Mr. Chalmers, what room is registered to

Mrs. Hensley?"

"Two twenty-eight," he brusquely answered.

"Why that's a lovely room, Mrs. Hensley." She honestly believed the woman would be happier there, and she intended to persuade her to stay put. "Did you notice how it overlooks the park on the northwest side of the hotel? Not only that, it's one of the few rooms with a private bath and outside balcony."

The woman gazed off in the direction of her room.

Julia lowered her voice conspiratorially and, despite the cloying smell permeating Mrs. Hensley's clothing, leaned toward her. "Don't tell anyone I said this, but when trying to sleep in a room overlooking the Pacific, the surf can be a trifle disturbing to anyone who wakes at the slightest sound. And in the late afternoon, the lowering sun can heat those rooms until they are stifling unless the doors are left open."

"Oh my, I am a light sleeper," she whispered back. "And I don't do well in too much heat." She lifted her chin. "I'll stay where I am."

Julia smiled. "I'm sure you'll be comfortable there. And, as I hope you've been made aware, your room has a wall safe for the security of your jewels." She darted a brief look at the woman's bracelet. "Or you're free to use the safe here at the desk, which is manned twenty-four hours a day."

"Thank you. I'll keep that in mind." Mrs. Hensley peered around at the floor. "Now where has my little Muffie gotten to?"

"Would Muffie happen to be a Yorkshire terrier?"

"Yes. Have you seen her?"

She located Alex and beckoned to him, trying not

to think how at home he appeared in her lobby.

He strode toward them, the dog lying peacefully on his hand, which he held at his waist.

"Oh, there's my baby." Mrs. Hensley folded the netting up on her hat.

Alex's step faltered, and his expression froze.

Julia swept an inquisitive glance between him and Mrs. Hensley.

"Thank you, sir." Mrs. Hensley reached for the dog, barely sparing Alex a look. "Come here, Muffie. Come to Mother."

The terrier sneezed delicately as Alex gently relinquished her. His expression remained frozen, his attention riveted on the woman. Julia felt a little frozen herself. Even if Alex knew the woman, why would his seeing her cause such a disturbing reaction?

Mrs. Hensley scratched the dog's ruff and made cooing noises to her. "Since my husband's death, Muffie is my only companion and such a comfort when I'm a long way from home." She raised the dog, turning her so they were nose to nose. "Aren't you, baby?"

Muffie yipped and licked her owner's nose.

Mrs. Hensley laughed and finally looked at Alex, his scar taking her aback for a moment. "You must be very good with animals, sir. Muffie isn't usually so trusting of a stranger." Mrs. Hensley tilted her head, then leaned forward as Alex took a step back. "Goodness, you so remind me of someone back home, though I can't think who." She let Muffie rest against her ample bosom. "Of course, whoever it is doesn't have, well, a scar. I would have remembered that.

Perhaps you're a relation of someone I know. Where are you from?"

"I move around a lot."

When he said no more, Julia wondered at his reticence. "Mr. MacLean recently arrived from Los Angeles," she inserted, ignoring the narrowed look he sent her way. "He is my guest here at the hotel, and Mr. Chalmers is registering him into a room this very minute. Aren't you, Mr. Chalmers?" Her unwavering gaze dared the clerk to defy her.

"Yes, Miss Fairbanks," he said, squeezing the words from between uneven teeth. Chalmers flipped open the large register, spun the book around, and jabbed a finger at the blank line. "Sign here, Mr. MacLean."

"MacLean. MacLean." Mrs. Hensley stroked Muffie's back and peered into the dog's dark brown eyes. "I am sure we've heard that name before, haven't we, baby? But from where?"

Alex turned away from the woman, grabbed the fountain pen from its holder, and signed the register.

Julia stared in fascination at the vein in his temple. It pulsed like a raging river pushing at its banks. If Alex was acquainted with Mrs. Hensley, why not admit it?

Despite wanting to know more, she shrugged the question off. She had more important matters to think about, such as her looming deadline and how to convince this drifter to stand before a minister with her, say "I do," and then leave. Whatever prior relationship he had with Mrs. Hensley made no difference to her. He would soon be gone.

Muffie whined.

"I can't recall either," the matron said to her dog. "Perhaps after a proper night's rest I'll remember. Let's go back to our room and dress for dinner, shall we?"

Muffie yipped, and Mrs. Hensley carried her "baby" to the gilded birdcage elevator. Julia noticed Alex watching the matron out of the corner of his eye. The elevator boy clanged the door shut and whisked his charges upward.

Chalmers shoved a key across the desk at Alex. "Enjoy your stay," he bit out.

"Thanks," he said, obviously preoccupied as he took the key. The clerk's blatantly rude behavior did not seem to affect him in the least.

Julia, however, could not let it go. She leaned across the desk and crooked her finger at her ill-mannered clerk.

His gaze flicked around the lobby, then he slowly bent toward her.

"Mr. Chalmers," she said, keeping her voice low, "if you wish to remain in my employ, you will change your attitude right now. I expect you to treat everyone who steps up to this desk with the utmost respect. That includes Mr. MacLean. Do you understand?"

He swallowed so hard his throat seemed to convulse. "Yes, ma'am."

"Good." She straightened and turned to Alex, intent on checking off the next item of business on her mental list—her proposal of marriage.

But he was gone.

She whipped around. Thankfully, he had only

gotten halfway to the bell desk, where Theo stood with his bag. She hurried after him.

"Mr. MacLean, please wait. There's something I wish to discuss with you."

He didn't stop.

"Mademoiselle Fairbanks!" her maitre d' called out from across the lobby. "I have need of you in the dining room. *Tout de suite!* Immediately."

She held up her hand to put the Frenchman off. Jacques Levesque's devotion to his job was exceptional, but anything to do with that job was an emergency to him, even if it was nothing more than having her check the spelling of the chef's specials on the menu. She focused her attention on Alex. When the grandfather clock on the stairway landing chimed six, she inwardly moaned as her deadline loomed ever closer.

At the bell desk's podium, Alex retrieved his bag from Theo and pressed a coin into the bellboy's palm. Theo tried to give it back, but he refused to take it.

Julia was touched by the generosity she doubted her guest and savior could afford. "Mr. MacLean," she said, coming up beside him, "I would like to speak with you."

He shifted his bag to his other hand.

"Mademoiselle!" Jacques, dressed in his black tailcoat, inserted himself between her and Alex and glowered down his beaked nose at her.

She reined in her irritation and impatience. "Jacques, is someone injured in the kitchen?"

"*Non*, but—"

"Is the dining room on fire?"

"*Non, non,* nothing like that," he answered, his accent pronounced.

"Then please wait for a moment."

Like a spoiled child in a snit, his mouth puckered prominently.

Theo scooted up to him and took his arm. "Why don't you come with me? Tell me all about it."

To her relief, he guided the Frenchman away. However, her thoughts were a scattered mess, like grains of sand being carried by the wind. She needed to approach Alex carefully, laying out her proposition just so. He would see the benefits to himself and ultimately, hopefully, agree to help her.

"Mr. MacLean, what I wish to discuss with you is important, but, as you can see"—she waved in Jacques' direction—"I have duties to attend to. Will you please dine with me this evening? The dinner service begins in less than an hour. We'll be able to talk more readily then."

He hesitated. "I don't think your fiancé would approve."

"Phillip has no say in the matter, nor is he here to object. I'm asking you to dine with me because … well, I wish to discuss a business proposition with you."

"Let me guess. You want to hire me as your bodyguard."

She opened her mouth, but no sound came out. The idea of a bodyguard had not occurred to her. In fact, from the time Phillip's telegram had arrived, she had barely thought about what her encounter with the flowerpot meant. "Uh."

"Sure. I'll meet you here at seven," he said. "Or shall I come to your rooms? You'd be safer that way. I assume you live on the grounds."

"I have an apartment on the second floor," she said, imagining Alex coming to her door like a suitor. But he was not her suitor. Nor was he thinking like one. He was, once again, trying to protect her. The warmth she'd felt while in his arms returned. She struggled to douse it. "I'll meet you here, in the lobby. Seven o'clock."

"As you wish. Until then, be careful." He tipped his head to her and strolled away, leaving her more uneasy than ever. Her pulse scudded along. She glanced around the lobby for anyone who might be watching her, who might be looking for his next opportunity to harm her.

Everyone seemed to be looking at her, and Julia hurried after Theo and Jacques.

Chapter Four

Alex waited in the Rotunda, eager to see Julia again even though he knew what he was feeling for her could go nowhere. He should have declined her invitation to dinner, but she needed a bodyguard, and he was available, unable to work at his trade. He didn't expect the job to last long, though. Her fiancé would likely take over the responsibility for her safety.

Tugging at the high collar of his single dress shirt, Alex tried to stretch another sixteenth of an inch of space into the neck. His wrinkled, faded, charcoal-gray jacket pulled across his chest, back, and upper arms. In Baltimore, before he developed a laborer's muscles, the suit had fit perfectly. His tailor would cringe to see it now.

He tried to ignore the sideways looks cast his way. The other guests, turned out in their finest evening clothes, were filing past him into the Crown Room.

He forgot about them the moment he saw Julia.

She descended the stairs as gracefully as any debutante, her dress a confection of pale pink satin.

Her face was radiant under the electric lights. He would've whistled if he could, but she had stolen his breath away.

Her hair was pinned atop her head, with loose, curling locks dangling the length of her neck. Each tendril shimmered and bobbed with her steps. Alex would have liked to touch her hair, feel its softness. He lowered his gaze to her bodice, and a different kind of softness tempted him. The bodice was molded to her breasts, and though it revealed only a modest amount of her ivory flesh, his mouth went dry. His feet felt cemented to the floor, as if they had become part of the foundation.

He wanted her. It was that simple. But she wasn't his for the taking, and somehow he had to tamp down this desire he felt for her. She needed his help until her fiancé arrived. Where the hell was Phillip Williamson anyway?

Julia approached, smiling warmly, but the closer she came, the more stilted her steps appeared. Alex saw the tension behind her smile. Was she worrying that Phillip would not approve of their meeting for dinner? Her gaze flitted away from him, alighting first on the diminishing line of guests entering the dining room, then on the night bellboy, and ending with the quiet registration desk, where another clerk had replaced the weasel.

Remembering how neatly Julia had dealt with Chalmers earlier, Alex had to admit she was no pushover. He admired her. A woman operating a place like this had to have intelligence, determination, and courage.

She stopped in front of him. Immediately, the alluring scent of orange blossoms surrounded them in a fragrant cocoon, tempting him with thoughts of spring and new life.

"Why, Mr. MacLean, you shaved," she said amidst the hum of muted conversations and the rustle of elegant skirts.

He rubbed his smooth jaw. "I took Dr. Dolan's advice and visited the barber."

"He trimmed your hair, too, I see."

"A little." Running his hand over the back of his head, he felt where his hair still covered his collar. "I kind of like it long."

"You look quite handsome." She said it with feeling, as if she meant it, but he could not accept the compliment.

"No, I look as ugly as ever. You, however,"—he let out a breath—"are stunningly beautiful."

A lovely flush moved into her cheeks.

He had always admired and appreciated beauty, be it in nature, the lines of a building, or the face of a woman. His Elizabeth, on their wedding day, had been the most beautiful woman he ever set eyes on. As his bride swept down the aisle on her father's arm, he'd pinched himself at the altar to ensure he wasn't dreaming. She had chosen him, Alex MacLean, to be her husband, and he had reveled in his good fortune. At their reception, most of the men had clapped him on the back, reiterating how lucky he was. They hadn't known the real Elizabeth any better than he had.

"Shall we go in?" Julia asked.

Out of reflex, he offered her his arm.

She took it, placing her gloved hand through the crook of his elbow. Her hand trembled as it touched him. Alex felt shaky himself, but he also felt at ease, not the least bit self-conscious with her. He realized that Julia Fairbanks had a calming influence on his emotions, but a very stirring influence on the rest of him.

Inside the Crown Room, he forced himself to look at the huge room instead of at her. Chandeliers shaped like crowns hung above tables covered with snowy white linens, decoratively folded napkins, shiny silver, and spotless crystal goblets. Conversations vied with music and the clink of silver against china. The heavenly smells of roasted meats and fresh-baked bread emanated from the kitchen. Alex pressed a hand to his rumbling stomach and hoped the string quartet, playing from the dais, covered the growls that announced his hunger.

"What do you think of the room?" she asked, the pride in her voice unmistakable.

He lifted his gaze to the high ceiling. Despite his protesting ribs, he leaned back further to admire and examine the incredible workmanship. "Exceptional. Is that sugar pine?"

"You know your woods, Mr. MacLean. As a carpenter, you'll also appreciate the fact that there are no nails in the ceiling. The panels are fitted together like a puzzle."

"Tongue and groove." He nodded, then peered from one end of the room to the other in awe. "There are no supports. What're the dimensions?"

She laughed. "My father would have liked you. He

never tired of discussing the hotel's design details with anyone. The Crown Room is sixty-six feet wide and a hundred fifty-six feet long."

"Impressive." She impressed him as well. Very few women of his acquaintance had appreciated architectural details the way he did. "Who was the architect?"

"There were three. The Reid brothers from Indiana—James, Merritt, and Watson. If you'd like, I can try to dig out their plans and show them to you."

"I would like that," he said, feeling a familiar spark of creative excitement. He had thought that spark long gone. "I've come across their work before. They're known for their railroad stations."

"Which you have undoubtedly passed through in the course of your travels."

Her teasing smile was so beguiling Alex felt as if he had just smacked into another hitching post. This was not good. He ought to excuse himself and get back on the road tonight, but he couldn't tear himself away from her. She made him feel things he had thought he would never feel again.

"Traveling is one way to see what others have done," he said. "A picture postcard is what first piqued my interest in the Hotel Grand Victoria. The job advertisement gave me a practical reason for coming here."

"Then I'm thankful for both of those items." As she peered up at him, a sudden, anxious intensity came into her eyes.

Was she remembering the danger that stalked her? He doubted she was experiencing the same inappropriate feelings for him that he had for her. No woman wanted a man with a face like his.

Abruptly she turned and motioned to the maitre d', the tall, slim Frenchman who had rudely interrupted them in the lobby earlier. "Good evening, Jacques. Would you have a front window table available for Mr. MacLean and me?"

He gave her a courtly bow, his earlier irritation with her apparently appeased. "But of course, mademoiselle. Follow me, please." He folded his white-gloved hands over his white satin cummerbund and strolled down one of the aisles.

Alex released her arm and motioned for her to go first. He was relieved they would be seated in a section far from Alberta Hensley. He had spotted her at a table near the string quartet. Just in case she looked over, he kept his face averted so she wouldn't see his good side and possibly remember him.

Julia strolled the length of the room, smiling and nodding to the guests who looked their way. She was the ultimate hostess and obviously felt at home in her role. The hotel would undoubtedly prosper under her guidance, provided the flowerpot assassin did not make another attempt on her life.

Jacques seated them at a candlelit table where the menu awaited them, then he departed. Outside the window, beyond the carriage drive and down an incline, lights glimmered on the smooth surface of the bay.

Before Alex could bring up the job of bodyguard, a young man in a spotless white apron arrived to fill their goblets with iced water. Next came a red-haired, freckly faced waiter bearing a silver mesh basket of bread buried in white linen. Alex hadn't experienced this kind of service in, well, just over three and a half years. Though he had not forgotten his manners, his hunger and the yeasty smell of warm bread drove him to excavate a slice while the waiter launched into a description of the chef's special offerings.

Julia removed her gloves and set them aside, then ordered the prime rib dinner and its accompanying side dishes.

"I'll have the same," he said, slathering fresh butter on another slice of bread. He considered ordering a good bottle of wine, a label and vintage he had enjoyed in his former life, but he was afraid he'd enjoy it too much. He needed to keep his wits about him, not only to control his desire for Julia, but to watch over her in case someone took aim again.

"Very good, sir." The waiter left, and they were finally alone.

Alex set down his butter knife. "My compliments to your baker. I haven't tasted bread this good in ages."

"You don't appear to have eaten in ages either."

"Breakfast was quite a while ago." He took another bite.

"I'm sorry." She looked abashed and needlessly moved one of her forks an eighth of an inch to the left. "I should have offered you something from the kitchen this afternoon."

"This was worth the wait. Have some." He pushed the basket closer to her.

"No, thank you. I'll … wait for dinner." She lifted her water goblet, but when she put it to her lips for a sip, her hand shook, and she quickly returned the glass to the table.

Alex kept chewing, watching her look everywhere but at him. She clasped her hands like a schoolgirl sitting at her desk, then unclasped them.

"Miss Fairbanks," he said, brushing the crumbs from his hands and sitting back, trying not to lose himself in the deepening blue of her eyes as they reflected the candlelight, "we might as well get down to business. You need me, and I'm available."

* * *

She certainly did need him. And it was, indeed, business, though not the business proposition he would be expecting to hear.

As the string quartet finished one melody and started another, Julia hauled in a deep breath. "Mr. MacLean, I am prepared to offer you a generous sum for your assistance."

"Oh?" He picked up his water goblet.

"I am able to pay you three thousand dollars."

His hand stalled halfway to his mouth. "That's a lot of money for a bodyguard."

She leaned forward and lowered her voice. "I'm not proposing that you be my bodyguard," she said as he began to drink. "I'm ... proposing marriage."

He choked on the water, coughing so hard he nearly knocked the goblet over when he plunked it back down.

She winced at the pain his coughing would cause his ribs. "I'm sorry. I should have waited for you to finish drinking." She ignored the inquiring looks from guests at nearby tables. "Are your ribs all right?"

Grimacing between coughs, he pressed a hand to his back. "Forget my ribs. Did I hear you right? You want me to be your husband?"

"Yes, I do." She silently groaned at her inadvertent choice of words.

He coughed one last time and cleared his throat. "Miss Fairbanks, you already have a fiancé."

"Call me Julia, please." Under the circumstances, it seemed only right that she let him use her given name.

"Talk to me, … Julia."

"I had a fiancé. The telegram I received was from Phillip. He broke his leg and can't travel." Before dressing for dinner, she'd sent him a telegram in care of the hospital in Denver, inquiring after him and offering to pay his medical costs and travel expenses. It was the least she could do.

Alex shook his head. "So instead of waiting until he can travel, you're throwing him over for me, a man you met only a few hours ago?" He sat back and folded his arms across his chest. "What's going on, Julia?"

"It's not something I like to talk about."

"You can't propose marriage to a man without explaining the circumstances."

"You're right, of course." She looked toward the lanterns of the boats bobbing gently at anchor in the bay. They calmed her, and she chose her words carefully. "I am trying to save my inheritance, my employees, and myself from an uncertain fate. When my father died suddenly last year, he left a will that stipulated I must marry within six months of his death or lose the hotel. The deadline is midnight Saturday,

ANN COLLINS

just over fifty-two hours from now. If I don't make it, the Hotel Grand Victoria will be sold to the highest bidder. The money will go into a trust fund for any eventual male offspring I may produce. My father wanted a son, you see, a male heir to run the hotel in his place. He failed. A grandson was his next hope."

"I think I'm glad I didn't meet your father." He pushed his knife further away. "Did your father's will also stipulate who would manage the hotel until your son came of age?"

"No." She allowed herself a tiny smile. "He would be extremely aggravated if he knew I put myself in charge."

"Your father was a fool. From what I've seen in the last few hours, you are perfectly capable of running this hotel on your own. You shouldn't have to marry."

Her heart beat faster at Alex's simply stated compliment, at his belief in her. He was different from most men, who thought women were only good for homemaking, intimate relations, and childrearing.

"Thank you for saying that, Mr.—"

"Alex," he broke in.

She nodded. "Alex. Your opinion, however, does not solve my problem. I need a husband."

He rubbed the back of his neck. "Under normal circumstances, I might be flattered by your proposal, but I have a feeling you're not being terribly picky at the moment."

Heat flowed into her face. "It was either you or a convicted murderer sentenced to hang."

"You really are scraping the bottom of the barrel," he said, a note of sarcasm in his voice.

Julia couldn't blame him for it.

He pointed to his scar. "This wouldn't bother you?"

"How you look makes no difference to me." He was, in fact, a good-looking man. She didn't mind the scar.

He tapped his fingers on the tablecloth. "Was your marriage to Williamson a business arrangement?"

"Yes. He agreed to do it for the three thousand dollars I mentioned before. He also agreed to several conditions. I have some stipulations of my own."

"I thought you might, although you're not really in a position to make demands," he said, diminishing her hopes of getting what she wanted. "Go ahead. Tell me."

Just then the waiter arrived with their dinner, two plates of perfectly roasted, juicy, pink prime rib, mashed potatoes, and string beans. Alex's stomach growled so loudly Julia felt a sense of relief. He wasn't likely to leave the table—and her—until he had eaten.

The waiter bowed to them and moved on.

Alex leaned down and inhaled the smells from his plate. He cut off a piece of meat and stuck his fork into it. "Feel free to keep talking while I eat."

Too nervous to swallow anything herself, she explained the rest of her proposition and the arrangements made with Phillip. "Tomorrow morning, in the presence of my lawyer, Phillip was going to sign a legal document stating that he would never seek any further financial remuneration from me. The ceremony is tomorrow evening, and upon its completion, Phillip was to receive his payment and leave the Hotel Grand Victoria for good. The same conditions would apply to you."

The forkful of mashed potatoes in his hand stopped in midair. "I'd have to leave?" When she nodded, he said, "But I just got here. I haven't even had a chance to explore the hotel yet."

She chewed on her thumbnail, hating to compromise. However, he was injured, and she had promised him a room until the doctor pronounced him fit. "In light of your injuries, perhaps we can come to an agreement on your departure date. But you can't stay too long. As I'm sure you can imagine, I cannot have my husband living nearby and working for me. What would people think?"

"What will they think if your newly wedded husband isn't around at all?"

"I can handle that."

"You have it all figured out, huh?" Alex shoveled in the mashed potatoes.

She blinked hard against a sudden surge of hot tears. "I've done my best in a situation I abhor. The will doesn't say that I have to produce any children, only that I have to marry. I have no intention of consummating my marriage. Intimate relations are not part of the arrangement."

He set down his fork. "You're not giving me much incentive. I would have liked to … know you better. I admit I'm very attracted to you." He shifted in his chair.

Julia tried to dismiss his statement. She had always attracted male attention. His was no different, she told herself, ignoring the flare of warmth inside her.

"Three thousand dollars should be plenty of

incentive," she said. "You came here in search of work." She glanced at the frayed cuffs of his shirt, then quickly focused on the goblet at his fingertips.

He picked it up and gulped down half the water.

Julia cringed. This was not going the way she had hoped. But how could a drifter not jump at an offer of three thousand dollars?

"I'm sorry," she said. "I'm in a bind, and the clock keeps ticking. I hope you'll give my offer serious consideration." Her legs began to shake, and she was glad they were concealed beneath her dress and the generous tablecloth. "For obvious reasons, I would appreciate an answer as quickly as possible."

"I will think about it." He kept eating, his eyes rarely moving away from her. Every so often he pursed his lips. She wished she knew what he was thinking. His expression told her nothing. At least he hadn't told her "no."

She picked up her fork and dipped it into the gravy-covered potatoes. She managed several bites while she tried to decide what more she could say or do to convince him. No shining revelations emerged.

When Alex finished his meal, she offered him the rest of hers. "I'm not hungry, and I would hate for it to go to waste."

"Pass it over."

She did, and he tucked into it as if he hadn't eaten anything yet. When he finished, he pushed her plate away and wiped his mouth with his napkin. "That was delicious. My compliments to the chef."

"I'll tell him when I see him later." She waited for Alex to say more, too afraid to ask him outright what she so needed to know.

He sighed. "Julia, money-wise, your offer is something not too many men would easily dismiss. However, money is not that important to me. Not anymore."

Her near-empty stomach seemed to drop to the floor. Oh, Lord, was he turning her down?

"I had money once," he continued. "Quite of bit of it for a while, but it was never enough for my wife. If I marry again, money will not enter into the equation."

She forced herself not to slump in her seat. Though she had wanted to learn more about Alex MacLean, Julia had not expected to hear it now, or that his marriage had not been as perfect as she assumed.

"Is there anything that you do want?" she asked in a last-ditch effort, trying not to sound as desperate as she felt. She held her breath.

He pulled his hands off the table, rolled his shoulders, and leaned from side-to-side, as if to ease the ache in his injured body, but also to give him time to formulate his response. Waiters flitted throughout the room, clearing plates and pouring coffee. While the string quartet took a break, conversations whirred. Boisterous laughter broke out at a table of eight.

"Miss Fairbanks," he said, "I think you should take a breath before you suffocate."

Her breath came out in a rush while heat flooded her cheeks. Despite her embarrassment, she felt a shiver of awareness dance over her flesh. She seriously doubted if, in the same situation, anyone else would have noticed she was holding her breath. Alex MacLean seemed much too observant where she was concerned.

"Better?" he asked.

She nodded, but as she waited to find out if there was any last hope for her, she felt as if she were suspended over a school of circling sharks.

"Julia, what I want is a marriage before God, a woman who loves me, and children. I admit that I'm a drifter, but I'm drifting toward the life I someday hope to have, a life with love and purpose and responsibilities. You and I want different things, and for that reason, I must decline your offer. I can't help you."

She sagged in her chair, feeling as if the hotel were sliding into the ocean, out of her reach. She had thought Alex might be the answer to her prayers, but prayers often went unanswered. She could not fault his decision, though. In fact, she admired his reasons for turning her down. He deserved the life he wanted. Oddly enough, Julia envied the woman he would one day marry, whomever she was.

"I'm sorry," he said.

She slowly scooted herself back up in her chair. "So am I, but I don't blame you. I was being selfish, thinking only of what I wanted. If you said vows with me, you wouldn't be free to marry the woman who's waiting for you somewhere out there." She waved her arm at the window, and a hollowness spread through her heart. She tried to convince herself it had nothing to do with Alex and everything to do with the rapidly growing prospect of losing her home.

"Not truly selfish." He shifted his goblet aside. "You're trying to look after the hotel and your employees. That's a heavy responsibility."

"For a woman?" she heard herself say, so accustomed to having her gender thrown at her whenever the subject of her hotel responsibilities came up.

"For a man or woman," he said calmly, disregarding her defensiveness.

She sighed. Alex MacLean was very different from other men, and nothing like her father.

"What will you do now?" he asked.

"I expect I will meet with a murderer destined to die on the gallows. He will have nothing to lose and a lot to gain if he has parents or siblings who could benefit from the money I offer. I can't give up until the deadline has passed."

Alex frowned, but Julia dismissed his expression when, over his shoulder, she glimpsed her maitre d' hurrying toward their table. She rose at his approach.

Alex stood, too, as a gentleman did, but with the sound of air sucked between his teeth. He put a hand to his side.

"Mademoiselle Fairbanks," Jacques said, out of breath, "your presence is needed in the lobby *tout de suite.*"

She grabbed her gloves. "What is it?"

"One of the chambermaids, a Madame Reynolds. She has evidently met with an accident."

Julia stepped away from the table, her heart pounding. "Is it serious?"

"I do not know."

"All right. I'm coming. Mr. MacLean, please stay here and enjoy dessert. Don't bother waiting for me. I won't be back."

"I'm coming with you."

She stepped in close to him and waited until he bent his head down to hers. Not wanting to be heard by the maitre d' or her guests, she whispered, "No, you no longer have anything to do with my problems. I am not hiring you as my bodyguard."

"I'm not asking to be paid." He brought his mouth close to her ear. "Julia, you need protection. I can't work as a carpenter right now, but I can earn my keep by watching after you, so get used to it."

She tried to ignore his moist breath tickling her ear. "You are not responsible for my safety."

"I think I am. I saved you once today. It would be irresponsible of me to let you walk into more danger. You take care of the maid. I'll take care of you."

His warm breath, deep voice, and bold intentions sent gooseflesh galloping across her body. She suppressed an urge to close her eyes, sway into him, and let him take care of her. She needed a good argument for refusing his protection. Once she wrestled herself back under control, her common sense prevailed. Someone was out to harm her, and having a bodyguard was the sensible thing to do.

"Come on then," she said. "We're wasting time."

Chapter Five

As Alex followed Julia through the Crown Room, he thought back over her unexpected proposition. It was crazy, but it had clarified for him what he wanted most—a loving wife and family. He found himself regretting that Julia could not be that woman.

She was kind and caring, considerate of others but also able to stand up to them when necessary. She had put her rat-faced desk clerk in his place without making a scene, and she had persuaded the insistent Alberta Hensley over to her way of thinking with barely a fuss. She had even persuaded him to see the doctor.

When he eventually moved on, Alex feared he would miss Julia. He might even regret declining her proposal, but agreeing to a marriage on her terms was out of the question. He wanted more from her than she was willing to give. Alex did worry, however, about her second choice. He knew firsthand how thoroughly a reputation can be savaged when anything to do with prison is involved. But she would do what she had to, and at least the man was safely behind bars, unable to take advantage of her or demand his conjugal rights.

They crossed the lobby toward a woman who looked like a snowman squeezed into a chambermaid's uniform. Above a ruddy face, curly wisps of reddish-brown hair stuck out wildly, her white maid's cap unable to contain them.

"Mrs. Reynolds," Julia said, "I was told there'd been an accident."

"Oh, Miss Fairbanks, I'm surely glad to see you." Huffing and puffing on each word, the chambermaid fanned herself with chapped, work-reddened hands.

Julia's gaze skimmed the woman from top to bottom. "Are you all right?"

"Only just. I nearly fell to my death, and that's no lie."

Alex frowned. If this accident had anything to do with the flowerpot incident, he wanted to know. He would do everything he could to keep Julia safe.

He stepped forward. "What do you mean, Mrs. Reynolds? What happened?"

For a moment, Julia looked as if he were intruding in her business, but then comprehension dawned. Though she glanced at the front entrance, she seemed to see beyond it to the attack this afternoon and the threat against her. Her hand trembled as she brought it up to her throat.

Mrs. Reynolds answered him. "On the service stairs at the other end of the hotel"—she pointed toward the Garden Patio—"when I were climbin' up to the fourth floor, my foot went crashing straight through one of them steps. Rotted it must be. I lost hold of my bucket, and my scrub brushes and soaps scattered every which way. Thank the Lord for that stairway rail. I grabbed it hard as could be and managed to save myself. If I'd been coming down those stairs, I'd have broke my neck for sure."

Alex opened his mouth to ask another question, but the woman heaved in a breath and went on. "Normally, I wouldn't have used them stairs at this time o' day, but this afternoon I left my favorite brush in the fourth-floor linen closet and wanted to get it back before one of the other girls got hold of it."

"Mrs. Reynolds," Alex said, "I'd like to see that step for myself. Are you up to showing me where it is?"

"Alex," Julia said, no longer trembling, "Mrs. Reynolds has obviously had a fright. I think she ought to sit down."

"I think she's made of strong stuff." He winked at the stout woman.

"But she could have been injured."

Mrs. Reynolds smiled, glancing between them like a spectator watching a match on the hotel's tennis ground. "I do come from sturdy stock, and I'm proud of it. I don't mind showing the gentleman, Miss Fairbanks. And you, of course."

Julia placed her hand on the chambermaid's arm. "Are you sure you're feeling well enough? I'd be happy to have Dr. Dolan look you over."

"I don't need no doctor, but I thank you for your concern." She patted the back of Julia's hand. "Besides, I need to gather up my cleaning supplies. I left a bit of a mess, though I doubt anyone'll be up there to see. That stairway's hardly ever used at night."

"Very well, then." She motioned for the chambermaid to lead the way. "We'll follow you."

Alex stayed close to Julia, swiveling his head in search of anyone who might be watching her or planning an imminent attack.

A few minutes later, after safely crossing the attractively lit central courtyard, landscaped with fragrant tropical plants, palm trees, and a decorative gazebo, they climbed to the third floor.

"Down this way," Mrs. Reynolds whispered as they passed guestroom doors.

Alex glanced over at Julia and saw the worry lining her forehead. Was she thinking about the step? Or had her mind returned to her marriage plight?

The chambermaid stopped and pointed up a narrow, half-hidden, dimly lit staircase leading to the fourth floor. "It's there, where you see my bucket."

Julia cautiously started up, but Alex grasped her hand and held her back. "Let me go first."

She looked as if she might argue with him, but then she closed her mouth, stepped aside, and let him pass.

On his way up, he dodged cleaning rags and an assortment of brushes.

Julia came right behind him. He heard the rustling of her dress and smelled the scent of orange blossoms. Alex wished she'd give him more space. His body was responding to her nearness, and he didn't need that kind of distraction, not when her life might be in danger.

He picked up the bucket and handed it to her. She set it down several steps lower, then closed the distance again. He crouched and examined the step, sorry he didn't think to bring a lantern for more light.

"Can you tell anything yet?" She leaned around him, so close their shoulders brushed.

He shifted away as nonchalantly as possible.

"Oh, my goodness. I can see for myself. The wood's almost completely broken through. How could a step rot so badly in a hotel barely ten years old?"

"I don't think it is rotted. It looks like the middle section may have been weak from the start and grown worse over time." He lowered his voice. "Mrs. Reynolds' weight is most likely the proverbial straw that broke the camel's back."

"Shush." She glanced at the woman gathering up her cleaning supplies. "Mrs. Reynolds, when you finish there, could you please ask the night maintenance man to cordon off this stairway and replace the step?"

"Yes, Miss Fairbanks. I'll be off in two shakes."

"Thank you."

Alex inspected where the wood had parted. The top edges were splinter sharp and uneven, except at the very end, which had him worried. Carefully, he ran his fingertips along that end. It was fairly smooth where it should've been jagged. A sticky, wet substance clung to his fingers.

"Have you found something?" She leaned over him. Loose strands of her hair brushed the back of his neck.

He struggled to concentrate on the step. "Yes, and it's not good." When he lifted his hand, white paint stained his fingers. "It's fresh."

A Matter of Marriage

"But that can't be right. I keep good track of the maintenance schedule—everything that's been done and everywhere the men have been working. These steps have not been painted recently."

He wiped the paint off on the step. "Move back a minute."

When she had done as he asked, he gripped one half of the board and hauled up hard on it, grimacing at the pain in his ribs. Nails squealed as they pulled free of the anchoring wood, but the section of step came up easier than it should have. Alex turned it in his hands and saw what he had been afraid of finding.

"Julia, this has been tampered with. The step was removed, almost sawn through from the underside, then nailed back down using the original holes." He turned the wood. "At this end, the wood was sawn through completely, no doubt by accident. The paint was used to disguise it."

She sat down with a thud. "Someone sabotaged the step."

Somewhere along the third-floor hallway, a woman giggled and a man laughed deeply. A door shut, muting their laughter.

Alex set the damaged board aside and sat down next to Julia, careful to keep their bodies from touching. "A job like this took time and nerve." As well as arrogance, he thought. "Do you use this stairway?"

Her face paled, giving him his answer.

"When would you have used it?"

She clasped her arms around her knees and hugged them to her. "In another hour or two, when I did my

89

last rounds of the day. At night, I walk through the main building. During the day, I also check on the departments set away from the hotel, such as the laundry and gardening shed." She swallowed visibly. "This was meant for me, wasn't it?"

He wished he could tell her otherwise, but hiding the truth from her would not keep her safe. "After what happened this afternoon, I think it's a logical conclusion. We can also conclude that the saboteur knows your routine, where you go and when you go there."

A visible tremor vibrated through her.

Alex started to put his arm around her, then thought better of it. "Did you report the flowerpot incident to Coronado's marshal?" The suitor who had never given up hope of a relationship with her, Alex recalled.

"No." She rubbed her arms, as if trying to warm herself. "I was distracted by my marriage problem, and I suppose I still didn't want to believe the danger was serious enough to alert Marshal Landis."

"Why haven't you asked him to marry you? If he was your suitor, like you said, he'd probably jump at the chance to help you out."

"I believe he would. He doesn't know about my predicament or that I have a wedding ceremony scheduled for tomorrow evening. If he had heard about either, he would have confronted me." Julia sighed. "Now he may be my best hope. There'd be no risk of scandal. He's a good and well-respected man. However, like you, Tom wants a real marriage. Unlike you, he doesn't approve of a woman running a business."

"You're a very persuasive woman, Julia. I expect you could bring him around to your way of thinking." Alex nearly gagged on his suggestion. Though he felt compelled to help her, marrying her off to another man irked him for some reason he refused to examine. "The marshal wouldn't want to see the hotel mismanaged by someone else. Coronado would suffer. No matter how he fits into your marriage situation, you need to let the marshal do his job. If whoever did this"—he aimed his thumb over his shoulder—"tries again and succeeds, you won't need a husband. Period."

Her eyes went bright with fear, and her body quaked beneath a violent shudder. This time, Alex could not keep himself from comforting her. He slipped his arm around her back and shoulders, never expecting her to accept what he was offering. She surprised him, though, leaning into his side and resting her head just below his shoulder.

She fit against him just right, and he held her a little tighter. He knew the moment wouldn't last, not once she gathered her courage and resolve again, but he liked holding her, liked having her depend on him. He worried for her even more. She was facing a clever, determined assailant who knew her schedule and had easy access to the hotel.

Alex believed it had to be one of her employees, someone Julia trusted. She was in terrible danger, but unless he could keep her locked behind a stout door, Alex feared he might not be able to protect her any better than he had his wife and son.

* * *

In her second-floor apartment, Julia waited with

Alex for Tom Landis, Coronado's marshal, to arrive. Unable to sit still, she paced the sitting room while Alex sat on the leather sofa, reading one of her father's dime novels. Each page crackled as he turned it. The sound both annoyed and reassured her. He was calm, the exact opposite of what she currently felt. Only when she had been seated beside him on the stairs, his arm pulling her into him, had she felt safe. His quiet, solid strength had seeped into her until she'd been able to stand on her own again, as she had always done. And would continue doing.

She did not want to depend on Alex, and yet, Julia knew that if he were not with her now, she'd be pinging off the walls or cowering in a corner. Someone definitely meant her harm. Had it not been for Mrs. Reynolds' chance trip upstairs, the worst might have happened. Now she needed the police to find and arrest whoever had sabotaged that stair. Until then, she would be vulnerable and worried just when she most needed to be strong and focused on the hotel and her marriage situation. After Alex's refusal, she needed a husband worse than ever.

Tom would certainly marry her before the deadline. And as head of the Coronado Police Department, all two members of it, he could keep her safe indefinitely. But he wanted children.

"What are you thinking?"

She jumped at the sound of Alex's voice, then scolded herself for being so jittery in the safety of her own apartment. "What?"

"I can see your mind working from here, debating about something. What is it?"

"For a man I barely know, you seem to know me quite well. I don't think I like that."

He shrugged. "If I knew you really well, I wouldn't have to ask the question that you haven't answered."

She lifted her chin. "If you must know, I'm giving your suggestion serious consideration."

"Which suggestion was that?"

"The one about marrying Tom. He's an upstanding citizen and keeper of the law. A marriage to him would not damage my reputation or that of the hotel's."

Alex threw the dime novel onto the coffee table. It slid to a stop next to the section of broken step. "Then I guess he's your best bet."

"Yes, but I'm worried about his ... expectations."

He rubbed his jaw without touching his scar. "You mean those 'intimate relations' you mentioned at dinner?"

"Yes. No." She told herself she wouldn't blush, but she couldn't stop it. "Sort of. I'm terrified of having children."

His eyebrows rose, but if he had planned to say anything, the loud knock at the door silenced him.

"That'll be Tom." Julia hurried to the door.

Alex rose, slowly and stiffly amidst the creak of leather.

She opened the door. "Tom, thank you for coming." He was nearly as tall as Alex. Though it was half past nine, he still wore his uniform. Not a crease marred the navy-blue fabric. Gold buttons and a seven-pointed gold star gleamed on his barrel-shaped chest. "I'm sorry to call you out this late."

"I don't mind." His usually stern mouth, most of it hidden by a full, sandy-colored mustache, softened. "It's good to see you, Julia. I've been wanting to come by. When you telephoned, I was glad to oblige. Any excuse to see you is a good one."

She blinked at him. An attempt on her life was a good excuse to see her? "Uh, come in, please."

Tom's penetrating blue eyes narrowed as soon as he spied Alex. However, he showed no reaction to Alex's scar other than a straightforward perusal.

"Who are you?" He slapped his gray cowboy hat against his left thigh.

"MacLean."

Julia hurried to make the introductions. "Tom, this is Alex MacLean, a … guest." He was not her employee yet, so she preferred the marshal view him as someone from a higher class. Tom would not have approved of her allowing a male employee into her apartment for anything other than maintenance tasks. "Alex, this is Marshal Landis."

He tipped his head. "Marshal."

Tom's gaze swung between her and Alex, his eyes still narrowed. Then he thrust out his hand and clasped Alex's hard enough, she observed, to squeeze the blood out of it. The marshal always liked people to know who was in charge.

Alex showed no outward sign of discomfort, and she started to worry for Tom's hand. Despite his size, he did not labor with his body the way Alex did.

"I've known Julia since she first came here back in eighty-seven," Tom said, his grip unchanging. "How do you know her?"

"We're more recent acquaintances."

She nodded in agreement, pleased by Alex's lack of specifics. Tom could take his response to mean they had known each other for months, or even years, rather than just a few hours.

"You have a good grip on you, MacLean."

"So have you, Marshal."

At an apparent stalemate, they released each other.

Relieved, she arranged herself on the overstuffed, upholstered chair at the head of the coffee table. Tom tossed his hat down beside the broken step and took the other sofa across from Alex. The men faced each other over the low table.

Tom turned to her. "So what's this nonsense about someone trying to kill you?"

Alex's hands clenched into fists atop his thighs. "Marshal," he said, before she could respond, "physical threats have been made against Julia. We expect you to take them seriously, not consider them 'nonsense.'"

She barely breathed even as tears pricked her eyes. No one on Coronado ever challenged Tom Landis. And no man, not even her father, had ever championed her like this. Alex had also included her in his statement, speaking as if they were together, of one mind.

Tom made no apology. "If there is a threat, I will give it the attention it's due. Julia, you were circumspect over the telephone. I need details. Tell me what happened."

"I'll let Alex explain, starting with the flowerpot that was thrown at me. He saw everything."

He described the incident, the unerring aim of whoever had thrown the flowerpot, and how he had grabbed her, rolling them both out of range.

A shiver crept up her spine, and Julia wrapped her arms around herself, unsure whether she was belatedly reacting to those frightening moments or remembering how it felt to be in Alex's arms, her body pressed to the length of his.

"But you never saw who threw it," Tom said.

"No," he answered. "I wish I had."

"Tom, Alex saved me from certain injury and possible death. The threat is serious."

The marshal pulled at his mustache. "What about this?" He leaned forward and touched the broken board.

She motioned for Alex to explain his findings. The marshal would take his opinion more seriously than hers.

"That came from an upper-floor service staircase Julia routinely uses at night. The stair, as you can see, was tampered with. The step gave way under the foot of a chambermaid, who fortunately wasn't injured."

Tom examined the freshly sawn and painted wood, then dropped the piece back on the table. "Julia, when are you going to give up this insanity of managing the Hotel Grand Victoria? It's not a job for a lady like you. And now it has become dangerous. You—"

She raised her hands, palms outward, to stop him, then remembered how much she needed him. "You may be right, Tom,"—she saw Alex purse his lips— "but you know how much I love the hotel. It's my home. I can't let just anybody take charge of it. Surely you can understand how I feel."

He squinted at her, and his mustache shifted from side to side as his mouth worked beneath it. "Well, I suppose. It is the only home you've known here."

Alex abruptly sat forward. "You can keep the damaged step as evidence, Marshal."

"I don't see a need for that. I know where to find it if necessary."

"Then how about you make a list of suspects."

Tom laughed. "That'd be a long list. Every man who works here, and a few who don't, would be on it."

Julia did not appreciate his laughter, but she forgave him. He was her best hope for an instant and upstanding husband.

A taut stillness came over Alex. "That would put you on the list, too, wouldn't it, Marshal?"

Julia cringed. What was Alex doing?

Tom grabbed his hat, jammed it onto his head, and stood up. "You saying I'd do harm to Julia?"

Alex slowly pushed to his feet. "You obviously don't want her running the hotel anymore than Chalmers, the desk clerk, does, and he's our prime suspect."

"I would never hurt Julia, or force her to do something she didn't want to do. She means a great deal to me, as she well knows." He turned to her. "Julia, if you'd just marry me the way I asked you to last Christmas, all your problems would be solved. No one would dare hurt my wife."

On shaking legs, she rose from her chair and swallowed hard. It was now or never. "Tom, I would—"

97

"She's already spoken for, Marshal." Alex strode to her side and linked his hand in hers.

Afraid she might be dreaming, she said and did nothing except school her face into an expression that kept her emotions to herself.

Tom's nostrils flared.

"Tomorrow," Alex added, "Julia will become Mrs. Alexander MacLean."

"The hell she will!" Tom thundered. "I don't believe it. I've heard nothing about this, and I would have heard." He thrust his index finger at Alex. "I've got half a mind to put you in jail for lying."

"Tom, you will not arrest"—she tasted the next two words on her tongue, liked how they tasted and spoke them—"my fiancé." An amazing sense of peace flowed into her, calming the turmoil that had been her life since the day Mr. Byrnes read her father's will to her.

"Julia, you can't be serious," Tom said.

"It's true, Tom. The ceremony is tomorrow evening."

Alex squeezed her hand. "You're invited, if you can be civil."

Tom sputtered, looking as if he were about to suffer a fit of apoplexy.

Alex went on. "Once Julia and I are wed, she will continue operating the Hotel Grand Victoria. I have no intention of interfering in her work unless her safety is at risk. From you, Marshal, we want your help in discovering the identity of whoever wants her dead."

Reminded of the danger, she shifted closer to him. She needed Alex's strength, and she wanted to believe that her future and the hotel's were no longer in question.

Tom's gaze whipped from their joined hands to their faces. "Something's not right here. How long have you and he been courting?"

"My wedding has been planned for some time," she said. Thankfully, only the Dolans and her lawyer had known the name of her husband-to-be. If Tom knew she was going to marry a stranger, he might put *her* in jail just to stop the proceedings.

"*Our* wedding," Alex added.

Tom's gaze darted between them. "I'm not convinced. Julia, with your father gone, somebody has to watch over you. Someone like me. And what I'm seeing is you promising yourself to a man you introduced to me not twenty minutes ago as a guest, but who looks like he can't afford a new shirt let alone a room here. What's the story?"

She lifted her chin a notch and gripped Alex's hand tighter. "I appreciate your concern for my well-being, Tom, but I don't have to explain my choice of husband to you."

"Marshal," Alex said, his eyes narrowed, "we'll show you out now. You'll want to get started on your investigation." He pulled her with him toward the door and opened it wide.

Scowling and grumbling, Tom stomped past them into the hall, then twisted around. "I'll start my investigation all right. With you, MacLean. Then we will see what's what."

Chapter Six

Alex shut the door behind the marshal, restraining himself from slamming it. "Overbearing ass. Give a man a badge and he thinks he can step on whomever he likes. If he spends all his time investigating me, he'll end up compromising your safety." He might even find what Alex had spent the last three and a half years trying to put behind him.

"Did you really mean it?" Julia asked softly.

"Mean what?"

"That you'll marry me."

"I wouldn't have said it if I didn't mean it, and I think you know that. Your search is over."

"But what about your dream of children and a wife who loves you?"

"I haven't given up on any dreams. I won't be abandoning you after the ceremony." He glanced at their linked hands and felt a kind of bond he had never shared with his wife. "We barely know each other, but I think we have a good chance together. Certainly better than what you would have had with him." Alex tilted his head toward the door. He avoided telling her how his heart had taken flight when she claimed him as her fiancé.

She tugged her hand free of his. Acting skittish all of a sudden, she opened the distance between them. Her behavior didn't bode well for their wedding night, or even the ceremonial kiss that would start their marriage off right, showing everyone in attendance that their vows were real. Alex could hardly wait to share a kiss with her, one befitting a bride and groom.

"Have you changed your mind?" He held his breath.

She plopped herself into the upholstered chair. "No."

He breathed again, more relieved than he expected. He truly wanted this marriage. In this storybook castle of turrets and towers, happily-ever-after seemed possible. Alex remembered the strange sense of belonging he'd felt upon his first sight of the hotel, and then again when Julia saw his scar and didn't flinch or turn away. Perhaps they had been fated to meet at the very moment when she needed him.

"But, Alex," she continued, "we are virtual strangers. With Tom, at least I knew what I was getting."

"Which is exactly why you didn't deny my claim to your hand."

She slumped deeper in the chair. "You're very sure of yourself."

"Am I wrong?"

"No."

"Julia, if we have a chance at a happy future

together, then we need to do everything we can to make our marriage work. If, however, after a suitable time has passed we discover we are not a good match, I'll go, leaving you with my name."

Her posture straightened. "Really?"

"You don't have to look so hopeful."

"Sorry, but it is what I've wanted from the first."

"Yes, well, we'll see how long that lasts." Alex looked forward to the challenge of wooing her.

"What about the money?" she asked.

"I won't accept anything I haven't earned as a carpenter. I won't be paid for being a husband and protector." He stepped up next to her chair. "So, are we going to do this?"

"We need to talk about children."

"Okay." Taking care with his ribs, he eased himself onto one of the sofas. "You said you're terrified of having them. I think most women are afraid of childbirth, but medicine has come a long way in recent years. Doctor Dolan should be able to appease your fears. Have you talked to him?"

She shook her head. "Childbirth is not what worries me most."

"If you're afraid you won't be a good mother, then I think I can quell those fears. From everything I've seen today, you're a compassionate, caring woman who can also maintain discipline. I believe you'll make a wonderful mother when the time comes."

Her breath came out on a shudder. The lamplight glistened on the moisture in her eyes. "Thank you for your belief in me. When I was a little girl, I dreamed of having babies of my own. Of course, in my dreams, they were going to be my playmates. I didn't have any brothers or sisters."

He nearly smiled at her revelation, but an expression of loss moved into her face.

"That was before I knew about the trials of childbearing." She scraped a fingernail over the chair's padded leather arm. "My parents and I lived in Philadelphia, where my father owned a small but successful hotel and tried to father a son. I was born, but apparently there were complications. I arrived three weeks early and was very small. Father said it was because I was too eager to enter this world. He said I lived because I had a stubborn streak as deep as the ocean."

Alex chuckled. "No one can dispute your iron will."

"I admit that I can be very determined, which I believe I got from my mother. She did everything she could to try and give Father the son he wanted, but she miscarried over and over." Julia dropped her gaze to the coffee table. "Each one of those tiny lives lost tore out a piece of her heart. After each loss, Mama suffered terribly from melancholia. My father ignored the problem while I sat beside her in bed, trying to be cheerful and make her feel better." A tear trickled down Julia's cheek.

Alex stifled the urge to wipe it away. "I'm sorry. That must've been very hard on you."

More tears leaked from her eyes. She did not look at him. "Even after Father sold the hotel and moved us to California, Mama kept trying. The worst came when I was seventeen." She dropped her voice to a whisper.

"My baby sister was born, and she was perfect, but she wasn't the boy Father had wanted. Mama hated to disappoint him yet again, but she was thrilled to finally have another child. She had gone against doctor's orders to get pregnant again. Not long after my sister's birth, Mama died of blood loss." She sniffed, pressing the heels of her hands to her face.

Alex wanted to reach out to her, gather her into his arms, but she seemed at home suffering by herself. He feared she wouldn't want his comfort, and saying he was sorry didn't seem enough.

"I felt like a ship that had been wrecked. It was horrible, but I had Lily. I named her for my mother, Lillian. Father hired a wet nurse, and I helped with Lily's care. She was the sweetest thing, so innocent, beautiful, and helpless. When she was two months old and sleeping in her cradle, I went to check on her. She … wasn't breathing," Julia said raggedly.

Alex flinched.

"I screamed and screamed. The doctor said it happened sometimes, babies dying for no apparent reason." She finally met his gaze. "Alex, I don't want to have children. I can't feel that kind of pain again. You don't know what it was like."

He knew exactly what it felt like. He considered telling her about Danny, his wonderful little boy, but even after more than three years, his wounds were too raw to bring out of hiding. Perhaps if he had been allowed to attend the funeral services, his sense of loss would not be so acute when his memories of Danny surfaced unexpectedly. He told himself he needed to move forward, not back. If he didn't think about

Danny, he was all right. He wanted children—boys to wrestle with and girls to show off, all of them racing each other to greet him on his return home from work. A family would complete him. He could not, however, disregard Julia's fears.

"We've both suffered losses," he said, his voice low. "I don't have any family left either. My parents are buried back in Maryland, in the little town where I was born. They've been gone a good while now."

He missed them, though. Even worse, Alex felt as if he had let them down. He had been born late in their married life, and they had spent the rest of that life working until their backs were bent and their joints stiff, scrimping on everything to see that he got the education they wanted for him, the education he had wanted as well.

He fiddled with a loose button on his suit jacket, thankful his parents hadn't lived long enough to witness his downfall and suffer the loss of their only grandchild.

"What were your parents like?" Her tears had stopped flowing. "I'd like to know about them."

"They were good people, and they had a good marriage. My father was a carpenter. He taught me everything he knew, but he always believed I could do more. As a child, I'd made structures out of wooden blocks and drawn pictures of houses and buildings on whatever scraps of paper I could find. The wall in my bedroom worked well, too, until my mother caught me at it one day."

A fleeting smile lifted the corners of Julia's mouth. Alex had to force himself to look at her eyes instead, which did nothing to lessen his attraction to her. Her eyes mesmerized him.

"No wonder you've shown such interest in the hotel's architecture," she said. "It's a shame you didn't become an architect."

"I did become one." He shrugged at the surprise in her face. "I went to school in Baltimore and ended up staying. I worked there for a number of years, met Elizabeth Ellingson—the woman who became my wife, and then ... lost everything, including my ability to design. That's when I took to the road."

"I'm sorry," she said softly. "Was she ill?"

He stared at the table, trying not to see the flames again. "No, she was ... trapped in a fire."

Julia clapped a hand to her mouth, but it didn't cover her gasp. "Your poor wife! Now I understand why you became a drifter. Losing her like that must've been devastating."

Julia didn't understand the half of it, but he wasn't ready to tell her the rest. "I've been tired of drifting for a while now. I want a home. A place where I belong."

"And you want a family." She sighed, a touch of resignation in the sound. "Every man wants a son. My father never gave up in his quest for one. After my mother died, he remarried to try again."

"I would be honored to have a son or a daughter, but not against your wishes or at the expense of your life. I'm not like your father."

She stared at him and said nothing for a moment, as though she were unable to speak. "Thank you," she whispered.

"Julia, there are ways to avoid conceiving a child."

"Yes. We can abstain from intimate relations."

He swallowed a laugh. "I wasn't thinking of that one. I'm not a priest."

She chewed on her lower lip. It was full and pink and … Alex tore his gaze away before he could reach out and touch the fullness of that lip.

"I suppose celibacy would be asking a lot," she said, avoiding his gaze. "Alex, I give you my word that I will do my marital duty, but just so there is no confusion, I wish to keep separate bedrooms."

Marital duty? She sounded as though lovemaking was something to endure, not enjoy. Julia Fairbanks had a lot to learn, and Alex thanked heaven he would be the one to teach her, starting on their wedding night. She could have her separate bedroom, but he doubted she'd keep it once he initiated her into the pleasures of "intimate relations." Just remembering her fascination with his bare chest in the doctor's office made him wish he wouldn't have to leave her tonight. Tomorrow night suddenly seemed a long way off.

"Julia, I will let you in on a secret. Intimate marital relations can be very enjoyable for both partners."

Clearly skeptical, she frowned, two vertical creases appearing above her nose.

He raised his right hand. "It's true, and I'll make a promise to you. In my arms, you will experience the ultimate satisfaction and enjoyment."

Her cheeks flushed. "I suppose we will see about that." She sounded as if she had laid down a challenge.

"Yes, we will." Alex could hardly wait to meet that challenge. He nearly smiled. "What time is the ceremony?"

"Six tomorrow evening. Here."

"In this apartment?"

She nodded. Her hands roved over her skirt, rearranging the satin folds. "For such a small affair, this room is as good as any."

"Julia, a private ceremony is one thing, hiding is another. I won't marry you in here."

"But I want to hide. I'm ashamed and embarrassed about this entire situation. I don't want the world"—she motioned toward the door—"to witness my humiliation."

"I would rather not be called your 'humiliation,' but I understand these circumstances were forced on you. It's only natural you'd rather not celebrate them." He scooted to the edge of the sofa. "However, a private wedding will raise questions. If we skulk around and marry on the sly, people are going to think you're with child."

She groaned. "I can't have people thinking that. I'd lose all the respect I spent the last six months struggling to earn."

"Then tomorrow you show the world a woman who is getting what she wants. Though I'd like to imagine I am what you want, I know—for now—it's the hotel. Your guests and employees will see a happy bride, just as they would expect. No one will be the wiser."

"Except for the Dolans. I told them the truth today, when I received the telegram from Phillip."

"I would bet your secret is safe with them. After more than three years on the road, I've become a good judge of character, and I trust them."

She nodded. "They are like family to me. I trust

them implicitly."

"Maybe they can help with the wedding arrangements. The gazebo we passed in the Garden Patio will be the perfect place for the ceremony."

Her pretty mouth tightened. "That's too public. Anyone could watch."

"Exactly. You'll be introducing me at one fell swoop, and your attacker will find out you're no longer alone. Anyone bent on hurting you will have to go through me."

She clasped her fingers so tightly they turned white. "You think the saboteur will try again?"

"I think we'd be foolish to drop our guard. Tomorrow morning, while the marshal is twiddling his thumbs trying to find out about me, I'll start my own investigation. I'll also spread the word about the ceremony. I expect you to do the same. Despite your shame and embarrassment, this wedding is going to be real."

She stood abruptly and swished her skirts past the chair. "Tomorrow is going to be a busy and difficult day. I believe I'll skip my rounds tonight and go to bed."

"Good idea. Skip your rounds tomorrow morning, too, unless I'm with you. Let's keep your assailant guessing."

"All right. No rounds." She started for the door. "I don't want to do anything foolish."

Alex took the hint and followed her. He walked slowly, though, thinking. For a woman who didn't want to do anything foolish, she was planning to commit herself to the height of foolishness—marrying a man she barely knew. "Julia, are you absolutely sure you want to go through with this?"

She stumbled, righted herself, and faced him. "You're not having second thoughts, are you?"

"No," he said quickly, his answer removing the panic from her eyes. "I like you, and I want to marry again. Awhile back, I even proposed to a woman up in Oregon, but she practically shuddered at the thought of seeing this"—he touched his scar—"every morning and night."

Julia studied his scar and shrugged, showing no revulsion at all.

Alex felt his heart clutch, then beat faster at the promise of happiness in front of him.

"Sometimes I wished I were ugly," she said. "Then I wouldn't attract so much attention. I'd rather be admired for what I do, not how I look."

"If those people knew you, they'd realize the beauty that captured their interest is nothing compared to the beauty inside you."

Her mouth opened slightly, and she licked her lips. Alex vaguely heard a clock ticking somewhere nearby. She swallowed, the movement tempting him to trail his fingers along the curve of her neck and beneath her ear. He imagined twining one of her decorative curls around his finger. And when her desire matched his own, when she leaned into him, he would kiss her. Their lips would—

She unlocked the door with a loud click.

He blinked, bringing himself back to reality. Disappointment nagged at him, and he comforted himself with thoughts of the wedding. He supposed he could wait until then for their first kiss.

Standing stiffly, all business now, she said, "Tomorrow morning, at eleven, my lawyer is bringing the marriage contract to my office."

"Do we need that?"

"I do. You're still a stranger, Alex, and I will do whatever I must to protect the hotel. You said money isn't important to you. Therefore, you won't mind signing away your rights, as my husband, to the hotel. I wish to remain the sole owner."

"That's fine with me. I don't want what's yours. I'll meet you at eleven. Will you arrange to have the gazebo area set up for us?"

"Yes. And I'll speak to Reverend Spencer about … the kiss. I know it's becoming more common to include a kiss in wedding ceremonies, but I wish to leave it out."

Alex felt like a boy who'd just had his lollipop stolen. "Wait a second. I was looking forward to that part."

"I'm sorry to disappoint you, but that gazebo will be a stage. Any kiss we share would be an act solely for the benefit of our audience, and I'm not an actress. They would know something wasn't right between us."

"If you say so." So much for starting their marriage off right.

"I do say so." She placed her hand on the knob and turned it. "I can't take any chances on something going wrong. The deadline is too close." She opened the door.

"Everything will work out. You'll see." He stepped

into the hallway. "Good night, Julia. Lock the door and don't let anyone lure you out. I'll see you tomorrow."

As he walked away, he heard the click of the lock and felt some sense of relief. She was safe for now. But as he headed toward his room, Alex remembered the danger Alberta Hensley posed. If she remembered him, she could dash his dreams of a future with purpose and love. Worse yet, she could ruin Julia's chance to keep the Hotel Grand Victoria.

* * *

Friday morning, Julia closeted herself with an account book in her small, paneled office beside the registration desk. The same disconcerting thoughts that had kept her awake most of the night continued spinning through her head. Alex had, once again, stepped in just when she needed him most.

He had rescued her from what she knew would have been a miserable marriage with Tom Landis. There was a price to pay, though. Alex intended to stay and try to make something real out of their arrangement. He intended to make love to her. Could his claim be true—that intimacy between a husband and wife could be enjoyable? Harriet, her stepmother, had described it as a duty that had to be "endured on a regular basis." Plenty of guests, however, especially the couples staying in the two Bridal Chambers, seemed to look forward to checking into their rooms and not coming out for hours on end.

Julia decided to reserve judgment on Alex's claim. At least he hadn't dismissed her feelings about childbirth and losing a child. When he mentioned how his wife had died, the sorrow in his eyes had touched a deep chord in her heart. They had both, indeed, suffered.

She gave her head a shake. With so much on her mind, it was a wonder she had slept at all.

Leaning forward, she forced herself to concentrate on the account book in front of her, but when she added up the latest food and beverage expenses for the fourth time, she derived yet a fourth answer.

She threw down her pencil, leaned her elbows on the hand-carved oak desk, and propped her head in her hands. Why was she even bothering today of all days—her wedding day?

Once again, her thoughts returned to Alex. Last night, they had begun getting acquainted. Learning about his past had intrigued her. His parents must have been special people, and he had obviously been close to them.

She smiled, imagining a very young Alex caught in the act of drawing on the wall by his mother. Her smile faded though when she recalled that he had lost his ability to create, which he had seemed born to do. Perhaps his marrying her and living a stable life at the hotel would put his past trials behind him, even allowing him to design again.

A knock at the door nearly sent her skyward. She thought first of Alex, then of her assailant, and then of her lawyer and his reason for coming. Her heart beat too fast. Maybe tomorrow, after today and tonight were done with, she would be her unruffled self again.

"Who is it?" she managed to call.

"Alex."

Her heart continued to pound, and she tried to calm herself with a deep breath. It didn't help. "Come in."

The door opened, and he entered wearing a clean work shirt and a pair of brown canvas trousers that had a few less patches than the pair he had worn on his arrival yesterday.

Julia tried another deep breath, but the air barely filled her lungs as thoughts of her imminent future flooded her head. Alex would be moving into her apartment tonight.

"Morning," he said. "I thought I'd check in with you before the lawyer arrives."

"I'm glad you did." She glanced at the wall clock her father had brought from Philadelphia. It read quarter to eleven. Mr. Byrnes would arrive soon, and she would be relieved to get the paperwork out of the way.

Alex eased himself onto the chair across from her, his lips pressed into a thin line as he moved.

She winced in sympathy. "I'm sorry. You're in even worse pain today than yesterday, aren't you?"

"I'm stiff, but that's to be expected." He shrugged. "I'll feel better as the day goes on."

"You shouldn't have pulled up that step."

Another shrug. "Probably not, but we needed to see the underside to know what we were dealing with. I told Theo about it this morning. He hasn't come up with any new suspects."

"I wish we had a longer list of specific names to investigate." She picked up her pencil and tapped it against the open account book. "Having grown up in hotels, I thought I was a good judge of character, but—"

"You are. You're marrying me."

She huffed at his attempt at humor, except that his expression was serious. Was he teasing her? "As I was about to say, apparently I am not a good judge of character because I have no idea who hates me so much he wants to harm me."

"Well, you know it's not me."

"If only it were you," she said, ignoring the lift of his eyebrows. "I would rather entertain the notion that a stranger was responsible for the attacks instead of someone I know and thought I could trust. To be honest, anyone, except you, could have been on that balcony."

He slanted a questioning look at her. "Are you saying we shouldn't have trusted Theo with so much information or asked for his help? He wasn't with you at the hotel's entrance, and he arrived at the scene shortly thereafter."

She carefully set the pencil aside and shook her head, unable to imagine Theo as her assailant. "No. I misspoke. Not just anyone could have thrown that flowerpot with such force or sawn through that step. Theodore Mulligan is strong for his age, but he is not a suspect. I have known him since the hotel opened, and he is as close to a grandfather as I have ever had. He has never shown me any disrespect, either before or after I took charge of the hotel. He's smart, efficient, and has a wonderful memory for the guests' names and room numbers. Best of all, he always wears a smile."

"I admire your loyalty to him and agree that he is

an unlikely suspect." A twinkle shone from Alex's eyes. "You see, Julia, we already agree on something. I have a hunch we're going to get along very well."

She crossed her arms. "We'll see." She would concede nothing until she knew him much better. "Shall we continue discussing our limited list of named suspects?"

"It hasn't changed." He shifted in the chair, as though trying to find a more comfortable position for his ribs. "Theo took me up to the room where the flowerpot came from. I didn't find any clues."

She closed the account book. "The culprit could be anyone who's been watching me closely enough to know where I might be at a given time."

"I believe so. Until he, or she, is caught, I suggest you vary your schedule and routes around the hotel."

"I will do that," she said, though she wished she didn't have to change anything, including her marital status. Though Alex seemed like the answer to her prayers, they'd met less than twenty-four hours ago. She hoped she would not live to regret her choice. And what if Alex regretted his choice? As far as she could tell, she was the one who would benefit most from their arrangement. She shoved her worries aside, reminding herself *one thing at a time*. "Have you been telling people about the wedding?"

"Just Theo. He said, 'Leave it to me,' and went straight to the biggest gossips on your payroll. Ten minutes ago, he informed me our news has spread faster than bees pollinating flowers. It's the hot topic in the housekeeping department, laundry, kitchen, engine house, dining room, and maintenance and gardening sheds. When I passed the registration desk, Chalmers even congratulated me, though his sincerity was questionable."

"It would be." Resigned to her fate, she moved her account book to one side of her desk, making room for the paperwork Mr. Byrnes would be bringing for their signatures. This evening, she would be saying her vows in front of countless members of her staff and whichever guests heard about the show taking place in the Garden Patio.

At least there would be no kiss for them to gawk at. Thank goodness she had made that clear to Alex last night, when she had very nearly lost herself and her resolve in his gaze and words. With genuine feeling, he'd spoken of the beauty inside her instead of what most people saw when they looked at her. He had wanted to kiss her. She was not so inexperienced that she didn't recognize when a man desired her. Fortunately, she had taken charge at the critical moment, sending Alex on his way. The moment she closed the door, however, she had felt a sense of regret, as though she might have missed something special.

Julia massaged her temples. Once again, too many thoughts swirled and pulled at her like a dangerous undertow in the sea. Her head ached. What was happening to her? She no longer knew what to think or how to feel.

"Have you started the ball rolling for our big event?" Alex asked.

"Yes. Reverend Spencer will be here at the appointed time, and lights will be draped around the inside of the gazebo. Other than that, I'm keeping everything simple, with a minimum of fuss and fanfare."

"All right. That's better than no fuss at all, hidden away in your apartment."

At a knock on the door, she rose. "That will be Jonathan Byrnes. He used to be my father's lawyer. Now he's mine." As she walked to the door, her light green dress rustled with each step.

Alex got up, too, though with a grimace. He rubbed one side of his ribcage. Julia felt terrible. He was suffering because of what he'd done for her, and tonight he was going to save the hotel and her. She owed him more than she could ever repay.

She let the lawyer in. "Mr. Byrnes, thank you for coming."

"I'm glad to be here." He removed his hat, hooked it on the rack, and smoothed his hand over the limited amount of hair he still had. "And I'm very glad your fiancé finally arrived. I was getting worried you might not make the deadline."

"So was I, but"—she motioned to Alex—"this is—"

"Mr. Williamson," the lawyer inserted, his smile stiffening as he took in the sight of Alex's face. Nevertheless, he stuck out his hand. "I'm pleased to meet you, and very happy you could help Julia out of her difficult situation. You will be amply rewarded."

"I expect I will," Alex said, shaking his hand. A corner of his mouth quirked upward.

Julia tried to ignore the kind of repayment she assumed was on his mind. "Mr. Byrnes, Phillip

Williamson met with an accident and couldn't be here. You will need to remove his name from the contract and replace it with that of Alex MacLean."

"Alexander Devlin MacLean," he said. "That's what I use on legal documents."

The lawyer pushed his spectacles higher. "Well, I suppose unforeseen setbacks do happen in these kinds of situations. I'm just relieved the deadline will be met. Shall we proceed?"

"Please." She motioned for him to take her chair behind the desk. Once the contract was signed, she would move one step closer to legally owning the Hotel Grand Victoria. Her home would never suffer from neglect, and her employees would not lose their positions.

After unbuttoning his gray frock coat, Mr. Byrnes sat down, withdrew a set of papers from his leather portfolio, and laid them on the blotter. Next he brought out a shiny gold fountain pen. "I'll just strike out Mr. Williamson's name and replace it with Mr. MacLean's."

Standing next to her desk, she eyed his careful penmanship. Alex stood beside her, so tall she felt as if the room had grown smaller. If not for the little window that looked out onto the Garden Patio, she might've been inclined to claustrophobia.

"There we go. If you'll both initial the change on each copy and sign at the bottom on the second page, we'll be done." He held the pen out to her.

She didn't take it. "Several more changes must be made as well."

"Oh?"

Alex shifted closer to the desk and to her, making her mouth go dry. He spoke to the lawyer. "The terms Mr. Williamson agreed to are different from what Julia and I have settled on." He outlined the new terms that specified he would be staying, giving their marriage every chance to succeed. The clause pertaining to her ownership of the hotel would not change.

Mr. Byrnes' eyes blinked owlishly behind his spectacles. The lawyer peered up at her with a troubled expression. "Julia, are you sure this is what you want?"

She almost laughed. Of course it wasn't, but what choice did she have? People were depending on her, and she loved the hotel. "Yes. I'm going to marry Alex."

"As you wish. I'll make the appropriate changes."

After more strikeouts, additions, and initialing, he presented them with two copies of the final contract.

Alex signed first, his signature bearing a creative flourish.

She signed next. Though her hand shook and the ink smeared slightly, Julia was relieved to get it done and move forward. After handing the pen to Mr. Byrnes, she pulled a velvet pouch from her skirt pocket. "Here." She gave it to Alex. "You're going to need this."

"What is it?"

"My wedding ring."

"Oh." He poured it into his palm. A small diamond set in gold winked up at them both. "Nice. Simple, but elegant. It suits you."

"Thank you. I'll be wearing that ring for a long

time, so I thought it should be something I liked."

"I don't suppose you got one for me, too."

She opened her mouth, but a moment passed before any sound came out. "No. Do you … want a ring?"

"Nah. I rarely wore the one Elizabeth gave me. When I worked with my drafting tools or the tools and materials on a building site, it always seemed in the way. It's gone now."

She relaxed. Running to one of San Diego's jewelry stores at the last minute was not on her agenda for the day. She did wonder about Alex's first wife, though. How had Elizabeth felt about his not wearing the ring she had given him?

He put her ring back inside its pouch and pushed it into his pants pocket. "So I guess that leaves us with the ceremony."

Mr. Byrnes slid his copy of the contract into his portfolio. "You've already procured the marriage license then. That's good."

She gasped. "Marriage license! Oh, no! I completely forgot." She had been so worried about finding a replacement for Phillip, she'd forgotten about the license.

Alex laid his hand on her shoulder. "Take it easy. Everything will be all right."

She spun away from him, and his hand dropped to his side. "No, it won't," she said, dismissing the expression his eyes, first of hurt, then of nothing, as though he had drawn a curtain in front of his feelings. She avoided thinking about the woman in Oregon who had rejected him so cruelly. "Things are already going wrong. We have to go to San Diego for it, and today is

Friday. The County Clerk's office is always busy. If we don't get in today, there's no hope. They're closed on Saturdays."

Mr. Byrnes looked between them, pinching his bottom lip together. "Julia, I agree that Fridays are notoriously busy in the clerk's office, but you have time. All is not lost. Not yet."

She felt like screaming. Why did this have to be so difficult?

Her lawyer stood up and looked between them again. "Well, don't just stand there. If you don't get going, there will be no wedding."

Chapter Seven

Eight minutes. Eight minutes until she would be late for her own wedding. While the sun neared the horizon and Mary and Kate Dolan bustled around her bedroom, Julia stood in front of the full-length mirror and tried to position her small bridal hat on her head, but she couldn't get it right. Her hands trembled so badly the pin slipped in her perspiring fingers.

Her nerves were beyond frazzled. Though the marriage license had been safely procured, the County Clerk's office had been worse than a Saturday night in August on the Grand Ballroom's dance floor. Then the ferry had been delayed due to engine trouble. On top of that, Alex had barely spoken to her the entire time.

She realized now that she owed him an apology. In her office with Mr. Byrnes, Alex had attempted to soothe her worries by placing his hand on her shoulder, but she had essentially snubbed him and his efforts to reassure her. Too wrapped up in her problems and deadline, she had continued to keep him at arm's length during the trip across San Diego Bay.

Despite her thoughtless behavior, Alex had remained nearby, looking out for her every minute, as if trouble might have followed them from the hotel. This was not how she wanted to start her future with him. He deserved better.

She tried again to pin the hat in place, without success.

"Mary, will you please help me with this?" She heard the pleading tone in her voice. Pressed for time and needing support, she had changed her mind and asked Mary and Kate to help her dress. After returning late from San Diego, she needed all the help she could get.

Mary clucked her tongue and took the pin. "Julia, if you're not careful, you'll prick herself and ruin your beautiful dress."

"Do you really think it's beautiful?" She touched the Brussels lace that was sewn over a modest white satin bodice. It reached from her waist to her throat and was tucked into a smooth, white, unadorned satin skirt. "It's only ready-made, and I never expected to wear it in public. I'm not sure why I bothered buying a dress at all, but I did, and I wanted something simple."

"Simple on you looks exquisite, so stop fretting. Now bend your knees so I can reach your hat."

Only moderately relieved about how she looked, Julia tried to think clearly as she watched Mary in the mirror. She knew she was forgetting something, but what?

"There," Mary said. "All set. Is there anything else?"

She attempted an inventory. "My shoes! Where are

my shoes?"

"They're right here." Kate picked them up from the floor in front of the bureau. Her eyes shone brightly from her freckled face.

"Julia, please," Mary said, "you must calm down."

"I can't. I'm going to be late. I just know it."

Mary patted her forearm, where the pompadour sleeve of her wedding dress narrowed. "It's perfectly normal for a bride to be late, so stop worrying."

"But there's nothing normal about this wedding." She held out one foot as Kate crouched like a lady's maid and slipped on her shoe. "The guests and staff might think I'm not coming at all because everything was arranged so quickly."

"They will think no such thing," Mary said as Kate slid the other shoe on Julia's foot.

Julia chewed on her thumbnail. "I should have checked on the patio and gazebo when I got back. And so many other things. Oh, Mary, I completely neglected the hotel today."

"Julia, my dear girl, stop. Tonight, you are off duty."

Kate giggled. "Tonight Julia's duty will be to her husband."

"Kate," her mother admonished, "don't be silly. Even though Julia said Mr. MacLean is not going to leave her immediately after the ceremony, this is still a marriage of convenience. She doesn't have to do anything she doesn't want to."

Uttering a groan, Julia considered locking herself in the apartment and never coming out.

Kate stood and pressed her hands to the waist of her

light blue dress. "She might want to, though. I saw Mr. MacLean this morning, and he is to swoon for."

"What are you thinking, Kate?" Mary smoothed a wrinkle in Julia's skirt. "The man's face is horribly scarred."

"Only on one side, and it's not *horrible*. In romantic novels, all the best men have been scarred in some way or another. A scar like his is a badge of honor. I wonder how he got it. Perhaps he saved a woman from being stabbed by her jealous lover. Or maybe he was injured in a terrible war somewhere."

"Sweetheart, you read too many novels. I believe the doctor and I will have to pay more scrutiny to your choice of books."

Kate ignored her mother. "Julia, how did Mr. MacLean get his scar?"

"I don't know, but he is self-conscious about it." She remembered when Dr. Dolan had attempted to examine the scar. "Your father asked him what happened, and he wouldn't say. I didn't want to distress him by bringing it up again."

"Maybe he'll confide in you after you're married." Kate slid a glance at her mother. "My parents tell each other everything."

"Which is as it should be," Mary said, in spite of fanning her rapidly coloring cheeks.

Since the moment Alex chose to stay, Julia had hoped he would confide in her. She wanted to know everything about him.

"Mother, stop blushing. I didn't say anything inappropriate." Kate smiled slyly. "Not yet anyway."

Mary's eyes widened. "Not at all, I hope."

Kate twirled in a circle, then leaned close to Julia. "Mr. MacLean, as a widower, is obviously a man of experience. Imagine what a kiss from him must be like."

Mary's mouth dropped open. "Kate!"

"Oh, Mother, don't be an old hen. Kissing a man like Mr. MacLean must be heavenly." She sighed dramatically. "I'm glad he's staying."

"Only if we are compatible," Julia said.

Kate continued as if she hadn't spoken. "Julia will have a real marriage, and she won't have to pretend to anybody or make up stories." She swished her skirt. "I can't wait to see him kiss her during the ceremony."

Julia started to shake her head, but the clock in the sitting room began chiming. Six o'clock. She froze. She was late, and yet she hesitated to go at all now that the moment was here.

Mary pulled a handkerchief from inside her sleeve and dabbed at her eyes. "Oh my goodness, the next time that clock chimes, you'll be a married woman. I can hardly believe it."

Neither could she. Maybe being homeless and penniless wouldn't be so bad. Maybe the new owners would care about the hotel and her employees as much as she did.

"Come on." Kate grabbed her elbow and dragged her toward the door.

"Wait," Mary said between sniffles. "Where's your bouquet?"

"I … don't have one. Oh, Mary, there's so much I didn't do. I didn't even arrange for music."

"It'll be fine, dear. All you really need is the

minister and the groom."

"Hurry up," Kate said. "Let's go."

Julia hastened from the apartment feeling as if she were trapped in the surf, her lungs burning for air. Each successive wave rolled her over and over, driving her deeper under the sea. She tried not to think about it. Soon she would fulfill her father's final decree, and the Hotel Grand Victoria would be legally hers. But the price was so steep. She was tying herself to a stranger.

* * *

Alex checked again that his new pewter-gray, lightweight wool frock suit was buttoned properly. It was, which left him with nothing to do but peer around the Garden Patio from his station at the bottom of the gazebo's stairs. Two sparrows chirped to each other from the branches of a fruit-laden lemon tree. Above, streaks of pink and orange tinted the twilight sky. Guests and employees lined the walkway railings along the upper floors surrounding the courtyard.

Alex examined the faces for anyone who looked out of place, whose expression betrayed hatred or malcontent. No one like that popped out at him in the diminishing light. He saw Theo, however, in a prime viewing spot on the second floor. The bellboy waved.

Alex nodded to him, then scanned the area again, this time for Marshal Landis and Alberta Hensley. He saw no sign of either of them, but that didn't mean they weren't there somewhere. Now that he was dressed like a man of means again, he worried that Alberta would recognize him. And that would not be good.

Reverend Spencer stood inside the lighted gazebo. The round-faced, black-robed minister wore a smile that stretched from one thick red sideburn to the other. It seemed the man enjoyed officiating at weddings.

Alex swallowed hard and fiddled with his new cravat. He could hardly believe he was about to say "I do" to a woman he'd known for a day—to any woman, for that matter. He still couldn't believe his scar didn't bother Julia to some extent.

"Quit fidgeting," Dr. Dolan said, standing beside him as his best man. "I didn't buy you that suit so you could wear it out the first time you had it on."

"I'm a little nervous. Two days ago, I never thought I'd be getting married again."

The doctor patted his arm. "You have a generous heart, helping Julia out of her predicament like this. We appreciate it."

"I'm not as generous as you think, Doc. I believe Julia and I have a good chance of making this marriage work. Of having a real relationship." At least, that's what he had thought before Julia whirled away from him in her office.

The doctor's eyes sparkled. "Well, if this isn't a most interesting turn of events." He laughed. "Welcome to the family." He shook Alex's hand. "My Mary and Kate will be delighted. Oh, here they come now." The doctor's smile grew. "And, oh my, look at Julia. What a beauty!"

Amidst the sweet fragrance of a nearby orange tree, Alex peered along the subtly lighted pathway, past palms and bird-of-paradise, fruit trees and blooming hibiscus. Mary and her daughter scurried forward, taking their places nearby. When Alex finally saw Julia, he forgot to breathe.

She stood at a bend in the path with the painted sky reflected in the white satin of her skirt. A lace-covered bodice hugged the curves of her waist and chest, enticing him with thoughts of what lay beneath. Her lovely face, and the luminous blue eyes he could only imagine at this distance, were framed by delicate, curling tendrils of ash-blond hair.

Alex couldn't tear his gaze from her. Julia Fairbanks, heralded by the muted sound of the surf, was about to walk down that path and become his wife.

But she didn't move.

Wringing her empty hands, glancing around at the growing number of spectators, she looked as if she might bolt. She had no father to walk her down the aisle, and it seemed she hadn't asked anyone else. No fuss or fanfare was right.

Alex almost left his station to go and get her himself, but then a man he'd seen working in the hotel's gardens hesitantly stepped up to her, offering her a bouquet of deep red roses.

The thoughtful gesture appeared at first to surprise her, then to calm her and strengthen her resolve. She gave the man a warm smile and started forward. The Crown Room's string quartet, seated behind a large hibiscus bush, began playing a soft rendition of the Wedding March.

Her steps faltered, and her head twisted toward the sound. The men had apparently taken it upon themselves, like the gardener, to make this evening special for her.

She regained her footing, and a quavering smile touched her lips. Her eyes glistened. Slowly, in time to the music, she made her way toward him. Her skirt and petticoat whispered with each step that brought her closer.

Alex's heart raced. His blood streamed through his veins. Judging from his body's reaction to her, he knew that Julia's insistence on having the kiss omitted from the ceremony had been a good idea. There would be plenty of time for kisses later.

Two steps away now, she passed her bouquet to Kate Dolan.

Alex stepped forward. She did not reach for him, though, and he kept his arms at his sides.

Dr. Dolan left them alone and joined his wife, who dabbed at her eyes and sniffed into her hanky.

Alex leaned down, nearly touching his cheek to Julia's loosely bound hair and the stylish hat barely covering her head. "You look stunning."

"Thank you," she whispered. "You look quite dashing yourself."

He studied her for any sign of a lie. To his amazement, he saw none. Since his injury, he had never expected to hear a woman honestly describe him as "dashing."

"Is that a new suit?" she asked.

"Compliments of the doctor. He insisted I dress appropriately for the ceremony and took me to the gents' furnishing store downstairs. I promised to pay him back, but he wouldn't hear of it."

"He's a kind and thoughtful man." She briefly

lowered her gaze. "A better person than I. Alex, I'm sorry for the way I treated you in my office. I was in a fretful state, and I pushed you away when you were only trying to help me."

He admitted he had not reacted well to her rejection. During the ferry ride to San Diego, he had begun to worry that marrying Julia was a mistake. But he had given her his word, and he would not go back on it. Her apology restored his faith in her and their future together.

"I promise I will always do my best to help you. I hope you'll remember that. Apology accepted." He held out his hand to her.

She took it, accepting him, scar and all.

The reverend cleared his throat and beckoned them to enter the gazebo lit with a golden glow.

She licked her lips. "It's time."

"Yes, it is," he said, more ready for this than he ever would have imagined.

Hand in hand, they climbed the stairs and took their places.

Reverend Spencer began the ceremony, preaching about love and marriage as the sky darkened into night. Alex's thoughts strayed to his first marriage and the huge church wedding Elizabeth's parents had insisted on. Of the five hundred eighty-nine guests present, only ten were people Alex had invited. James Barrett, his school friend and business partner, had been his best man, but their partnership could not withstand the events that subsequently changed Alex's life forever.

"Mr. MacLean?" Reverend Spencer prodded.

He jerked his attention back to the minister. "What?"

The man stroked one sideburn. "The correct response is 'I do.'"

"Sorry. I do."

The minister continued, then waited for Julia to answer the same question.

"I do," she whispered.

Reverend Spencer squinted one eye. "I'm sorry. My hearing's not as good as it once was. Could you repeat that, Miss Fairbanks?"

"I do!" Her resounding reiteration made the gallery titter. She cringed.

Alex suppressed a chuckle.

"Very good." The reverend grinned like the sales clerk who had sold Dr. Dolan the new suit. "Please face each other and join both hands."

Alex took her hands and squeezed them. Marrying Julia was a new beginning for him. With her, his life would have purpose and the prospect of happiness. It might even have what he wanted most—love.

The minister intoned the vows that Alex happily repeated. "I, Alexander Devlin MacLean, take thee, Julia Ann Fairbanks, to be my wedded wife, to have and to hold from this day forward, for better, for worse, for richer, for poorer, in sickness and in health, to love and to cherish, till death us do part. This is my solemn vow."

She made her vows as well, though she stumbled on the part about loving and cherishing him.

"The ring, please," the minister said.

Alex released her hands, fumbled in his coat

pocket, and brought out the ring she had given him this morning. He handed it to the minister, who said words over it and gave it back.

As Alex lifted her left hand, he felt her trembling. "Don't worry," he whispered, gently working the ring onto her third finger. "It's almost over."

She drew a shuddery breath. "It's only just beginning."

The minister spoke again, and Alex repeated the words. "In token and pledge of the vow made between us, with this ring I thee wed, in the name of the Father, and of the Son, and of the Holy Spirit. Amen."

Reverend Spencer blessed them, raised his voice and said to all the onlookers, "I pronounce that they are man and wife together, in the name of the Father, and of the Son, and of the Holy Spirit. Those whom God hath joined together, let no man put asunder."

Applause and cheers erupted from everywhere. Mary sobbed.

As Alex was about to turn and lead his bride back down the stairs, the noise abated and Reverend Spencer's voice boomed out, "Mr. MacLean, you may kiss your bride!"

* * *

Julia froze, staring at Alex as he stared back. He looked as surprised by the minister's declaration as she felt. Simultaneously, they faced Reverend Spencer.

He slapped a hand over his mouth. "Dear me, I didn't mean to say that. I'm sorry. It just came out. Habit, I suppose."

Julia heard Kate giggle behind her, then Mary shushing the girl. From one of the balconies came a yipping sound—Muffie, the little Yorkshire terrier.

"You don't have to do it," the reverend quickly added. "I'll just introduce you and that will be that." He raised his arms and peered around. "Ladies and gentlemen, I present to you Mr. and Mrs. MacLean."

More applause greeted his announcement, but then a man with a deep, reverberating voice shouted, "Kiss her!"

Several other voices joined his, beginning a chant. Hands clapped in a rhythmic beat that left no question as to what everyone wanted.

Julia wanted to disappear under the gazebo until the crowd dispersed. Once again, others were forcing her to do something she preferred not to do. At the very least, her first kiss with Alex should be saved for a private venue, but choosing not to kiss him now would disappoint her guests and employees and lead to questions she didn't want to answer.

"It's up to you," he said to her.

The chanting and clapping continued.

"Go ahead. I'll try to act convincingly." Though she told herself she wouldn't feel anything, a traitorous flutter of anticipation made her pulse take flight.

"I'll try to do the same," he said, a twinkle in his eyes. He encircled her waist with his arms, pressing his warm palms against her lower back.

An expectant hush fell over the crowd.

He pulled her gradually closer. "Mrs. MacLean." He spoke the words, acknowledging their bond for life. Then he smiled, widely and warmly.

Staring up at him, captivated by the smile she had never seen, Julia felt as if rational thought had been knocked right out of her head. His smile transformed his entire being. His face seemed to glow with an inner light. Tiny golden flecks glinted in the brown of his eyes. His prominent scar seemed to fade away. He laughed, the sound deep and warm and catching her off guard.

Dizzy, she grabbed his upper arms for support. His hold on her thankfully tightened. Without him, she felt sure she would have fallen down the stairs and landed in a heap of white satin.

His smile grew as he peered down at her.

Her breath hitched, and for the first time since she met Alexander Devlin MacLean, she feared her heart might be in more danger than her life.

His head lowered, and his mouth covered hers, tenderly at first, then with a growing sense of possession. His hands pressed deeper into her back, forcing her hips, stomach, and breasts against his solid build.

Too shocked by the sensations swirling within her, she did not react at first. But then a tiny, uncontrollable quiver swept over and through her. She might have even made a sound, though she couldn't be sure. Alex smelled of raw masculinity and the ocean air. She closed her eyes and opened herself to him, willfully kissing him. Their lips melded together, mouths meeting, opening, exploring, and tasting.

She let her senses take over. Her hands, as though of their own accord, slid up to his shoulders and the back of his neck. She lost track of everything but the man holding her hard against him, tantalizing her with his lips and tongue.

Sometime later, whether seconds or minutes she had no idea, Julia registered the sound of Reverend Spencer coughing and clearing his throat. She also heard loud cheers, whistles, and laughter echoing around the courtyard.

Her eyes popped open. She broke off the kiss, bringing her hands to rest on Alex's rapidly rising and falling chest. She tried to catch her breath.

He peered down at her, his eyes so dark with desire that she trembled. What had she done, losing herself first in his smile and then in his kiss? Kate had been right. A kiss from Alex MacLean was heavenly. She had not needed to act like a stage performer. But what must her guests, employees, and minister think of her after such a passionate display? Some of them might call it wanton.

Her face flamed, and she pushed away from ... her husband. "That's enough." She had to think of the hotel and her reputation.

He blinked several times, as if he had been as lost in their kiss as she. His arms dropped to his sides, and he stepped back. The cool evening air rushed in where she had been warmed and protected by his touch and body.

Julia quickly discovered that she already missed his touch, and that frightened her. This man was her husband. Tonight they would share her apartment. Once inside, they would be alone, on their wedding night.

A chill skittered over her. She wasn't ready for this, not at all, not when she had yet to recover from a single kiss. Fear overwhelmed her tingling senses.

Already, she felt as though she were losing what she had fought so hard to become—an independent woman. She had lost herself in a kiss, and she was afraid of one day wanting to do whatever she could to please Alex, just as her mother had done with Father.

Julia silently moaned. What was she going to do?

Chapter Eight

"One last toast, my friends." A bit unsteadily, Dr. Dolan held his champagne glass out to the bottle-carrying waiter working his way around the table set up especially for the wedding party.

The Crown Room buzzed with talk of the ceremony two hours after the fact, and the string quartet continued to play melodies associated with love.

Alex did not accept more champagne. Despite the celebration, he had drunk very little. A threat against Julia's life still existed. As her husband and protector, he intended to keep her safe. What he really wanted to do was whisk his wife upstairs to the safety of her apartment and finish what they had started in the gazebo. With that one kiss, she had permanently awakened his long-dormant urges. He wanted her more than ever. She'd been a passionate partner, soft and yielding, yet also demanding, as hungry as he.

In the end though, she had pulled away. Alex had seen in her eyes how stunned and dismayed she was at her behavior. During dinner, she had tried to keep some semblance of distance between them, but her attempts had failed, thanks to the maitre d'. Jacques had placed their chairs so close together her tantalizing wedding dress brushed Alex's leg every time he or she moved.

Mary Dolan and her daughter, both smiling broadly, lifted their glasses for another of the doctor's toasts.

Julia's smile appeared less than genuine, though she raised her glass, too.

"Ladies and gentlemen," Dr. Dolan said, "I present this toast to our Julia. As of tonight, the Hotel Grand Victoria has a long and rosy future ahead. I also offer this toast to Alex, who made it all possible, and who we welcome with open arms."

"Thanks, Doc." Alex started to sip from his glass.

"Wait," Mary said, her eyes as bright as her husband's. "I have something to add." Giggling, she raised her glass higher, her hand weaving. "To many more kisses and a future filled with beautiful babies."

Champagne sloshed out of Julia's glass, landing on the remains of the small wedding cake her pastry chef had baked for them.

Kate laughed. "Mother!"

Alex lowered his glass. Wanting to reassure Julia he hadn't forgotten her fears, he said, "Mary, it's a little early to be thinking about children."

"I know, but children are so very precious." She smiled affectionately at her daughter, and they clinked glasses.

He felt Julia squirm, heard the rustling of her dress. She set her glass back on the table.

"Yes," he said, "they are extremely precious." He tried not to think about Danny, didn't dare if he wanted to keep his composure. He reminded himself that tonight was a new beginning for him. "Julia and I will do what's right for us."

The doctor raised his glass higher. "And that is as it should be. Julia, you made the right choice of man." He drank down every last bubble of his champagne.

She darted a glance at Alex. "I … believe I did," she said, but she didn't drink.

"Good stuff," the doctor said, then smacked a noisy kiss on his wife's cheek.

"Harold!" She playfully pushed him away. "Not in public."

He grinned. "I'll kiss you anywhere I please, my love." He lifted her pudgy hand and settled his lips against her fingers.

She giggled. "That tickles."

He smiled, then looked toward the doors and cupped a hand to his ear. "I do believe I hear the Friday night orchestra tuning up." Swaying slightly, he stood and pulled his wife to her feet. "What do you say we all adjourn to the Grand Ballroom for a bit of fancy footwork?" He winked at Mary.

She blushed like a schoolgirl. "Are you sure you remember how to dance, old man?"

"I will gladly show you how much I remember." He tucked her arm in his.

Kate stood beside them and rolled her eyes. "Mother, you know exactly how much he remembers. You danced with him two weeks ago."

Mary's blush deepened. "I was just teasing him,

Kate. We like to tease each other. You'll understand that someday." Eyes glinting, she exchanged a knowing look with her husband.

Alex stood, too, envying the doctor and his wife. Might he and Julia someday share such feelings for each other? He hoped so. It would take work, though, and they needed to be able to trust each other. Without trust, they would have nothing, and there was so much Julia didn't know about him. But did he have the courage to confide what he wanted to forget?

"Doctor," he said, "I think Julia and I will call it a night."

She jumped up so fast her chair toppled over. "But I want to dance."

Alex picked up her chair, knowing a stall tactic when he heard one. He started to worry about the night of lovemaking he had planned. He wanted a willing bride in his bed, the same woman who had kissed him without reserve in front of hundreds of people. "You do?"

"Yes. Yes, I do."

"Then we'll dance." He took her arm and steered her past the Dolans, out of the dining room.

"Wait up, Alex," the doctor called out. "Take pity on a stout old man."

He glanced over his shoulder. "We'll meet you in the ballroom."

Dr. Dolan waved them away. "Go on then."

They crossed the Rotunda, passed by the reception desk, and strode down the hallway.

She tugged on his arm. "You don't have to walk so fast."

He slowed. "I thought you were eager to dance."

"Not really, but I suspect you already knew that."

He shrugged, then nodded. "It wasn't difficult to figure out."

"Today has not been easy for me, but I am grateful for what you've done, Alex. The hotel is safe now. I'm also grateful for the way you handled Mary's toast about … babies."

"You're welcome on both counts. Whether we choose to have children or not is nobody's business but ours. However, you might ease your fears by talking to Dr. Dolan about the medical side of things."

"I'll … think about it," she said as they entered the circular Grand Ballroom.

Couples sat at small tables, stood in groups, or whirled around the dance floor. Other guests watched from a gallery above. An orchestra played on stage, and as Alex led his wife toward the dance floor, the band broke off their song, swiftly changing to a rendition of the "Wedding March."

He felt Julia wilt a bit, then shore herself back up as men and women uttered congratulations or acknowledged them with a smile or nod.

One rosy-cheeked man got up from his chair and lifted his glass to them. "Are you going to christen the Bridal Chamber yourselves?" He roared with laughter.

Her steps faltered.

Alex steadied her. "We'll leave that room to the paying guests," he answered for her. They didn't need the Bridal Chamber. Julia's apartment—their home— would do just fine.

They finally reached the dance floor, and the

orchestra segued to a waltz. He took his wife into his arms and spun her around with him, their steps perfectly matched, their bodies moving as one. Beneath the press of her fingers against his shoulder, his flesh grew hot.

As the melody ended and another began, Dr. Dolan cut in, saving Alex from having to excuse himself or dragging Julia upstairs. He danced with Mary and then Kate, grateful for the chance to cool down. But then he was paired with his wife again.

She settled into his embrace as if she had never been gone, as if she belonged there. He held her closer, leaning his head against the softness of her hair, happy that she'd stowed her hat in her office before dinner. Her sweet scent enclosed them in a world of their own, and Alex couldn't help but remember the honeyed taste of her mouth. Damn, but he wanted her.

Three torturous dances later, he stopped them near the edge of the floor. "Let's go home."

"We are home," she said, feigning innocence.

"You know what I mean. Upstairs, to the apartment."

She tensed. "You go ahead. I have some things to do."

"What things?"

"Well, everything I didn't get done this afternoon because we had to go to San Diego for the marriage license."

"Your duties to the hotel can wait until tomorrow. Tonight, everyone, including me, expects you to put hotel matters aside. Besides, you're not going anywhere unless I accompany you. Have you forgotten someone around here wants you dead?"

She tensed. "I'd like to forget it, but I haven't."

"Your safety comes first, Julia."

"Thank you." She let go of him. "We might as well go upstairs then."

He offered her his arm.

She stared at it a moment, inhaled deeply, and let her breath back out in a rush of air. She slid her arm through his with a minimum of contact.

Leading her from the ballroom, Alex kept his expression neutral, no longer sure whether the night he'd been eagerly anticipating would happen.

* * *

Julia climbed the stairs to the second floor. Every part of her body hummed with her awareness of Alex as he walked beside her. On the dance floor, in his arms, she had almost forgotten that her husband was a stranger who undoubtedly expected a wedding night. She had let the music and his agile strength and elegant steps sweep her along until, heaven help her, she had wanted him to hold her closer and tighter. She'd wanted to dance with him forever.

But now reality returned. They were about to enter her apartment, and she had a duty to perform as his wife. She trusted him to do what he said was possible to avoid conceiving a child. He had not dismissed her fears, speaking up for her when Mary had made her toast about babies. Julia's trust in him had grown.

Outside the apartment door, they stopped. Alex pulled a key from his coat pocket.

"Where did you get that?" Her refuge was no longer her own.

"Theo slipped it to me during dinner, after he put my belongings inside." He inserted the key in the lock and opened the door.

The sitting room was lit, compliments of Theo, no doubt. She spied Alex's battered traveling bag beside the nearest sofa. It belonged in her father's old bedroom.

She started to go inside, but Alex held her back. "What?" she asked.

"Don't you want me to carry you over the threshold?"

"No. Under the circumstances, that would be silly." Their union was far from a real marriage. "Besides, you're not to lift anything heavy. Doctor's orders, remember?"

"You're not heavy."

His eyes had darkened again, and her heart started to hammer. "Nevertheless, you are not going to carry me over this threshold." She stepped inside.

"I guess I won't." He closed the door and locked it, the decisive click making her flinch. He set his key on the parlor table, then unbuttoned his coat and loosened his cravat, as if it were perfectly natural for him to begin undressing in front of her.

"Your room is there," she said quickly, pointing. "Mine is there." She pointed in the opposite direction. "We each have our own bathroom with water closet." She mentally thanked the hotel's architects for that. She wanted her privacy.

"Then I'll move into my room and make myself at home." He ambled over to his bag and picked it up. "Then perhaps we could … talk."

146

Talk, indeed, she thought, her legs beginning to shake.

"Will you be needing help with your dress?"

"No! I mean, no, thank you. I can get out of it myself. I will … see you afterwards."

"All right. Whenever you're ready. Oh, and just to put your mind at ease, I have what we'll need to avoid conception."

Her cheeks grew hot. "I am glad to hear that." She gulped. Now she had no reason whatsoever to deny him his rights as her husband.

"Do you want me to come to your room?" he asked.

"No, I'll come to you."

"It won't be awkward for you, being with me in your father's former room?"

"I'll be fine. Several months after my father's passing, I cleaned out his things, replaced the furniture, and had the room repainted." Consummating their marriage in her father's old room would not be any more awkward than the entire situation already was.

He shifted his bag to his other hand. "Okay. See you in a little while then." He sauntered away and disappeared into his room.

When she tried to move, Julia felt as if her legs were made of wood. Hobbling into her bedroom, she switched on the electric lights in the wall sconces and tried to get hold of herself. Alex had kept up his side of their arrangement, now it was her turn.

She could do it. In fact, the sooner she did it the better. She would offer herself to him, and a few short minutes later, their first time together would be over.

Her duty for the night would be done, and she could return to the privacy of her own room. Julia ignored the little voice reminding her of Alex's boast that she would enjoy their intimate relations.

She toed off her shoes and unfastened the buttons at her nape. Fatigue from her lack of sleep began to set in. Try as she might, contorting her hands and arms, she could not reach the rest of the buttons. Spent, she let her arms fall to her sides and dropped her chin to her chest. She needed help, and the only help available was Alex.

She uttered an unladylike curse. Well, she might as well give in now. She would let him become her husband in every way, and she'd find out if his claims about lovemaking were true.

Squaring her shoulders, she left her room, crossed the apartment, and knocked lightly at Alex's door.

It swung open, and he stood shirtless in front of her, the top two buttons of his pants unfastened.

Her mouth turned to sand.

"I didn't expect you so soon." He folded his bare, muscular arms over his bare, muscular chest. Even worse, he smiled. She wished he wouldn't. She tended to forget herself when he smiled.

She tried to find her voice. "I, uh, can't reach the buttons on my dress."

He chuckled, the sound making her insides quiver. "Turn around."

She did, her legs wooden again.

His deft fingers started where she had left off and slowly moved down. They brushed her skin where the edges of the dress fell open.

Julia could barely breathe. She stood perfectly still, trying to quell the little tremors spreading over her body. How did he manage to touch her so lightly yet send ripples of feeling flowing to the very tips of her fingers and toes?

When he stopped, she managed to ask, "Are you … finished?"

"That depends."

"On what?"

"On how much further you want me to go?" His breath and words feathered across the bare skin above her combination camisole and corset.

She shut her eyes at the sensation. Her normally rational brain felt as if it were floating in a thick fog. "I … don't understand."

He skimmed kisses along the top of her spine, and her head dropped forward, seemingly of its own accord. "Would you like to come in?"

Shivery from his seductive touch, she slowly turned and glanced from his warm gaze to the wide bed. The reality of her situation flooded back to her. She was not married to a man she loved, but she was about to give herself to him anyway, because it was his right as her husband. She also owed him for her future at the hotel.

She nodded, the movement like a woodpecker's. "Yes, I will come in. I want to get this over with as quickly as possible so I can go back to my room and sleep. It's been a very long day."

Instead of stepping aside, he rubbed his jaw. "Julia, making love to you for the first time will not happen 'quickly.' It will be slow and sensual, every moment and movement to be savored. You're a passionate woman. You proved that when we kissed."

"I suffered a moment of weakness. I don't expect it to happen again." She told herself she didn't want it to happen again, but standing in front of this man—her husband—with his chest hair gleaming under the electric lights and his rich brown eyes looking so knowing, she felt her resolve eroding like Coronado's beach during a winter storm.

"You enjoyed that kiss as much as I did." His long, dark lashes lowered over an amused glimmer. "And when we make love together, you will enjoy that even more. Like our wedding kiss, our mating will go on and on, but even that won't be enough."

Instead of laughing at his outrageous talk, she trembled. "I don't think so. Now let's just do this before I lose my resolve."

He dropped his hand to the waistband of his dress pants, which now seemed to fit more snugly across the front. The moment Julia realized why, she whisked her errant gaze back up. Her cheeks burned with embarrassment while her lower body pulsed. What had she been thinking to look down there?

He pursed his lips, then released what sounded like a groan and a sigh. "Julia, I know I'm going to regret this for the next few hours, but I'm sending you back to your room. When we consummate our marriage, it's going to be because you want me as much as I want you. Tonight, nothing is going to happen between us."

"But—"

He covered her lips with his fingers. "We will, eventually, make love. I think I can promise you that.

The time and place are what will remain in question."

She curled her hands into fists. Not knowing when it would happen was even worse than doing it now, when she didn't want to but was resigned to letting it happen.

He leaned down, cupped one side of her face with his hand, and pressed his lips to the other side in a tender, lingering kiss.

Her knees went soft. Any hope of whirling away from him, exerting some semblance of control over herself and the situation, deserted her.

He straightened, trailed the pad of his callused index finger along the line of her jaw, and said, "Good night, Mrs. MacLean. Sleep well."

With that, he stepped back and closed the door.

Breathless, staring at the wood grain just inches away from her nose, Julia didn't think she would sleep at all. Alex had given her a reprieve, but one she wasn't so sure she wanted anymore.

* * *

Alex leaned against the bedroom wall as hot and hard as he had ever been for a woman. Sleep would not come easy tonight, but he had done the right thing by sending Julia and her alluring innocence away. He didn't want her coming to him out of obligation. He wanted her in his bed as a willing marriage partner— because she wanted him, scar and all.

Only then would she be his.

Chapter Nine

Dressed in a pastel-blue shirtwaist and skirt, Julia sat at the small dining table in her apartment and attempted another bite of toast, but she had no appetite. Every time she heard Alex moving around in his bedroom, she jumped. Hearing him taking a bath had sent her imagination soaring to places she didn't want to go. At least, that's what she kept telling herself.

His door opened.

She stiffened, her spine as rigid as the pilings holding up the boathouse on Glorietta Bay. Her fingers clamped down on the triangle of toast. It crumbled, dropping onto her plate.

"Good morning, Mrs. MacLean." He came up behind her, placed his hands on her shoulders, and leaned over her.

When she dared to look up at him, tipping her head back, he kissed her forehead. She struggled not to close her eyes. If she lost the struggle, she would end up picturing him taking her into his arms and passionately kissing her on the mouth.

"Did you sleep well?" he asked, coming around the table and sitting down across from her. He wore his faded work clothes.

"No," she admitted, relaxing a bit now that he wasn't touching her.

"Me either." He leaned his forearms on the table. "The doctor was right about a hot bath, though. I can move better now."

"He'll be glad to hear it." She lifted the silver coffee pot. "Coffee?"

He nodded. "Thanks."

As she poured him a steaming, fragrant cup, she noticed his gaze roaming over the china platters kept warm by silver covers. There was also a linen-lined silver basket filled with toast and breakfast rolls, as well as a pitcher of orange juice—everything her kitchen staff had thoughtfully provided for a hungry couple the morning after their wedding night.

He lifted one of the silver covers, revealing crisp bacon slices and scrambled eggs. "Mmm. Smells good. I don't suppose you cooked this up yourself this morning."

"No, it's all courtesy of my breakfast chef and his staff."

"You didn't go down there alone, I hope."

She heard the concern in his voice and liked it. "No, I promise you I am taking the threat against my life seriously, I used the annunciator. One of the waiters responded, and when he came to the door, I ordered breakfast. He returned with a lot more than I asked for."

"Nice of him. And them. I'm starved." He served himself a generous helping of everything, took a bite of roll, and glanced at the apartment's small, but serviceable, kitchen. "Do you cook?"

"I know how. When I was growing up, I often spent time in the hotel kitchen, first in Philadelphia and then here, watching and learning from the chefs." She picked up her glass of orange juice and took a sip. "I don't usually bother, though. If I don't eat in the Crown Room, I have the chef prepare something that can be delivered to my office. Or here."

"It's a good arrangement. Elizabeth and I had a cook by necessity. I would've wasted away otherwise. My wife, uh, first wife, couldn't boil an egg and didn't care to learn. In the five years we were married, I don't think she entered the kitchen more than a handful of times."

"What was she like, if you don't mind my asking?" She was grateful for the opening Alex had given her. She wanted to know more about his past and was curious about her predecessor.

His eating slowed. "She was beautiful, with dark hair and big brown eyes, but she was also spoiled, the only child of an old, powerful, and rich Baltimore family." He put down his fork and took a sip of coffee. "When she set her sights on me, I was 'over the moon,' as they say. She had poise, beauty, breeding, and connections. I'd grown up poor in an insignificant little town and was only just starting to make my name as an architect. One of my buildings had won an award. Elizabeth was at the ceremony, and we were introduced." He shook his head, and he wasn't smiling.

"What?"

He picked up a slice of bacon and ate half. "It seems so long ago now." He finished the rest of the slice. "I was young and foolish, and she bewitched me with her looks and background and consuming interest in me. I fell in love. I thought everything would be perfect. We'd be together, and her parents—the Ellingsons—would praise my architectural accomplishments and services to their well-to-do friends." A faraway look came into his eyes.

Julia wondered what he was seeing. "What happened?" she quietly asked.

His gaze came back to her. "Nothing turned out the way I expected. Elizabeth accepted my marriage proposal, but her parents disapproved of me. I was a nobody to them, and always would be. They tried to keep us from marrying. Even offered me money." He laughed, the sound hollow. "Funny, isn't it? You offered me money to marry you. They offered me money to walk away."

She winced. No wonder he had adamantly refused her monetary offer. "You obviously didn't take their money."

"No, and they couldn't talk Elizabeth out of the marriage either. What I didn't know then was that she had set her mind on having me, as if I were a doll or puppy that she wanted but was being denied. Eventually, as always, she got her way. I didn't know how until about a year after we were married, when I experienced for myself what turned out to be legendary amongst the servants in her parents' home.

She threw a tantrum, shouting and screaming and throwing things around the room." He stared at a crumb on the white tablecloth.

Julia carefully folded her napkin and laid it on the table. "That must've been a nasty shock to you."

"I was more disillusioned than anything. And I was disappointed in myself for not seeing her character clearly." He drank down his entire glass of orange juice. "You and I, after less than two days, are more compatible than Elizabeth and I ever were." He picked up his fork and slowly finished the last few bites of egg.

She had to admit they were getting along well. Maybe their marriage could work. Julia didn't want to think what might have happened if he had not agreed to marry her when he did. He deserved more from her than just her thanks.

"Did Elizabeth want children?" she asked.

He pushed his plate away, a mask seeming to slide over his features. "What are your plans for the day?"

His sudden change of subject took her aback. Had he said enough about his first wife? Or did he prefer to avoid the subject of children and the family he had hoped to have? Feeling guilty about denying him what he wanted, Julia avoided the subject, too. "I intend to catch up with my paperwork and do my rounds. What about you?"

"I'll take you on your rounds, then do some investigating. I want to find out if Tyler Wolff is in the area. If he is, then we can assume he's still interested in acquiring the hotel and is therefore a suspect."

She got up as well. "You'll need to go to San Diego

then. He's staying at the Heritage Hotel, or he was, at any rate."

"I'll try there first."

"While you're in San Diego, I'd like it if you could stop into Marston's Department Store and purchase some new clothes, both for your job as carpenter and for evenings in the hotel. You can charge everything to my account."

"No. I'll buy what I need after I've worked some."

She crossed her arms over her chest and tapped her fingers against one elbow. "Alex, you know I have a reputation to uphold. If you plan to stay here as my husband, you must be presentable. You're welcome to leave if you object."

"Nice try, but I'm not going anywhere. You might as well bury whatever hopes you harbor on that point."

She sighed. It had been worth a try, half-hearted though it was. "Then you'll go shopping?"

"I'll get enough of what's needed so I won't shame you. You can take the costs out of my future wages. I don't want your money."

"It's not charity, Alex. You're my husband."

"I'll earn my own way, same as you're earning yours by managing the hotel. I assume you can understand that."

"Yes, I understand." After teetering on the brink of destitution, she understood very well.

"Elizabeth couldn't," he said, his tone one of resigned acceptance. "She had no concept of the value of money or work. She spent and spent, with no regard for the amount I was earning. When I complained, she said she'd ask her daddy for help, even though she knew I didn't want a single penny from him."

Julia dropped her arms to her sides. She had married a proud man, and the more she learned about him, the more she found to like about him. "I'll keep an accounting of your purchases and deduct the costs from your earnings. Will that suit you?"

"Yes. Thank you."

"Good." She strode to the annunciator and pressed it. "A waiter will be here in a few minutes to clear away the dishes. After that, I'd like to do my rounds."

"I'll be ready."

As would she. For two nights in a row, she had neglected the hotel. Everything needed checking on, but she also welcomed the opportunity to spend more time in Alex's company, maybe even to feel again what she had felt last night on the threshold of his room.

* * *

Thirty minutes later, Alex accompanied Julia downstairs. He told himself he was not a coward for veering away from telling her more about his life in Baltimore. She had a right to know, but the losses and humiliation he had suffered were buried deep within himself. Bringing them out into the light would be heaping one painful episode onto another, like a cascade of water hitting rock after rock on its way to the pool at the bottom, where he'd be pushed under. Not only that, his past might act like a poison, tainting his hopes for a future filled with love and maybe even family.

Walking with Julia, Alex concentrated on her and the present. He wished he were back in bed and that she were beside him. Waiting until she wanted him as much as he wanted her was going to try his patience and fortitude. Maybe he could nudge her toward a quicker decision in his favor. He smiled to himself. During Julia's rounds, he would get to explore the hotel and study its architecture, as well as search out the best spots for a man and woman wanting a little privacy. If he found a spot with promise, he believed he could entice Julia into taking advantage of it.

They crossed the Rotunda, and she immediately went to speak with the weasel at the registration desk about the number of guests due to leave and arrive. Alex stood close enough to listen to their discussion and intimidate Chalmers if the clerk showed her any disrespect.

The man, Adam's apple bobbing, glanced over at him several times and stayed on his best behavior.

"Thank you, Mr. Chalmers," she said. "I'll check with you again later."

"Yes, Miss Fair—" His gaze shot to Alex. "I mean, Mrs. MacLean."

Alex winked at him, took Julia's elbow, and led her away. "Where to next?"

"The laundry."

On their way out the front door, Theo was coming in, pushing an expensive leather trunk on his cart. He tipped his pillbox hat to them. "Morning, Mr. MacLean, Mrs. MacLean."

Julia greeted him with a self-conscious smile.

Alex leaned down to the bellboy and lowered his voice. "Any news for us?"

Theo pushed his spectacles higher and glanced

around the lobby. "Not much, I'm afraid. Mrs. Reynolds spread the news about her near fall after stepping on a rotted stair. No one has said anything about it being sabotaged, so whoever did it is keeping quiet."

"As will we," Julia said.

"Anything else?" Alex asked.

"Well, the biggest news, of course, is your wedding. Everyone is talking about"—he pulled his head into his shoulders like a turtle—"the kiss."

She grimaced, color flowing into her fair face. "I'll never live that down."

"I'd rather you didn't," Alex said. "It was a great kiss, which is why everyone is gossiping about it."

A short laugh, quickly covered up, escaped from Theo's mouth. At Julia's pointed look, he cleared his throat. "Sorry. There is one more thing you should know. Marshal Landis has been wandering around the grounds asking a lot of questions. Mostly about you, Mr. MacLean."

Alex glowered. The man's jealous preoccupation could endanger Julia. "He's wasting his time, time that should be spent searching for Julia's assailant." He shoved a hand into his pants pocket. "Theo, later on, I'm going over to San Diego. I'd appreciate it if you could check on my wife every so often while I'm gone."

"Happy to do it. But now, I'd better be off." He tapped his cart. "Mrs. Trouville in three-sixteen is waiting for her trunk."

They let him go and headed outside, across the carriage drive and lawn, toward the red brick smokestack rising above the hotel's engine house and laundry.

Alex, eyeing their surroundings and anyone that looked suspicious, put his arm around Julia's waist.

She instantly halted on a patch of the freshly cut lawn. Her eyes were narrowed, but not from the sunlight shining into their blue depths. "What are you doing?"

"Showing whoever might be watching that you are under my protection." It was one of his reasons anyway.

"Just walking with me in public will accomplish that, so you can take your arm away."

"Is it so unpleasant to have my arm around you?" He stroked her side with his fingers, feeling her shirtwaist and corset and wishing neither was there.

Her chest rose suddenly, and she released a shaky breath. "Let's go. I have work to do." She started walking again, faster this time, but she didn't push his hand away.

Alex kept his expression bland, but inside, he was smiling. Perhaps tonight would be the night.

Outside the laundry's door, she said, "This shouldn't take long. I just need to converse with the head laundress and find out if there are any problems."

"I'm in no hurry, and I'll be coming inside with you."

"I seriously doubt I'll be in any danger here, but, since I am 'under your protection,' I will accept your presence."

"Madam, you have no choice but to accept it." He pushed open the door for her and followed her rigid back and stiff neck inside.

Five women, their sleeves rolled to their elbows and their brows damp from the steamy heat, worked amongst mounds of table linens, towels, and sheets.

"Hello, Mrs. Benedict," Julia said over the noise of machines filled with water, suds, and soiled laundry.

The woman whom Alex assumed was the head laundress turned, her hand lifting frizzy brown hair off her moist forehead. A wide grin broke out across her plump face. "Hello to you, Mrs. MacLean. That's a right-sounding name, if I do say so myself. And this must be Mr. MacLean. Congratulations, sir. Congratulations to the both of you." She did not seem at all put off by his scar. Perhaps she'd been warned about it.

"Thank you," Julia said, her smile appearing brittle to him.

"Good to meet you." He shook Mrs. Benedict's hand. "Today I'm getting an insider's tour of my new home."

"It's a grand place to call home." The older woman waved her chapped hands. "I'm sorry not to have seen your ceremony last night, but I didn't feel it'd be right for a group of laundresses to show ourselves inside the hotel. All us girls heard it was real nice though. Especially the end part, if it's not too forward of me to say." She glanced meaningfully between him and Julia.

Alex chuckled. "Mrs. Benedict, I'll be honest with you. That was my favorite part of the ceremony. Mrs. MacLean's too, though you won't catch her saying so."

The laundress laughed outright, and giggles emanated from the women folding the linens. One woman, her arms as thick as small tree trunks, heaved a clean load of dry sheets out of a machine and into a large basket.

Julia fanned her face. "Mrs. Benedict, you would have been welcome at the ceremony. All the girls would have been. Please forgive me for not extending a personal invitation."

"Ah, you're most kind, Mrs. MacLean." She waved a hand in dismissal. "But you're not here to discuss your wedding. I have good news for you today. Everything's in order. No broken-down machines. Just a mountain of laundry to get done."

"So I see, but I know you'll manage, as always. We'll let you get back to work. Good day." She strode to the door, opening it herself before Alex could open it for her.

He waved back at the ladies and followed her out to the sound of giggles and chatter behind him. "Nice group of women," he said, taking up his position beside her, though he didn't touch her this time. "Even though you're in charge, they're comfortable with you. I don't think we have to worry about any danger coming from that quarter."

"I feel terrible that they excluded themselves from attending the wedding."

"You're a good person, Julia Fairbanks MacLean. Elizabeth would have been appalled to have a group of laundresses anywhere near her wedding."

"These women are hard workers and deserve respect. I just wish our wedding kiss wasn't such a big topic of conversation. Hearing about it first from Theo and now from them is terribly embarrassing."

"Just grin and bear it," Alex said, remembering his youth. "That's what my father used to say."

"Easier said than done," she responded, "but good advice. I think I would have liked your father."

"He would've like you. My mother, too."

They walked in silence for a minute, Alex wishing his parents had gotten a chance to meet her. Unlike Elizabeth and her parents, Julia would have welcomed his family.

"Where are we headed now?" he asked.

"The north side of the park. That's where the groundskeepers' shed is."

"Lead on."

They strolled past the doctor's cottage to the Paseo del Mar, a concrete walkway overlooking the long, crescent-shaped stretch of beach. A light breeze rippled the ocean and stirred Julia's hair. The tide was out, and Alex breathed in the pungent, salty smell, enjoying it as several women with parasols shading their faces sauntered past in the other direction. Blue sky touched the horizon, and a lone steamship puffed into the channel to San Diego Harbor. Farther out to sea, a two-masted topsail schooner cruised southward. Square sails and triangular sails reminded him of Baltimore and its famed clipper ships of an earlier decade.

"Your father chose the perfect setting for his hotel," Alex said, noticing that the westerly breeze had loosened a lock of Julia's hair from its pins. Before he could think about it, he tucked the flowing strands behind her ear.

She froze for an instant, then darted a look at him as she kept walking. "You are taking liberties, Mr. MacLean."

"If you don't like my touch, all you have to do is say so and I'll stop. I expect you to be honest with me, though."

She didn't answer immediately. "I suppose, if I'm honest about it, I don't mind it too much. I'm just not accustomed to being touched like that. And certainly not in public."

"Then you might as well get used to it. I'm an affectionate man."

She licked her lips and stared straight ahead. "What were we discussing? Oh, yes, the hotel's setting. There wasn't much here when we started building. Just sand and scrub, rabbits and birds. Bringing in all the materials was a logistical chore unto itself."

"I can imagine." He smiled, looking forward to touching her with more affection. "I've worked on similarly difficult projects."

"Hotels?"

"One. Mostly I designed city buildings suitable for offices. I did, however, try to give them some aesthetic flair. My last project was a mansion on the Chesapeake Bay. The owner had no artistic ability whatsoever, but he admired and appreciated art, and he allowed me a lot of creative freedom, which I enjoyed." Alex had never gotten to finish that one, though.

"Do you think you might design again?" she asked.

"I ... don't know." He looked out at the sea, his

steps paced to hers. Waves curled in toward shore, and a formation of seven pelicans skimmed the foamy tops. "I hope so."

She waved him to the right, into the park. Low bushes circled by colorful flowers marked the locations of wrought-iron benches. Pepper trees were scattered here and there, and a grove of pines filled the park's center. A bushy-tailed squirrel scratched and scampered its way up a nearby trunk.

"San Diego is a growing city," she said, "as you may have noticed. There will be a lot of opportunities for a talented architect."

"'Talented?' You've never seen my work."

A sea gull cried out above them before wheeling away toward the sea. "You won an award, didn't you?"

"Three, in fact. The other two after Elizabeth and I married."

"Then you must be talented." She said it matter-of-factly, as if there were no question. Alex felt as if his heart were expanding. Julia had faith in him as an architect—a talented architect—even when he no longer had faith in himself.

As they entered the deserted pine grove, he took her hand and stopped her, stepping in front of her. "Thank you," he whispered, "for believing in me." He leaned down and kissed her gently, sweeping his lips over hers.

He both heard and felt her sudden intake of breath. When he looked into her eyes, he saw her indecision. Alex urged her toward the decision he wanted by kissing her more soundly, tracing the tip of his tongue over her lips until they parted.

"We … shouldn't," she whispered back, even as her arms came around his waist and her mouth opened wider, allowing him in.

He wrapped her in his arms and pulled her flush against him, wanting to feel all of her, wishing they were in a far-off forest where he could lay her on a soft bed of moss and make love to her with utter abandon.

He deepened the kiss, and he heard her moan softly into his mouth. But he also heard something else, an insistent yapping noise that was rapidly growing louder. Also growing louder was a woman's voice calling out, "Muffie! Where are you, baby? Come to Mother."

Alex lifted his head. "Damn."

Julia peered up at him, looking dazed and bewildered. "What's wrong?"

"We have a visitor." He aimed his chin at their tiny interloper. Muffie's belly scraped the lush grass as she trotted over to them. Big brown eyes stared up at them. "Any second now Mrs. Hensley will discover us, too."

"Oh, my goodness." Julia quickly stepped back, smoothed her shirtwaist and skirt, and patted her hair. "I knew this was a mistake, but you are a hard man to resist. Do I look all right?"

"You look beautiful." Not nearly kissed enough, though, he silently lamented. "And it wasn't a mistake."

Alberta Hensley emerged from around a tree, her chest and breath heaving. "There you are, you bad dog! Oh, Mr. and Mrs. MacLean, I didn't expect to see you. I did wonder why Muffie veered off the walkway during our stroll. She has obviously taken a liking to you."

Alex turned slightly so that his scar would be what she saw when she looked at him. Maybe then she'd keep her eyes on Julia instead.

"She's a sweet dog," Julia said, perfectly composed. She bent down and picked Muffie up.

The Yorkshire terrier gave a light-hearted yip.

Mrs. Hensley, her lilac water scent overpowering the pines, withdrew an embroidered hanky from her pocket and patted the sweating folds of her neck with it. "She's as sweet as can be, but she is loving your spacious hotel grounds a little too much. I simply can't keep chasing after her like this."

"Do you have a leash?" Julia asked.

"I do, back in my room. I must get into the habit of using it." Mrs. Hensley relieved her of the dog. "Before we go, I must say how much I enjoyed your wedding ceremony last evening. It was very special. I'd never attended an outdoor ceremony before."

"I'm glad you were able to join us," Julia said, the perfect hostess.

"Well, you two make a lovely couple." She glanced up at Alex and pursed her lips. "I still can't get over how much you remind me of someone back home. I just wish I could recall who."

Alex shrugged to keep himself from grimacing. Or running.

"Where is it you're from, Mrs. Hensley?" Julia asked, glancing between them.

"Baltimore. Wonderful city. So much culture and

society."

"I've never been there myself." She shot a quick and questioning look at Alex.

He tensed, and Muffie yipped.

Mrs. Hensley stroked the dog's ruff. "Yes, baby, we're going. I know you're thirsty." She gave them a distracted wave. "See you again."

She set off with Muffie in her arms, and they quickly disappeared into the trees.

Julia turned to Alex and propped her fists on her hips. "You know her, don't you?"

He hesitated, their kiss part of the distant past, no chance for renewal. "I ran across her a few times."

"Why won't you acknowledge your acquaintance with her?"

He shoved his hands into his back pockets. Alberta Hensley knew enough about his past to ruin him in the West, finishing what his wife's parents had started in the East.

"She's a close friend of my former in-laws, whom I want nothing to do with. I don't want to hear about them or think about them. Let's go." He took her by the elbow. "We have rounds to finish." He glanced around the park. "Where's the damn gardening shed?"

She motioned straight ahead, a confused and wary expression in her eyes.

Alex didn't look at her again. He knew he should say something to put her at ease. He ought to explain all the reasons behind his antagonistic feelings toward his in-laws, but he couldn't.

Not today. Maybe not ever.

Chapter Ten

Sitting at her desk during Alex's shopping and reconnaissance trip to San Diego, Julia entered the hotel's most recent expenses into the ledger. She tried to focus on the rising cost of beef, which would necessitate changes on the dining room menu and bring on the wrath of Chef Leuven, but her mind kept returning to the scene in the park.

She should not have let Alex kiss her out where anyone could have seen them, but, heaven help her, she had been powerless to resist. Thank goodness Muffie and Mrs. Hensley had arrived when they did, except that their appearance had subsequently raised troubling questions about Alex. There was no denying his deep-seated anger toward his in-laws. She had heard it in his voice. But what she knew so far of his in-laws didn't seem to warrant such anger. There must be more to it, but he was being secretive, which reminded her that she had married a drifter without references—a stranger.

Julia laid down her pen, rested her elbows on the

desk, and rubbed her eyes. Life was supposed to have gotten simpler after her marriage, not more complicated. The man she married, the man who had protected her, was worthy of her trust. She felt it in her heart. He was a good man. Why, he hadn't even taken advantage of her in the privacy of her apartment. And his pride had kept him from wanting her to pay for his clothing.

Her office door squeaked open, and she jerked her head up, half-expecting Alex to appear as if conjured from her thoughts.

"Mr. Wolff," she said through a tight jaw, masking her surprise and trepidation. Was he behind the flowerpot and sabotage? She did not get up. "It is customary to knock on a closed door."

"I'll try to remember that," he said, entering the office and offering no apology. He closed the door.

She ground her teeth at his arrogance and maintained a wary eye on him. Hopefully somebody had seen him enter her office. If he was her assailant, he wouldn't dare harm her here, would he?

"I had hoped I wouldn't see you again," she said. "Shouldn't you have returned east by now?"

"I did." He removed his black fedora, revealing dark, wavy brown hair.

His face was striking, olive-complexioned with hazel, old-beyond-his-years eyes, as if he had experienced more than most men his age. Julia couldn't help but think, yet again, that there was something familiar about him.

He dropped his hat on her desk and sat down across from her, making himself at home. "I took care of my most pressing business matters and came back here to handle the one that was pending."

"Nothing is 'pending' between us."

"Oh, but there is. I want the Hotel Grand Victoria, and you are going to sell it to me."

She picked up her pen, the only potential weapon at hand. The man's single-minded determination astonished and frightened her. He did not know when to give up and move on. How far might he go to get what he wanted?

"Do you not understand the meaning of the word 'no,' Mr. Wolff? I told you before, the Hotel Grand Victoria is not for sale."

"Under the right circumstances, everything is for sale."

"What do you mean by that? Under what 'circumstances'?" Was he implying responsibility for the attacks against her, telling her she would remain in danger until she signed over the hotel? She gripped the pen more tightly and wished Alex were with her. He would not be happy when he found out no one had stopped Tyler Wolff from waltzing into her office. From now on, she was going to lock the door.

"Oh, you never know. Circumstances can change quickly, necessitating other changes." He plucked a piece of lint off the fine black material of his cutaway suit. Woven into the lightweight wool, silvery silk threads shimmered like a spider's web. "Congratulations on your recent marriage, by the way."

"How would you know about that? The announcement won't appear in the newspaper until tomorrow."

"Gossip travels quickly, Mrs. MacLean."

It certainly did, she thought, especially if the gossip was being paid for. Did Mr. Wolff have an informant in her midst?

"I'd like to meet your husband," Wolff said, examining his manicured fingernails, then buffing them against his jacket. "He would undoubtedly find my offer of great interest."

"He would not. If you and he were to meet, he'd tell you the same thing himself."

"Maybe. Maybe not."

"Mr. Wolff, why do you want the hotel so badly?"

He rubbed at the bridge of his slightly crooked nose, the only imperfection she discerned in his looks. "For investment purposes, of course."

"Of course." She didn't believe him for a minute.

He got up and wandered over to the three framed photographs on the wall. One showed the hotel shortly after its completion, another showed it under construction, and a third showed her father breaking ground with a shovel.

"Though many banks are still suffering the effects of the Panic of Ninety-three," he said, studying the photographs, "the depression is, for the most part, fading from people's memories. In time, the economy will grow stronger and people will begin spending their money on travel again."

"And I will be waiting for them."

"I think not." He chuckled, then touched the frame holding her father's photograph. "Who's the man with the shovel?"

"Lloyd Fairbanks, my deceased father."

"You don't look anything like him."

"Mr. Wolff, as I'm sure you can understand, I have work to do." She tapped the ledger with her pen. "Please go. And don't come back."

"Ah, Julia, I had hoped you would make this easy on yourself. Now I'm going to have to do things the hard way."

Wolff's implied threat and his use of her given name sent an icy chill up her spine. She struggled to keep her composure. "What is that supposed to mean?"

He scooped his hat off the desk. "Good day."

The instant the door closed behind him, she jumped up, locked herself in, and quaked like a frightened puppy. She wanted Alex, needed him, but she also hated needing him. If only she could handle Wolff on her own, but she didn't know how, and she had already come to depend on Alex.

Too much, she feared.

* * *

Julia paced the increasingly small confines of her office, accomplishing nothing while waiting for Alex's return.

When someone knocked, she clapped a hand to her heart. "Who's there?" she called out.

"It's me," came his welcome voice. The doorknob shook as he tried to let himself in.

"I'm coming." She breathed a sigh of relief, but not as deeply as she would've liked. She hadn't managed a truly deep breath since before Wolff's arrival. She unlocked the door and swung it open, more relieved than she wanted to admit when Alex stood in front of her with an armload of packages wrapped in brown paper. If his arms had been empty, she might have flung herself into them.

He frowned, his broad forehead creased like freshly raked sand. "Has something happened?"

"Yes. No. I mean, first, get me out of here. Please. I feel like a caged animal. I want to walk on the beach."

"All right." He dumped his packages onto the chair and motioned her out the door.

With Alex behind her, she hurried through the hotel grounds and scrambled down the pathway to the beach. The surf was higher than yesterday, the waves rolling in and crashing down under the now-overcast sky. No one was bathing, the sea too rough and its temperature too cold.

She hastened her steps until reaching the end of the path. Not until she stood in the sand and stared at the ocean's horizon did she finally succeed in drawing a full, satisfying breath. It smelled of the sea, and she held it in for a moment before releasing it on a long sigh.

"Feel better?" Alex asked.

"Much better. Thank you."

"What happened?" He removed his shoes and socks, stuffing the socks inside.

She started walking toward the waves. He fell into step beside her, his shoes dangling from one hand. "While you were checking up on Tyler Wolff," she said, "he was checking up on me. He paid me a visit."

He slapped his shoes against his thigh. "Dammit! I should've been here."

A sea gull cried out above them. "You couldn't have known."

"I did know he'd gone out. The bellboy I talked to at his hotel didn't know where, though. Did Wolff threaten you?"

"Not specifically," she answered, turning north when they reached the high-tide line, "but I felt threatened just the same. He wants the hotel, and he intends to have it. I don't know what he has in mind, but I do think he's paying someone on my staff for information. He knew about our marriage." She felt better already, sharing her fears with Alex.

"Did he seem like he might be behind the attacks on you? I found out he returned to San Diego two days before the flowerpot was thrown."

"It's possible, but I don't know for sure." She skirted a mound of glistening brown kelp brought up by the waves and tide. Alex stepped over it. As they kept walking, they approached five spindly legged sandpipers probing the wet sand. Every few seconds, a wave would chase them up the beach, then they'd follow the foamy water back down. When she and Alex continued forward, the birds took flight, landing on another patch of wet sand.

"He probably didn't do it himself," he said. "He's a wealthy man and would've hired someone who can get close to you, possibly whoever's passing him the information about you. Did you ask why he wants the hotel so badly?"

"He claims for investment purposes." She shrugged as the breeze carried the spray from a large wave far enough to mist their faces. A shell crunched under her shoe.

"You think there's another reason?"

"It's just a feeling, but, yes, I think so. I just wish I knew what."

"I'm tempted to confront him," he said, "except that we don't have any evidence against him. And if he is behind the attacks, we'd be tipping our hand, letting him know we suspect him."

"Then I don't know what to do."

They walked on in silence, passing a little boy of about three who was playing in the sand, safely away from the surf. He wore a navy blue sailor suit with large, bright red buttons. He scooped dry sand into a tin pail, then poured it out. His mother, in a pink skirt and white shirtwaist, stood close by, smiling down at him.

Julia glanced over at Alex. He was watching the little boy, an expression of such painful longing and sadness on his face that her throat tightened. Suddenly he tore his gaze away from the boy and stared at a packet ship sailing past the islands off the coast.

Continuing their walk, leaving the child and his mother behind, Julia heard the boy say, "I'm gonna get some water."

"No, sweetheart, you stay here." There was a pause, followed by, "Joshua! What did Mama say? Come back!"

A woman's scream split the air.

Julia whirled and gasped

A wave had picked up the child and was pulling him off the beach. Joshua lay like a turtle on its back, his little legs and arms flailing as he tried to keep his head up in the surging mass of white water. He disappeared.

Her stomach clenched. She shrieked, "No!"

Alex had already dropped his shoes and was racing into the waves.

Julia ran to the boy's mother and threw her arm around her shoulders in an attempt to calm her, but also to keep her from trying to go after her son. Wearing sodden skirts and battling high waves, the woman would certainly drown.

Joshua's mother's screams turned to sobs. She clung to Julia as they watched Alex desperately searching for the child in the roiling and numbing water.

"He'll find your boy," Julia said, praying she spoke the truth.

Alex stood waist-deep in the surf. Waves battered his already battered body. He turned in circles, looking everywhere, reaching into the water, but coming up empty-handed. Every few seconds he dove under. Each time he surfaced with nothing.

Joshua had vanished beneath the endless procession of waves. His abandoned pail was half buried in the glistening sand. Water streamed around it.

Julia saw a growing panic in Alex's face. His movements became jerky, perhaps partially due to the cold water.

Trying to control her own panic, she scanned the surf for the tiniest bit of color that didn't belong to the sea. She had no idea how much time had passed, but she didn't think it could have been more than two minutes.

Joshua's mother moaned and keened. "My baby. Where is my baby? He can't just disappear."

She held the woman more tightly, trying to comfort them both. "Alex will find him. My husband will find your son."

"He just wanted some water in his pail. I should've gotten it myself."

Julia blinked away the burn of tears and continued watching Alex struggle against the crashing waves, against what was quickly becoming a hopeless mission. A murmuring crowd gathered, but she didn't look at them. No one else risked entering the surf.

A flash of red in the foaming water caught her eye.

"Alex!" she shouted, releasing the woman and running toward him, oblivious to the water soaking her shoes and hem. "There!" She pointed to where she'd seen the color, the red of the sailor suit's buttons. "Five feet that way!"

He dove under. Another wave broke over where he had been standing.

She backed herself out of the water, waiting and praying.

Alex surfaced with the boy.

A cheer went up from the crowd.

Joshua, sputtering and coughing and crying, clamped his arms around Alex's neck.

Carrying the boy, Alex trudged out of the surf, then collapsed to his knees, trying to catch his breath.

Julia rushed to his side, knowing how difficult his breathing must be with his injured ribs. Both he and Joshua were shivering.

Joshua's mother, sobbing with relief, stumbled

forward and tried to grab her son.

Alex didn't relinquish him. Not right away.

Julia thought she saw a tear rolling down her husband's face. She couldn't be sure, though. Too much saltwater dripped from his hair. Whether he was overcome with emotion or not, she knew that a large piece of her heart now belonged to Alexander Devlin MacLean. If he kept on like this, protecting her and saving small children, she might very well fall in love with the stranger she had married.

When Alex finally released the boy, Joshua let go, too. The boy reached for his mother and cried harder. She hugged him close, then carried him farther up the beach and set him down.

Julia helped Alex to his feet. "Are you all right?"

"I … will … be." His wet clothes stuck to his body. He continued to shiver.

Dr. Dolan emerged from the crowd, wrapped a towel around Joshua, made a quick examination, and pronounced him "a strong lad." He patted the boy on the back and turned to his mother. "Right now, madam, your son needs a hot bath and a good rest. Some warm milk with chocolate would go down well, too. I'll stop by the kitchen and bring a cup to your room."

"Thank you, Doctor," the woman said. "Would you please watch Joshua for a moment?" Before the doctor could respond, she rushed toward Alex and threw her arms around him. "You saved my son. I thought I'd lost him, but you brought him back to me. Thank you. I'll never be able to repay you, but you will always be in my prayers."

Julia blinked back tears.

Alex seemed at a loss as to what to say. He looked relieved when she let go and ran back to her son.

"I, uh, need to find my shoes." He walked away, leaving Julia alone.

Letting him go, she retrieved Joshua's pail from its sandy grave and carried it up the beach. The crowd began to disperse. Several of the men complimented her on her eagle eye. A woman said, "Without you, that little boy might still be underwater."

"Thank you, but my husband is the true hero. He's the one who deserves your praise."

The men and women gave him that praise as soon as he rejoined her, shoes in hand. Several men clapped him on the back, failing to notice that each well-meaning thump made him grimace.

"Well done, sir," one man called out.

Julia inserted herself between Alex and the others, put her arm around his back, and protected him from their compliments. It was the least she could do after all he had done for her and Joshua. If, indeed, he was keeping secrets from her, she hoped he would find a way to trust her as much as she trusted him.

* * *

Finally warm again, Alex eased himself out of the claw-foot tub and wrapped a linen towel around his hips. The ocean had been numbingly cold. He hadn't felt it at first, too intent on his search for Joshua and the race against time. He hadn't known how long the boy could hold his breath or if he had managed to gulp some air between waves. Thank God Julia glimpsed his clothing when she did.

Alex didn't know if he could have endured another child dying just out of his reach.

While in the surf, frantically searching for Joshua, he had seen flashes of his own son, first as Danny had stood at the window begging to be saved, then as the smoke and fire swallowed him whole. Danny had disappeared as suddenly as Joshua.

Forcing the agonizing thoughts away, Alex opened the bathroom door and stepped into the bedroom to dress. Spread over the bed were his new clothes. Julia must've had his packages brought up, opened, and laid out for him.

He chose one of his new sets of work clothes, dressed, and entered the sitting room. "Julia?"

"In here," she answered from her room.

At the threshold, he stopped and peeked in. The room was simply furnished, with a bed large enough for two, a linen-covered bureau, a dainty French writing desk, and shelves weighted with books, shells, driftwood, and framed photographs of two women, one who could only have been her mother.

Alex leaned in farther. To his surprise, Julia was sitting in a rocking chair by the window, sewing the hem of one of her dresses. He was impressed. Elizabeth would have never considered taking up needle and thread for anything as practical as mending an item of clothing.

"Come in," she said, resting her hands on the dress covering her lap.

He felt his eyebrows lift. "You're inviting me into your bedroom?"

"You are my husband."

"Yes, well, not in every respect." He stepped inside. "Not yet, anyway."

She swallowed visibly but didn't look away. "I see you found your new clothes. Theo delivered your packages. I laid them out and gave him your other clothes to be laundered. I hope you don't mind."

"Not as long as you didn't tell him to throw them out."

"They're not mine to dispose of. I had hoped, however, that you would wear one of your new suits this evening. I thought we could do my rounds early and then dine in the Crown Room."

He leaned against the bureau. "To be honest, I'd rather stay in tonight, away from any more demonstrations of appreciation." He put a hand to his aching back. If he kept going the way he had since his arrival at the hotel, his body would never heal.

"Of course. I should've thought of it myself. Word will have definitely gotten around by now. It's likely a reporter from the local newspaper will want to interview you."

"Not interested." He examined her sterling silver-backed hand mirror. "I don't want to talk to any reporters."

"But you're a hero, the only person who jumped into the surf to help Joshua. And you stayed in that freezing water because you refused to give up. Everyone will want to hear from you. You saved a child's life."

He returned her brush to the bureau. "I don't want to think about any of it. I certainly don't want to talk about it to some reporter." He hated how close they had come to losing Joshua. "What's the chef's special tonight?"

She jumped up and tossed the dress on the chair. "How can you just put it out of your mind like that? I can't begin to tell you how grateful I am to you for saving him. I don't know how I would have faced his mother if you hadn't pulled Joshua out alive."

"If it hadn't been for you, I would have failed." Again. He started for the door. "I'll be in my room putting my clothes away. Call me when dinner arrives. And order a bottle of wine with it. I'm thirsty." At her room's threshold, he paused and looked back. "After dinner, I'll be going to bed early. Alone."

While standing in the surf, helpless to find Joshua, Alex had felt wave after wave of guilt threatening to drown him. For over three years, mired in self-blame and suffering, he had tried not to think about Danny, essentially wanting to forget his own beloved son. He had married Julia to start his life over, hoping to find love and have other children. Alex groaned as he crossed the apartment. He had betrayed his little boy, and he did not deserve happiness.

Chapter Eleven

Despite her exhaustion, Julia lay awake. Dinner with Alex had been like eating alone. He had barely said a word, even after drinking nearly the entire bottle of wine himself. In fact, he had become quieter, as though turning inward, brooding about something he refused to share with her.

When he'd said good night, he hadn't even tried to touch her, let alone kiss her. She had discovered she wanted his affectionate and stirring touches.

An odd, unidentifiable noise made her sit up straight in bed. The sound had come from somewhere in the apartment.

She listened hard, trying to hear over the sudden hammering of her heart. Had her attacker dared to enter her refuge?

The noise came again, this time mixed with a loud muttering—Alex's voice.

Relieved but concerned, she slid out of bed and tiptoed into the sitting room.

The ramblings continued, but with his door closed,

she couldn't make out what he was saying. She crept closer and put her ear to his door. He kept mumbling, his bed frame creaking and bedclothes rustling.

Worried for him, she knocked lightly but received no response. The sounds inside continued. She opened the door and switched on the lights. "Alex?"

His eyes were shut tight. His body thrashed from one side to the other. He was shirtless, the sheet and blanket tangled around his lower body.

She winced at the vivid coloring of his bruises. He was surely in pain, yet he didn't wake. His incomprehensible muttering rose and fell, louder and softer. Was he feverish after his plunge into the ocean?

He moaned, pausing in his movements. She pressed her hand to his forehead. Perspiration dampened her fingers, but his flesh was cool. She breathed a sigh of relief.

"Alex, wake up." She shook his shoulder.

Eyes still closed, he suddenly screwed up his face and shouted, "No!" He drew the word out for what seemed an eternity, like the howl of a coyote.

Gooseflesh spread over her body. In anguish and astonishment, she watched as tears squeezed out of his eyes. What could he be seeing that was so terrible it brought him to tears in his sleep?

Abruptly every muscle in his body seemed to tense. "Danny!" he cried out.

She shook him harder. "Alex! Wake up!"

His eyes blinked open, and his body went limp. He peered up at her, then glanced around. When his gaze returned to her, he said, "Julia?" as if questioning who she was and where they were.

"Yes. Are you all right?"

His eyes cleared. "Why are you here?"

"You were having a nightmare."

"Oh. Yeah." He grabbed the covers, tugged them free of his lower body, and pulled them halfway up his torso. "I remember."

When he didn't explain, she said, "It must have been awful. You were thrashing around quite violently."

He only shrugged.

She felt a wrenching pang in her heart. Why wouldn't he confide in her? She was his wife.

"Who's Danny?" she asked.

His eyes locked on hers.

"You shouted that name. It obviously means something to you."

He rolled onto his side, facing away from her. "Switch off the lights on your way out please."

She didn't move for a full ten seconds. An empty, hopeless feeling overwhelmed her. Eventually she made it to the door and turned out the lights. Under the cover of darkness, she said, "All right, Alex. Keep your secrets. There's no reason for you to trust me with them. After all, our marriage was nothing more than a business arrangement."

She shut the door, fought back the tears stinging her eyes, and forced herself to walk calmly to her room.

* * *

Alex stood behind his closed door the next morning and breathed in the smells of bacon and sweet rolls. Despite his hunger, he remained in his room, trying to come up with a way to apologize to Julia for turning

187

his back on her. She deserved better from him, especially after her efforts to keep the well-wishers on the beach from clapping him on the back.

Though she'd only been trying to help him late last night, Alex felt as if she were prying into his past, a past he didn't want to talk about. He had relived enough of it during his nightmare.

Leaning forward, he pressed his forehead against the coolness of the painted wood. For several months, the nightmare had left him alone, but last night it returned with a vengeance, reminding him of his failure to protect his son. Julia had every right to know who Danny was, but talking about him was excruciating.

If Alex did speak of him, he feared that the pain he had kept to himself would trickle out at first, then rush like a flood through a narrow canyon. He didn't want anyone to see him that way, most especially Julia.

Straightening, he finally opened the door, no closer to a solution. He walked through the sitting room and into the small dining area. She was seated in the same chair as yesterday, a barely touched piece of toast on her plate. She held a coffee cup with both hands.

He cleared his throat. "Good morning."

She didn't look up. "Morning." Her voice sounded deeper than usual, and there was nothing welcoming in her greeting.

Alex dropped onto the chair to her left and tried to think of something neutral to say. "Smells good."

She took a sip of her coffee, still not looking at him.

He gave in, hating the coldness he knew wasn't her. Normally, she could warm a room just by being in it.

He had hurt her by refusing to answer the simplest of questions.

He pressed his palms to the tabletop. "Danny was my son."

For a moment, she didn't move, but then the cup in her hands started to shake. Afraid the steaming coffee would slosh over the rim and burn her, Alex took the cup from her hands and carefully placed it on the saucer. He steeled himself for the inevitable, the truth he had to tell, about Danny anyway.

"He died in the same fire that took Elizabeth's life, as well as a servant girl's. He was four."

Her hand flew up to her mouth. "Oh, Alex. When I told you about my baby sister, I said you couldn't know what it was like to lose a child, but you do know. Too well. I am so sorry." She placed her hand over his forearm. "Losing him in a fire …" She shook her head. "I can't even imagine."

"It's best you not try." He sucked in his stomach, attempting to maintain control. "I see it enough for the both of us."

Her fingers gently closed on his wrist. "Your nightmare last night?"

He nodded, afraid to say more.

"Tell me."

"I'd rather not."

"Please don't keep something this important from me. Despite the reasons we married, I am your wife and you said you wanted to stay. If you choose to keep your past from me, it will always be a wall between us."

She was right. He knew that, but—

"Please, Alex." She covered his wrist with both hands. "What happened?"

He drew a deep breath, stared at a covered platter without really seeing it, and remembered. "It was … a Thursday night. Elizabeth and I were arguing, again, about money. She wanted to redecorate the house that I hadn't wanted in the first place. Her parents bought it for us as a wedding gift. That way they could keep Elizabeth, their only child, close to them. We were three houses from theirs, and I hated the influence they had over her, and then over my son once he was born."

He closed his eyes as the memories emerged—his in-laws telling him how his own son would be raised, as if he had no say in the matter.

"Alex?"

He opened his eyes.

"Go on," she prompted.

He breathed in, then out. "Maintaining and staffing a house that big was more than I could afford with a wife who constantly spent money on herself. I told her we would not be redecorating, that I'd been looking for houses in a more affordable neighborhood. She threw the biggest tantrum I'd seen yet. Bottles of perfume and powders and I don't know what else went flying, crashing and breaking against the walls. There was no talking to her when she got like that. I didn't even want to be in the same house with her, so I left. I went for a walk. When I got back, the house was on fire."

"I don't know what to say." Her voice was filled with compassion and sorrow.

He didn't want her sympathy. Her hands on his

wrist were enough to undo him if he didn't keep a tight rein on his emotions.

"Later," he said, "I learned the fire had started in her room. Her tantrum had most likely continued after I left. The kerosene lamp on her dressing table may have been knocked over, the flame igniting what she'd spilled."

"The poor woman." She stared at the browned toast on her plate, shuddered, and jerked her gaze back up to him. "Where was Danny?"

He swallowed hard. "Upstairs. Asleep in the nursery on the third floor. He …"

She waited. "Don't stop. I know this is painful for you, but please don't stop."

He scraped a tiny patch of tablecloth with his blunt fingernail. "I haven't talked about Danny since I left Baltimore."

"Then you need to do so. The only way I was able to move forward after Lily's death was to remember the happy moments I had with her—the first time she smiled at me or how she would fall asleep on my shoulder. Having had Danny for four years, you must have many treasured memories of him."

He nodded slowly. He did, but they were trapped, only occasionally sneaking out to surprise Alex with their poignancy. But then his failure and loss would smack him so hard he'd nearly double over with the pain. The happy memories would vanish, scurrying back to their hiding places.

"Will you tell me just one?"

"No. His death overshadows them all. He suffered and died because of me. My argument with Elizabeth led to the fire, and I couldn't save him when I had the chance." He pulled his arm from beneath her hands. "Danny was trapped by the fire. From the street, I saw him at the dormer window. It was closed. Locked too tight for his little hands to open. I tried to get into the house, up the stairs, but the fire was too fierce." He lowered his head.

"What did you do?" she whispered.

His heart pounded, his mind taking him back to that night. "I climbed the tall sycamore in front of the nursery. Its branches nearly touched the house. But it was an old tree."

When he didn't go on, couldn't go on, she got up, moved behind him, and put her arms around him. Her face pressed against his neck.

At her touch, Alex felt tears leaking unbidden from his eyes. He had trouble speaking. "No. Don't hold me. I'll never get through this if you do."

She held him tighter. "Yes, you will. You don't have to keep everything to yourself. Tell me the rest."

He struggled to regain his composure, but the tears kept coming, the first real tears he had shed after his family's deaths.

"Danny was crying for me, shouting for help between coughs. His small fists beat against the glass."

Her arms tightened on him even more, and Alex tried to keep talking through what he recognized as sobs coming from himself. He was glad Julia wasn't facing him.

"I was so close. But the fire was closer. One moment Danny was there, the next he was gone, devoured by smoke and flames. I couldn't give up, though. I shinnied across a stout branch and reached for the edge of the roof below the window. The branch cracked. Broke. I was falling through space, helpless to save my son."

She pressed her cheek to his good cheek. Her face was as wet as his, and their tears merged.

"I'm so very sorry," she said, a quiver in her voice.

"This"—he traced the ugly, raised ridge of his scar—"was my souvenir that night. On my way down, a branch ripped open my face. Every time I look in the mirror, I'm reminded of how I failed my son."

Her fingers touched the line of his jaw. "Alex, you risked your life for your son and nearly lost it in your efforts to rescue him. You did everything you could."

"But it wasn't enough." He pulled her hand away from his face. He didn't want her comfort, didn't deserve it.

"Sometimes our best is not enough. Yesterday, though, you saved Joshua. You saved his mother from suffering as you have, from blaming herself for not acting differently when she had the chance. At that moment, she could not foresee the consequences of her son's desire to fill his pail with water, just as you could not foresee a fire starting because of your wife's tantrum."

Her rational comparison made sense, but he couldn't let go of his guilt. "Rescuing Joshua doesn't change how I feel about Danny's death." He pushed his chair back, forcing her to step away.

"No, of course it doesn't, but you can't raise a wall against him, as if he never existed. He lived, and he'll go on living in your heart if you let him. Do you have a photograph of Danny? One we could put up?"

He stood. "I don't have anything. Nothing was left."

"There must be something. Perhaps his grandparents have a toy that he played with. Or maybe they have a photograph you don't know about."

"The Ellingsons hold me responsible for the deaths of their only daughter and grandchild. I wasn't even allowed to attend the funerals. If the Ellingsons saved any kind of memento, I'm the last person they would give it to. Nothing I could ever do would change their feelings about me." And nothing they would do could ever change his feelings about them.

"Perhaps if I contacted them on your behalf."

"No. I don't want your help, Julia. You can't fix this. Or me." She had no connection to his old life, and he intended to keep it that way. "I should not have married again. I don't deserve to start over."

He turned from her stunned gaze, strode back to his room, and shut the door.

* * *

Four days later, Julia was working behind the registration desk, spelling Chalmers while he ate his midday meal. Theo usually filled in for him, more versatile than any of the other bellboys, but both he and Tilden were currently escorting a family of six and their luggage to their rooms.

She turned to the wall of pigeon holes and checked that the keys had been placed in their correct slots. The lobby was quiet, and she took her time with the simple task. Every so often, she rubbed her eyes, tired from too many nights spent lying awake, her thoughts like a whirlpool. They swirled from her hotel responsibilities to her faceless assailant patiently awaiting his next opportunity to Tyler Wolff and his implied threats to Alex and his withdrawal from her.

Her heart ached for her husband. He blamed himself for the loss of his wife and son, and he was punishing himself. Starting his life over with her, finding the possibility of happiness, must seem to him like a betrayal of his family—a selfish act. He was so used to suffering alone, not even able to grieve with others at the funerals of Elizabeth and Danny. Julia couldn't comprehend the kind of power his in-laws must have in their church and community to be able to deny Alex the final good-bye he had needed to say to his loved ones.

Before his admission, she had thought she understood his sadness, but she'd been very wrong. He had been keeping much more of himself, his emotions, and his past locked inside.

After he'd unburdened himself, she had thought they would grow closer as a couple, but she'd been wrong. Though he continued to watch over her, escorting her whenever she did her rounds or left the hotel, he rarely touched her. Their stolen kiss in the park had not been repeated. It now seemed like a dream.

Julia missed his touch, more than she ever thought possible. Last night, as she lay awake, she had seriously considered slipping into Alex's room and climbing into bed with him, to be close to him, offer him comfort, and show him he was no longer alone. But she'd been too afraid to act on it. In his current frame of mind, he probably wouldn't have welcomed her, and that would have hurt and humiliated her.

"Thank you, Mrs. MacLean."

She whirled to find her desk clerk standing behind her. "Mr. Chalmers! I didn't expect you back so soon."

He pulled his watch from his waistcoat pocket and clicked it open. "I was gone twenty-eight minutes."

"My goodness, where did the time go?" she said, amazed to have been so lost in her thoughts. "I'll leave you to your work then. Awaiting me is a stack of restaurant expenses to go through."

As she came around the desk, a tall, spare man wearing a dark plaid frock suit and carrying a brown leather case marched across the Rotunda. His nose was sharply hooked, reminding her of a hawk. She elected to leave the man to Mr. Chalmers, but then she overheard him speaking to her clerk.

"Good afternoon. I am looking for Mrs. Julia Fairbanks MacLean," he said in a no-nonsense manner. "Please direct me to her."

"Mrs. MacLean is just there."

She turned to see Chalmers pointing at her.

"Much obliged." The man approached her. "Mrs. MacLean, is it?"

"Yes, what can I do for you?"

"Kenneth Atkins, First California Bank. I am here on a matter of urgent business. Is there somewhere we could speak privately?"

She suppressed a puzzled frown, as well as a wrinkling of her nose. He smelled of money, as if he, personally, had counted the bank's assets that morning.

"Of course. My office is just around here." As she preceded the bank representative, Alex entered the lobby from the Garden Patio. She stopped and beckoned him over. "Alex, this is Mr. Kenneth Atkins. He's from First California Bank, where I do the hotel banking. Mr. Atkins, this is my husband, Alexander MacLean."

"Mr. MacLean." The banker looked down his nose at Alex's work attire and eyed his scar warily, but he shook hands with him. "Congratulations on your recent marriage. I read the notice in the newspaper. Are you managing the Hotel Grand Victoria now?"

"No, the hotel is my wife's domain."

"I see."

Julia heard the disapproval in the banker's voice, but his opinion was no different than most men's, so she didn't bother to challenge him. She loved how easily Alex spoke of her position, completely accepting of it. "Mr. Atkins wishes to speak to me on an urgent matter. Would you join us?"

"Happy to."

They filed into the office. She perched on the edge of her chair while Alex shut the door and leaned against it. He folded his powerful arms over his broad chest. The banker cast him another wary look, then seated himself across from her, his leather case lying flat on his lap.

"Mrs. MacLean, I won't waste your time with trivial small talk. As I'm sure you know, the legal agreement between First California and your father included a clause protecting the bank should the borrower die before the term of the loan expired or the loan has been paid off."

No, she didn't know. "I'm afraid I was not aware of that clause. What does it say?"

"It spells out First California's option of calling in the loan. We have decided to exercise that option. Full payment is due next Thursday, one week from today."

She nearly fell off her chair. The room spun, and Julia thought she might be sick. Suddenly Alex was beside her, his hand on her shoulder. When the room finally righted itself, she found her voice. "But that's nearly eighty thousand dollars."

"Seventy-nine thousand four hundred twenty-three dollars and twenty-eight cents, as of today. A considerable sum, and one we are no longer prepared to carry."

"But we've never been late on a payment. How can you do this?"

"Mrs. MacLean, this is obviously a shock to you, but if you had read the loan document, you would have known this was a possibility."

She should have known, but she had been too wrapped up in her efforts to take over the hotel's management and find herself a husband.

Alex squeezed her shoulder. "What if she applies to have the loan extended?"

"Despite the hotel's timely payment record, First California's board of directors feels that immediate repayment is the best course of action. We are still suffering the effects of the Panic of Ninety-three, and we'd like to get out from under them. In addition, the board does not believe a woman can be trusted to run an enterprise as large as the Hotel Grand Victoria."

"Why, the narrow-minded—" She broke off when Alex squeezed her shoulder again, but she fisted her hands in her lap. The men running First California Bank wanted a man in charge of the hotel. Just because she wouldn't play by their idea of the rules, they were going to force her out one way or another.

"Mr. Atkins," Alex said, "your news has shocked both my wife and me. As you can see, she is especially distressed. There must be a solution the board will accept. A smaller loan maybe. Or larger payments."

"The board has made its decision." He unbuckled the flap of his case, pulled out a single sheet of paper, and laid it on her desk. "Next Thursday's date is underlined, as well as the amount due."

"But I can't pay that," she said, looking at him and the paper through the blur of unshed tears. "The Panic hit us, too."

He latched his case. "I'm sorry."

She leaped up. "No, you're not. You could care less about my feelings and what losing the Hotel Grand Victoria will mean to me and everyone who works here. You're not sorry. Not one bit."

The banker stood, his chin high. "Good day to you, Mrs. MacLean, Mr. MacLean." He walked out.

The moment the door closed behind him, she collapsed back into her chair, her head in her hands. She was going to lose the hotel. After everything she had done, including marrying a perfect stranger, she was going to lose her home.

"Oh, Alex, what am I going to do?"

He turned her chair, knelt in front of her, and took her hands in his. "We'll think of something. There's time."

"A week? But that's nothing."

"It's about five days more than you had when you needed to find a husband."

A short, unexpected laugh popped out from between her sniffles. "It is, isn't it?" She leaned forward, resting her head against his shoulder, relieved to have him touching her again.

He rubbed her back, and she made a little sighing noise as his comfort and support seeped into her. She didn't want to move, but then she felt herself being pushed away.

He cleared his throat. Twice. "You had better get busy. I suggest you look for another bank to take over your loan." With that, he got up and left the office.

She slumped in her chair, wishing he were still with her. Whenever he stood by her, giving her his support, she felt anything was possible. But he had walked out, leaving her with the responsibility of saving the hotel. She supposed she couldn't blame him. From the beginning, she had made it clear he wasn't to interfere with her work. The Hotel Grand Victoria belonged to her.

Imagining the hotel in someone else's hands, Julia fought off her tears and reached into her bottom drawer. She pulled out the *San Diego City Directory* and turned to the page marked "Banks." One of them would certainly see the potential of financing a resort as renowned as the Hotel Grand Victoria. Wouldn't they?

Chapter Twelve

Seated alone at the breakfast table, listening to Alex dress in his room, Julia pushed her half-finished plate away. After yesterday's lack of success with the banks she had contacted, her scrambled eggs, toast, and even the fresh-squeezed orange juice tasted like paper. The life she had planned was spiraling away from her. No bank in San Diego, Los Angeles, or San Francisco was willing to loan her the money she needed to pay First California.

The last bank officer she'd spoken to had summed it up for her by saying, "Mrs. MacLean, few banking institutions will risk such a large amount of money with economic conditions at their current level. And they will never risk it on a woman."

The only bright spot in her morning thus far had been the delivery of the hotel's architectural plans. She looked forward to presenting them to Alex. She hoped they would cheer him up and bring back the man she thought she had married.

Hearing his door open, she scooted her chair back

and stood to greet him. He was dressed in his old work clothes, though Dr. Dolan had not yet permitted him to take up a hammer or saw. She had spoken to the doctor herself about Alex's state of health, as well as the subject of childbirth and its inherent risks. She had begun thinking about what she had said to Alex, how important it is to remember the precious moments he'd had with Danny. Yes, the pain of losing his son, and her pain of losing Lily, had been devastating, but what if Danny and Lily had never existed?

"Morning," he said, a wary look on his clean-shaven face.

"Good morning." She twisted her fingers together, feeling an unaccustomed shyness with him. Yesterday in her office, he had held her hands and comforted her, but since then, he had only reluctantly taken her arm as they walked together.

He stopped a good five feet away. His gaze skimmed over her white shirtwaist and pale blue skirt, then settled on her fidgety hands before moving up to her face. "What's going on?"

She stilled her fingers, disappointed that he continued to keep his distance. She supposed she could take charge of matters by marching up to him and giving him a good-morning kiss, but could she possibly compel herself to initiate such intimacy between them? She chewed her bottom lip.

"There's obviously something on your mind," he said.

She sighed, unable to make the first move. "Yes, two things, in fact. One, there's no need for you to accompany me downstairs and on my rounds this morning. I'm going to stay in my office and contact the largest and richest banks in New York, Boston, Philadelphia, and wherever else I can think of."

"Sounds like a good idea." He pushed his hands into his pants pockets. "I can do your rounds for you. And since Dr. Dolan won't let me work, I was thinking I'd inspect the building for areas needing attention."

"That's a wonderful idea. I'd appreciate having your trained eye look over the woodwork. However, I think you might enjoy doing something else first." Feeling like a little girl about to present a secret gift to someone special, she grinned. "The second thing on my mind is a surprise for you."

His head tipped to one side. "Oh yeah?"

She went to the sitting room closet and brought out the long roll of papers.

Interest flared in his eyes. "Are those the Reid brothers' plans?"

"Yes. Mrs. Russell, my head housekeeper, delivered them earlier. They were in a storeroom with the old registers." Hugging the plans to her chest, she carried them to the coffee table and carefully set them down. "You can indulge your architectural interest in the Hotel Grand Victoria to your heart's content."

Alex didn't move, just stared at the roll of papers.

Her smile waned. "Don't you want to see them? I thought you'd be pleased."

"No, I mean, yes, I do want to see them, and I am pleased. It's just that … I'm a carpenter now, not an architect."

She didn't understand his reluctance. From the day

of his arrival, he had been interested in the hotel. He had admired it, asked questions about it, and explored it. Had he seen enough?

Trying to keep her disappointment to herself, she glanced at the clock on the wall. "I need to go. You don't have to look at them if you don't want to. Just leave them be. I'll return them to Mrs. Russell later." She started for the door.

"Julia, I—"

"Don't worry," she interrupted with a wave of her hand. "Finding them wasn't any trouble." She strode to the parlor table and grabbed her key. "I'll see you later. Don't look for me at lunch, though. If I'm hungry, I'll order something from the kitchen."

He said nothing, and she didn't turn around.

She let herself out, struggling to hold her emotions in check. Apparently Alex's interest in the building's architecture had faded. Maybe he wanted to punish himself more by taking to the road again, locking his memories of her away and moving on. She told herself she ought to be glad he might be leaving. That was what she had planned to have happen since the day Mr. Byrnes read her father's will to her.

But Julia knew she didn't want Alex to go. She wanted him in her future.

* * *

Shortly after one o'clock, Alex stepped into the hotel's bar. The room smelled of good liquor, cigarettes, cigars, and pipe tobacco. It was a fitting place to try and forget how much he knew he had disappointed Julia with his lukewarm reaction to her surprise. The sudden appearance of the hotel's plans had caught him off guard, even scaring him. He hadn't looked at real architectural plans in years, and he wasn't sure how he would feel if he studied these.

He still didn't know.

For an hour, he had sat on the sofa, staring at the rolled-up papers. How could he enjoy looking at someone else's work when he could no longer do that same work, work he had once loved?

Settling himself on a tall stool at the bar, he glanced around. A bearded man dressed in a dapper frock suit sat alone three stools away from him, nursing a beer. At the far end of the room, eight men dressed in hunting jackets and tall boots were seated at tables that had been pushed together.

One fellow exhaled a cloud of cigar smoke and slapped his nearest companion on the back. "Harvey, don't lie. That rabbit jumped out at you so quick you nearly shot yourself instead of him."

The group erupted in laughter and more backslapping. Harvey laughed as loudly as the rest.

Alex turned to the bar.

"Afternoon, Mr. MacLean." The bartender, an older man with a waxed handlebar mustache as wide as his face, wiped his hands on a towel. "Welcome. I haven't seen you in here except during Mrs. MacLean's rounds."

"I'm doing her rounds today, and this is my last stop." He had also inspected sections of the hotel's exterior for damage from the sun and salt air.

"Then you've worked up a thirst. What can I get you?"

"Beer, please."

"Coming right up."

"No rush."

With plenty of time to spare, Alex admired the room's clean lines and masculine decor, then ran his fingers over the handcrafted mahogany bar. It was a work of art, though he doubted many of the bar's patrons ever thought twice about it. A pencil and several sheets of hotel stationery lay in front of the empty seat next to him. A previous customer had apparently been writing a letter.

Alex picked up the pencil. For something to do, he began drawing aimlessly—lines, squares, and cubes.

"Here you go." The bartender placed a tall, brimming glass of beer on the bar.

"Thanks." Alex took a deep swallow. "Mmm."

"Only the best at the Hotel Grand Victoria."

"So I've been told."

A roar of laughter went up from the hunters.

Alex tipped his chin toward them. "Did I miss a hunting party?"

"Yeah, over on North Island. It happens pretty regular. The guests hunt rabbits and whatever else they can find in the brush over there. Then the kitchen chefs cook it up for them. Any extras go on the menu's evening specials."

"Not a bad deal." With the pencil in one hand and his glass in the other, Alex drank again, enjoying the beer's slightly bitter taste.

The bartender strolled away when the bearded man sitting alone signaled for a refill.

Alex scribbled while he drank, paying no mind to what he was putting on paper. Out of nowhere, a memory of himself and Danny flowed into his head. They were sitting together at a child's small table in the nursery, both of them drawing on paper. Danny made artful scrawls that Alex incorporated into the façade of building. His son had laughed with delight.

Alex smiled at the memory, enjoying it, surprised not to feel himself engulfed by pain.

The hunters continued to rehash the glory of their kills and the disappointment of their near misses.

"Hey, you have real talent."

Alex glanced over to see the bearded patron now sitting on the stool beside him.

The man pointed at the stationery. "Are you an architect?"

Alex stared at the paper, amazed to discover that a building had emerged from the geometric shapes he'd been absently sketching. The drawing mixed a decorative colonial Spanish design with the style of an Indian pueblo he'd seen in the New Mexico Territory. "Uh, no, carpenter."

"You're probably a heck of a carpenter, but with some architectural training, I suspect you'd be a real asset to San Diego's building community." The man stuck out his hand. "Liam Howard."

"Alex MacLean." They shook hands. "Are you staying at the hotel, Liam?"

"Not me, no. I'm only a ferry trip away. I live in San Diego. Originally, I'm from New Jersey. Today I'm meeting some friends who're visiting from Chicago. They're upstairs readying themselves for our outing. I decided to wait in here, which I haven't minded a bit. Good beer and good company."

"How true." Alex tapped his glass against Liam Howard's and they both drank. "What line of business are you in, Liam?"

"Building, as you might have guessed. San Diego is growing fast, and that means opportunity."

"So I've heard." Alex remembered Julia saying something similar. With their living situation up in the air, he considered the opportunities a growing San Diego could offer him. If Julia didn't get a new loan, she would either lose the hotel or have to sell it immediately. In either case, they would have to find another place to live.

Liam nodded. "I can tell you understand what I mean. In San Diego, there are no limits to what can be accomplished."

"I like that." If Julia did find another bank to loan them the money, he'd be working for her, and that wouldn't go down nearly as smoothly as this beer was. Working for a capable and proficient woman was one thing, working for his wife was another. He didn't want to be dependent on her for his wages. Besides that, being married to the boss would put him in a difficult position with the other employees. He'd be better off working at a job away from the hotel. "Liam, I might be looking for some carpentry or construction work pretty soon. May I look you up?"

"By all means. I'm always in need of a good man, though you really ought to think about architecture." He lifted his glass in the direction of Alex's drawing, then glanced at the bartender, who waved at someone entering the room.

Alex peered over his shoulder and met Theo's gaze.

The bellboy made his way to Alex's side.

"Mr. MacLean, sorry to interrupt, but I was instructed to tell you your wife needs to run an errand."

"Thanks, Theo. I'll be right there." He slid off the stool. "Wish I could stay and chat, Liam, but my wife is waiting. It was good to meet you." He started away from the bar.

"Wait!" Liam called after him. "What about your drawing?"

Alex glanced back at what had begun as nothing more than the scribbles of a man in need of a drink and distraction. Those scribbles had turned into the rough design of a new building, something he had never expected he'd be able to do again.

He stepped back to the bar, picked up the sheet of stationery, carefully folded it several times, and slid it into his pants pocket. "Thanks. Maybe I do have a future in architecture."

He followed Theo out of the bar, his step lighter than when he had entered. He felt a bit like his old self again. His talent and ability hadn't been lost forever. They'd only been lying dormant. He had thought about Danny without suffering stabs of pain. The sweet memory had made him smile and want to remember more of the happy times they'd enjoyed together.

Alex found himself wanting to share his news with Julia. Having her in his life was undoubtedly the reason for the headway he'd made. He imagined himself taking her in his arms, spinning her around, and telling her how she and Danny had helped him design again. She would smile and hug him back and

...

Alex's excitement faded. What was he thinking? She wouldn't want to hug him after the way he had greeted her surprise for him this morning. Or after he'd been purposely pushing her away, just as he'd been doing with his memories of Danny for the last few years. Could Julia forgive him? Would she even want a guilt-ridden husband who continued to keep information about himself from her?

Since she hadn't wanted a real husband in the first place, he had his doubts.

* * *

While she waited for Alex, Julia glanced around the Rotunda, making sure everything was in its usual good order. Her gaze bounced from the marble floor to the dark wicker chairs to the polished spittoon and three guests chatting near one of the Oriental sideboards. Everything looked fine. It was she who felt as if something were off. She attributed the feeling to this morning's awkwardness with Alex about the Reid brothers' plans.

He arrived from the direction of the hotel bar, looking pleased about something, but also troubled. When he stood in front of her, she noticed beer on his breath and the clinging smell of cigar smoke. She didn't mind. He was a man, and he ought to spend time in the company of other men.

"I'm sorry to bother you, Alex, but I've finished contacting the banks and need to go to the laundry. I don't want to take any unnecessary chances by going on my own."

"I don't want you taking any chances either, and

it's no bother. I'd be angry if you didn't call on me."

She had known that, and she didn't want to cause or allow anything else to come between them. "Theo reported seeing Tyler Wolff roaming the grounds. We should perhaps be especially careful."

The muscles in Alex's jaw tightened. "Wolff's family name fits him well, the way he keeps prowling around your territory, wanting to take it over."

"I have to agree. I thought about telephoning Tom Landis and having Wolff removed, but the man wasn't doing anything illegal. Since this isn't a private residence, I didn't think I could have him arrested for trespassing."

"Marshal Landis would rather arrest me for trespassing on you."

"I know." She had heard from several people that Tom was still asking questions about Alex and making no progress at all in the investigation of whoever was after her. "I'm sorry he's such a sore loser."

"He's a damn fool." Alex grunted and started for the front door. "Tell me what's happening in the laundry."

She fell into step beside him. "One of the washing machines has broken down. A note was left on the registration desk."

"Why are you checking on it personally?" he asked as they crossed the veranda. "Send one of the maintenance men from the engine house to fix it."

"I could do that, but I wanted to assess the problem first and see how far behind the laundresses are in their work."

They descended the stairs and emerged from

beneath the portico into the sun. Julia breathed in the sea's ever-present salt tang, glad to be outside.

Alex looked back and up at the hotel, obviously searching for potential signs of trouble. Despite their current difficulties, her husband continued to watch out for her, and she felt safe with him at her side.

"If the broken machine is the same one that has been acting up for some time," she continued, "I need to decide whether to attempt another repair or order a new machine."

They crossed the carriage drive and stepped onto the lawn. A small brown rabbit hopped across the grass and disappeared beneath a cluster of shrubbery bordered by yellow marigolds. Though the gardeners wouldn't be happy about the rabbit, Julia smiled.

"Well, I wouldn't go spending any money on a new machine until you know if the hotel is going to remain in your hands."

Her smile faded. "You needn't remind me of my dilemma. It's very much on my mind." Locked in her office for the last four and a half hours, she'd thought of little else.

"Did you have any luck with the banks?" he asked, his gaze roving the grounds. A sea gull squawked above them and wheeled away.

"I contacted the biggest banks in the Midwest and the East. Several turned me down flat, but two loan officers knew of the hotel and asked for more information. They are considering my request."

"That's something anyway."

"I told them I was the owner. I didn't tell them I was also the manager."

"Oh."

She kicked a wayward leaf as they approached the circular fountain in the center of the lawn. Water spurted out of the mouths of three sizeable copper fish. A green patina covered their scales. "I should have told them, shouldn't I?"

"Not necessarily. The hotel is a reasonably good investment for any bank. If their officers want to make certain assumptions about the manager, that's up to them."

She was relieved to hear his opinion. She was also pleased about freely and comfortably discussing hotel problems and issues with him. If only conversations about their relationship and his past could be as easy. She suppressed a sigh.

"Enough about my morning," she said. "How was yours?" She deliberately didn't mention the hotel plans.

Alex peered over at her, his brown eyes gleaming with pleasure. Her heart skipped a beat. When he smiled, her stomach seemed to somersault. He appeared genuinely happy.

"The morning didn't go all that well to start with," he answered. "I chose not to look at the Reid brothers' plans. I just couldn't, not when I thought I'd never be able to do that kind of work again."

"Oh, Alex. I'm sorry. I didn't even think of that." No wonder he had avoided them. Seeing what others had done so successfully, what he could no longer do, would have been unbearable.

"Don't be sorry. All that has changed." His eyes gleamed more brightly. "Take a look at this." From his pocket, he extracted a folded sheet of paper and handed it to her.

She opened it, revealing a simplified sketch of what looked to her like a handsome Spanish-style building on hotel stationery. "It's very nice. Where did you get it?"

"I drew it. It's my own design. Julia, I can design again. Even better though, I didn't slam the door on a happy memory of Danny and me drawing together."

"Oh, my goodness! That's wonderful news." He was beginning to heal. She held up his sketch and twirled around with it. "We'll frame this and put it up in the apartment."

He laughed. "It's not that good."

"I think it's beautiful, but what it represents is more important. That's what we'll be honoring." Just as she brought the sketch back down, a gust of wind snatched it out of her hands. "Oh!"

The paper didn't fly far. Hurrying after it, she danced a quick little sidestep and—

A shot rang out, reverberating off the hotel. Birds took to the sky. A horse entering the drive spooked, nearly unseating its rider.

Julia registered it all as a burning sensation ripped into her side. She twisted, tripped, and fell, pitching forward. Her hands broke her fall. Lying on the grass, she turned her head, saw Alex's sketch, and reached for it before it could blow away.

"Leave it!" he shouted, the rampant fear in his voice frightening her.

She grabbed the paper anyway, curling her fingers around it, triumphant until the pain in her side worsened and stark realization penetrated her senses. Her assailant had finally hit his target.

Chapter Thirteen

Alex's heart beat like a sledgehammer swinging against his ribs. He dove for Julia, grabbed her under her shoulders, and dragged her to cover behind the fountain.

Blood blossomed on the left side of her waist, terrifying him. His wife had been shot, but instead of considering her own safety, she had rescued his design. What the hell had she been thinking?

She lay on the grass beside him while he crouched below the rim of the fountain's solid cement bowl. The dark red stain on her white shirtwaist grew. He needed to get her to Dr. Dolan fast. "Julia—"

"Here. Take this." She tried to press the sketch into his hand.

"Forget the drawing! It's not important."

"It is," she said through a grimace of pain. "Put it away. Keep it safe."

"Dammit." They were pinned down by a sniper, Julia possibly bleeding to death, and she was more concerned with his sketch. He seized the paper and shoved it into his pocket. "There. It's safe. Now I'm taking you to the doctor."

"No! Alex, it's too dangerous. He could still be out there."

Alex knew who she meant, the anonymous man he was tempted to kill with his bare hands, if the snake had the courage to come out of hiding.

"I don't think I'm badly hurt," she said. "We can wait."

"No, we can't. I won't take that chance. You're bleeding."

He risked a look around the fountain to try and spot where the gunman might be, if he was still in place, but several towers, assorted rooflines, and hundreds of windows and flowerboxes offered too many possibilities for concealment. Hopefully he was gone. The shot had already attracted a group of people to the front veranda, including Theo.

"The note," she said. "It must have been a ruse. Chalmers was in the gents' room when it was left on the desk, and I know the handwriting wasn't Mrs. Benedict's. I assumed one of the other laundresses had written it."

"We'll worry about that later. Right now, we have to go."

"But I don't think I can walk, and you're not supposed to lift anything heavy. Leave me here while you get help."

Air hissed through his teeth. "First my drawing, now me. Julia, think about yourself for a change. You could bleed to death if I leave you behind." Nearly shaking with his fear for her, he leaned in close, his face just inches from hers. "I won't leave you behind. I won't lose you, too."

"You're not planning to take to the road again?"

"No. My place is with you. So don't you dare die."

She touched his scarred cheek. "I won't," she whispered. "I promise."

"I expect you to keep that promise. Now forgive me for hurting you, but there's no other way." He lifted her into his arms as gently as possible, wincing at the pain from his bruised ribs.

She squeezed her eyes shut, and her mouth tightened into a thin line, but she made no sound.

Tightening his grip on her, he lurched to his feet and started running. In case the sniper had them in his sights, Alex used the few bushes and palms as cover and altered his course with intermittent zigs and zags.

No shots rang out, but he didn't slow until he reached the doctor's cottage. Theo was holding the door open for him, the elderly bellboy out of breath from racing him there. His face paled at the sight of Julia's blood fanning out over her shirtwaist. Alex suspected he looked pretty pale himself.

Dr. Dolan was standing in the doorway of his office when Alex carried her inside. Mary Dolan stood at the bottom of the stairs, her hands pressed to her cheeks.

Alex gasped for breath and words. "She's been shot. You have to stop the bleeding."

"Mary," the doctor said, all business, "help get Julia's clothes off, whatever's in the way."

"Yes, dear." Mary followed them into the office. "Oh, my poor Julia."

"I'll be all right, Mary. Don't worry."

"Hush," she said. "Save your strength."

Alex carefully laid her on the examining table.

"Is there anything I can do to help?" Theo asked, a tremor in his voice. He was standing in the doorway, gripping the doorjamb.

"No," Dr. Dolan answered. "Except close the door."

"Wait." Alex flicked a look at Theo while Mary began unbuttoning Julia's skirt. "Telephone Marshal Landis. Tell him Julia was shot. We don't know who did it, but with Tyler Wolff in the area, he should be considered a suspect."

"I'll tell the marshal."

Alex nodded. "After that, go to the laundry and find out if one of the girls sent a note about a broken washing machine. Come back when you've got answers. I'm not leaving Julia, but I will find whoever did this."

And once he did find him, if Marshal Landis failed to do his job and arrest the snake, Alex vowed to take justice into his own hands.

* * *

Julia gritted her teeth against the pain as Mary cut her stained combination camisole and corset away from her wound, leaving the rest of her modestly covered. She heard water running and the sound of Dr. Dolan washing his hands at the sink. Alex stood at the head of the examining table and brushed her hair back from her face, over and over.

She peered up at him, at her husband, the man who had risked his life bringing her to safety. He was also the man she ... loved.

She didn't know when she had fallen in love with him, but she realized now that her heart belonged to Alexander Devlin MacLean. There were so many reasons to love him—his kindness and caring, his intelligence and protective nature, his solid strength and support for her position as manager.

He was a rare individual, a special man who had endured tremendous loss, suffering, and self-imposed guilt, but who had also survived in the end, risking a marriage of convenience to keep her from making the biggest mistake of her life, tying herself to Tom Landis. In helping her, Alex had allowed her to meet her father's deadline. Even if she ultimately lost the hotel to the bank, she would not be losing everything. She had Alex.

She reached up and took his hand in hers. "I'll be fine. I'll be back in my office this afternoon."

"Oh, no, you won't. You'll be in bed, resting, and not only to recover from your wound. I know you haven't been sleeping well."

She wished she could deny his statement, but the dark circles under her eyes told the indisputable truth.

"Stop moving, Julia." Dr. Dolan bent over her side as Mary busily arranged the hem of Julia's skirt and petticoat more modestly over her ankles. "Let's see what we've got here." He gingerly wiped away the blood with linen toweling and visually examined her wound. "Well, you're right. You'll be fine. The bullet grazed you, and the bleeding has nearly stopped. You don't even need stitches."

Mary clapped a hand over her heart. "Oh, my goodness. What a relief. Thank heavens the gunman was a poor shot."

"On the contrary, Mrs. Dolan," Alex said. "Julia sidestepped at the last second to chase after a piece of paper she'd dropped."

Mary sucked in her breath. "Oh, dear."

The doctor blinked several times.

Only now grasping how close she had come to death, Julia felt a chill travel throughout her body. She gripped Alex's hand tighter, trying to stay calm.

"I had better get busy cleaning this wound," the doctor said. "There are some threads from your shirtwaist and camisole in it and some splinters of boning from your corset. To reduce the risk of infection, I'll need to get them out. This will hurt a bit, Julia."

"I can bear it," she said, preparing herself.

Dr. Dolan flicked a glance at Alex. "If you'd rather not watch, you're free to wait out in the hall."

"I'm not going anywhere. Julia, squeeze my hand as hard as you need to."

She nodded.

"Very well then. Here we go." Dr. Dolan began probing her wound with a pointed pair of tweezers.

She locked her teeth, clutched Alex's hand, and concentrated on breathing. She was grateful Alex insisted on staying, but she felt bad that he was subjecting himself to witnessing her pain. A grim expression made the tendons in his neck stand out like ridges in the sand.

"Doc, are the chances of infection high?" He laid his other hand across her forehead, as if checking for fever even at this early stage.

"There's always a possibility," he answered, continuing with his work, "but I keep up on the latest methods of medical hygiene. The advancements over the past twenty years have been most illuminating. I was particularly fascinated by Pasteur's germ theory of disease."

"Yes, but how likely is it that Julia will contract an infection?"

Dr. Dolan looked up. "Alex, you are putting the cart before the horse. There's no need to worry at this point, and probably not at all. Her wound is not serious, and the likelihood of infection is low. I am taking every precaution against it, and I will check on her regularly."

Alex let out a deep, audible sigh. "Thanks, Doc."

Twenty minutes later, after she had endured the application of a stinging, strong-smelling antiseptic solution, Dr. Dolan pronounced her wound clean and ready to be dressed. Mary helped him gather up what he would need.

Julia gave Alex his hand back, and he shook it out.

"You are stronger than you look." He smiled, relieving her of the worry that she might have hurt him.

At the sound of a light tapping on the door, Alex went and opened it a few inches.

"How's she doing?" came Theo's voice.

"Good. She's going to be fine. Absolutely fine."

"Thank God," the bellboy said. "I did like you said. Marshal Landis has been notified about what happened, and he's gone in search of Mr. Wolff. I went over to the laundry next. None of the laundresses sent a note about a broken washing machine. All the machines are working fine."

Julia lifted her head from the cushioned table, and her gaze locked with Alex's. "Someone deliberately sent me out there to be shot." She lay back down. What had she ever done to deserve such enmity?

The door closed as Theo left, and Alex's footsteps thudded across the floor on his way back to her. She rolled her head to the side and watched him approach, noticing his shirt for the first time. Across his stomach, her blood stained the faded blue cotton. Her stomach rose and dropped, as if she had just climbed a wave and plunged down the other side.

Alex, following her gaze, grabbed the shirt with both hands and ripped upwards. Buttons popped and fabric tore. With his chest bare, he wadded the ruined shirt together and wiped the bit of blood that had soaked through to his skin.

Seeing him shirtless again, she momentarily forgot why she was lying there.

Mary mumbled several incoherent words, then thrust out her hands and took the shirt from him. "I'll put this in the rubbish bin and get you one of the doctor's clean shirts." She hurried out.

Dr. Dolan prepared a dressing, gently pressed it to her wound, and secured it with a length of gauze wrapped around her middle. "There. That should do it. The wound will ooze, so I don't recommend removing the dressing. I'll check it tomorrow. Don't take any baths until I say so."

"All right, Doctor. I'll be a good patient."

"You won't need to curb your usual activities, but I

do recommend you get some rest. You are looking tired, Julia."

"I'll make sure she stays in bed," Alex said.

"Then I won't worry."

Julia sighed, feeling like a prisoner in her own home. However, she had to admit it was nice to have Alex take care of her. Could he ever love her the way she loved him?

Mary bustled back in with a clean shirt and closed the door behind her. "Here you are."

She helped Alex into it, her hands smoothing the fabric over his muscular arms, which pushed the width of the long sleeves to the limit of their seams. The shirt was also too short for his tall frame.

Julia stifled a laugh at the amusing spectacle.

"Oh, my," Mary said, trying to make the sleeves fit better, "you are a strapping fellow, aren't you? I noticed it that first day, but—"

"Mary!" Dr. Dolan snapped the linen towel he was holding.

Mary's hands paused on Alex's arms. "Yes, dear?"

"Let Alex finish the job himself."

Eyes twinkling, her mouth threatening a smile, Mary stepped back and dropped her hands to her hips. "Why, my dear Dr. Dolan, I haven't seen you this jealous since—"

"I am not jealous." He harrumphed and shuffled off to the sink.

Mary winked at Julia, refastened Julia's clothing, and covered her with a light blanket.

Alex managed to button the borrowed shirt most of the way up the front. The width was enough to accommodate the doctor's well-fed stomach.

The chest hair exposed in the V below Alex's collarbones captured Julia's gaze. She rather wished Mary had not returned so quickly to clothe him.

The door flew open, crashing against the wall.

Julia jerked her head up and stared in amazement as Tom Landis shoved an impeccably dressed and stumbling Tyler Wolff through the doorway. His fedora dropped over his eyes and fell to the floor.

"Marshal!" Dr. Dolan stepped in front of her, blocking the newcomers' view of her. "What do you think you're doing? This is a medical office, not a jail cell."

"I've apprehended a fugitive," he said, puffing out his massive chest. His star of office was polished to its usual high shine. "I caught him boarding the ferry."

Julia leaned out to see around the doctor.

Wolff had his back to her as he scooped up his hat and glared at the marshal. "I am no fugitive." He straightened his clothes. "Now will you please tell me why you dragged me off that boat?"

Tom Landis glared back at him. "To arrest you for the attempted murder of Julia Fairbanks ... MacLean." He jerked his head toward her.

Dr. Dolan stepped aside.

"What?" Wolff spun around. "Julia? My God! Are you all right?" The concern in his voice and the sincerity in his eyes floored her. He strode toward the examining table, but Alex stepped into his path. Wolff leaned from side to side to see around him. "What happened?"

"As if you didn't know," the marshal said.

"I don't."

"She was shot," Dr. Dolan said while Mary placed two pillows under her head. "Fortunately the bullet only creased her side."

"I didn't shoot her. Julia, I swear."

"That's 'Mrs. MacLean' to you," Alex said.

Wolff scrutinized him from top to bottom. "You must be the husband."

"I am."

"Well, Mr. MacLean, I had nothing to do with hurting your wife."

Julia wanted to see Wolff better. "Alex, let him come closer."

He shifted over, but only after curling a hand around the man's upper arm. "Try anything, Wolff, and you'll lose the use of this arm permanently."

Wolff stared at him, eyes narrowed, then tipped his head in acknowledgement. "Understood, but know that I have been wrongly accused. Marshal Landis, did you find a gun on me?"

Tom took his hat off and slapped it against his thigh. "You could've thrown it in the bay. You had ample opportunity."

Wolff's shoulders went back, and he seemed to stand taller. "I never had a gun to begin with. Why would I want to kill Jul— Mrs. MacLean?"

She propped herself up on one elbow. "To carry out your threat. You want the Hotel Grand Victoria, and you told me yourself you'd have to 'do things the hard way' because I wasn't cooperating."

"I was talking about the bank! I went to First California's manager and suggested the board of directors find a way to call in your loan, which would force you to sell. I am no killer. I am a shrewd and patient businessman who doesn't need to resort to violence to get what I want."

She laid her head back, trying to process what he'd said and formulate a response. The man willingly admitted he had purposely put her ownership of the hotel in jeopardy. Did she dare believe his claims about not resorting to violence?

She studied his unrepentant expression. "You succeeded very well at your game of business, Mr. Wolff. The bank did call in my loan, and, as I'm sure you know, I can't afford to pay it."

"Call them off, Wolff." Alex's hand tightened on his arm.

He winced. "I can't. My suggestion was a foregone conclusion before I ever made it. First California was hit especially hard during the Panic, and their recovery has been slower than most of the other banks that survived. To sustain their bank, the board of directors needs whatever money they can get out of this hotel."

Julia felt as if she were deflating like a balloon. She believed him. She'd seen firsthand the signs that not all was well at the bank. The building's interior hadn't been kept up, and fewer employees worked there now.

"Mr. Wolff," she said, "did you pay one or more of my employees for information about me and the hotel?"

"I did, and I don't apologize for it. In any business, accurate information is the key to success. I used two of your more disgruntled male employees, whom I met after spending some time in The Privateer, one of the taverns frequented by your staff."

"Tell me their names."

Dr. Dolan laid his hand on her shoulder. "Julia, perhaps you should interrogate the man another time. You ought to rest."

"Doctor, I want to know who betrayed me."

Wolff hesitated, then shrugged. "Chalmers and Levesque."

"Jacques?" She could easily believe Chalmers a traitor, but her maitre d'? Until now, she had attributed his occasional lack of respect to his temperamental disposition.

Alex's voice filled the silence. "Did you pay one of them to kill Julia?"

"No!" Wolff yelled. "How many times do I have to tell you? I wouldn't hurt her. I offered to buy the hotel, not steal it. Though, by rights, it should be mine."

She exchanged astonished looks with Alex, Mary, the doctor, and Tom. "Yours?"

"Yes, mine. Lloyd Alwin Fairbanks was my father."

Julia couldn't make a sound.

Mary gasped loud enough for all of them.

Everyone's face but Wolff's registered surprise and disbelief.

Julia swung her gaze back to him. Really looking at him, she was rendered mute a second time. Now she knew why he looked familiar. His eyes, the shape and hazel coloring, were her father's eyes.

He pointed at her. "That would make you, Mrs. MacLean, my half-sister."

A bubble of hysterical laughter popped out of her.

This was priceless. Her father had wanted a boy more than anything else. Over and over, he had tried to father one when, in truth, he already had one.

"My father didn't know about you, did he?"

Wolff's expression closed down on itself. "No."

Marshal Landis stepped forward. "Julia, you can't believe what this man says. He's trying to swindle you. If he didn't shoot you, I'll arrest him for something else."

"I appreciate your offer, Tom, but I do believe him. Look at his eyes. His chin, too. They're the same as my father's were."

Everyone stared at his face, which reddened under the scrutiny.

Questions whirled in her head, and another bubble of inappropriate laughter burst from her. She clamped down on it long enough to ask, "How old are you?"

"Twenty-seven."

"Two years older than I." He would have been conceived before her parents married. At least her father had not betrayed her mother with another woman. "Regardless of your age, if Father had known about you, the hotel would have been yours. He longed for a son."

Tears leaked from her eyes at the irony, and she began to cry from her heart. Her mother had died needlessly, trying to give Father what he already had. Why hadn't Wolff made himself known before now?

Julia gulped air but couldn't draw enough.

Alex dropped to his knees beside her and grabbed her hand. "You're freezing."

"It could be shock," Dr. Dolan said. "Everybody

out. Now."

While Mary spread a heavier blanket over her, Alex rubbed her hand between both of his. "It's all right, Julia," he said, a catch in his voice. "You're going to be fine. You have to be fine."

Chapter Fourteen

Julia awoke to her dark room and the sound of Alex's low-pitched snores coming from her rocking chair. The moonlight entering through the window silhouetted him, and she guessed he must have been as tired as she to fall asleep in the chair. He had been sitting there when she'd dropped off late this afternoon after he and Dr. Dolan installed her in her bed with orders to rest.

Trying not to wake him and careful not to dislodge the bandage under her modest white muslin nightdress, she got up and tiptoed into the water closet. When she came back out, the snores had ceased and Alex was sitting up.

"How are you feeling?" he asked.

"Good. Refreshed and hungry." Standing beside her bed, she switched on the lamp and glanced at the clock.

"What time is it?" he asked, surveying her modest nightdress with more attention than seemed normal.

When she realized the lamp behind her was

revealing her body to him, she quickly stepped aside. "Just after ten. Have you been in that chair since this afternoon?"

"No, your chef sent dinner up a few hours ago." Feet bare, he stood and stretched. Dr. Dolan's shirt had been replaced with one of his own, and it pulled across his chest as he raised his arms. "I ate it in the other room so I wouldn't disturb you."

"Is there any left?" she asked, dragging her gaze up to his face.

"Enough. Beef and barley soup, 'to strengthen your blood,' I was told. I'll heat it up and bring it to you. There's fresh bread, too."

"Alex, I'm perfectly able to eat at the table."

"I can see that, but, if you'll recall, I promised Dr. Dolan I wouldn't let you out of bed. You scared us when you couldn't catch your breath."

"I know. I scared myself. My emotions got the better of me. I couldn't stop thinking about my mother. If my father had known he had a son, Mama might still be alive today." Avoiding further thoughts of her parents and half-brother, she started for the door.

Alex stepped in front of her. "Julia, I intend to keep my word to the doctor. Please get back into bed."

She peered up at the implacable expression on his face. This was the man she loved, the man who wanted to stay with her and who had risked his life to carry her to Dr. Dolan. The temptation to touch him was too strong to deny. She pressed her fingertips, then her palm, against the center of his chest. Beneath her hand, his heart beat strong and fast, faster than she expected.

"What are you doing?" His hand came down on

hers, and his brown eyes glimmered with golden specks that flashed in the lamplight. His intent gaze ignited a scorching heat deep inside her.

"I'm ... not sure."

Inhaling his masculine scent, she realized her appetite for food had fled, replaced by a hunger for her husband. She loved Alex, and she wanted him to make her his. Until they consummated their marriage, they wouldn't truly be husband and wife.

She licked her lips and stepped closer to him. Beneath her hand, his heart pulsed faster, encouraging her. "I will go back to bed if you will join me there."

His brows rose. "Are we negotiating the terms of a possible wedding night, Mrs. MacLean?"

"No. Tonight I want nothing to do with terms or contracts. I do, however, want you to be my husband in the most intimate way possible. Show me that your claims about lovemaking are true."

His eyes seemed to darken. His chest rose and fell with the deep breath he took and released. "Oh, Julia." Her name came out on a sigh. "You don't know how much I want to do just that. I've wanted you from the very first, but"—he gritted his teeth and slid his hand out from between their bodies—"you're hurt. I won't risk aggravating your wound."

Staring up at him, she silently refused to let him be his gallant self and walk away. "I'm not in any pain. This"—she lowered her hand to her wound—"is no worse than a scraped knee. If it worries you, though, we can be extra careful." She reached up and cupped his jaw. "Please make love to me, Alex. Make me your wife."

He groaned, as if struggling with himself. "What about your fear of pregnancy? The sheathe we need to prevent conception is in my bathroom. I'd have to leave you for a minute."

"I don't want you to go anywhere, Alex." Not now. Not ever. She lowered her hand to his shoulder. "I'll always be afraid of childbirth, but when I recently spoke to Dr. Dolan about your recovery, I also discussed my fears with him. He said I am a 'very fit specimen of womanhood,' and there's no reason to think I'll suffer the same complications my mother did."

"What about the possibility of … losing a child?"

"Through you, your Danny, and my sister, I've realized how important it is to cherish whatever limited time we have with the ones we love. We have to risk our hearts to enjoy the greatest rewards—love and family. Do you still want children?"

"I always wanted to give Danny brothers and sisters. I loved being a father. Playing with him was the highlight of my days. Now that I've let him back into my life, I'm no longer starting over. I'm moving forward, and I'd like to give fatherhood another try."

"I'm glad. I think you must be a wonderful father."

"A word of warning. I'm going to be an extremely overprotective father."

"I won't mind that a bit." She trailed her index finger the length of his scar. "Thank you for marrying me."

"Thank you for asking." His lips came down on hers, gentle and warm. She reached around his neck, and his arms came around her back. He eased her against him, careful not to touch her wound.

Julia melted into his embrace and answered his kiss. It deepened, their tongues dancing in rhythm. She relished the solid feel of his chest. Farther down, a certain prominent part of him pressed intimately against her. The knowledge that she was the woman he desired made her body tense with mutual desire. Julia threaded her fingers into his hair, giving herself up to him and the love in her heart.

Time came to a standstill for her, the clock only beginning to tick again when Alex stepped back from her. His breathing was harsh and loud in the quiet of her bedroom. She wanted him to come back to her, to take her in his arms again and kiss her even more thoroughly. She wanted to feel his gentle but callused fingertips grazing across her flesh.

"Are you leaving?" she asked, desperation in her voice.

"Not on your life." He began to unbutton his shirt.

Her relief and longing made her limbs shake. Their wedding night was only just beginning.

She watched him in fascination, her attention riveted on his fingers and the widening expanse of muscled flesh. Her fingers tingled, as if they wanted to touch him, but she kept her distance, admiring him under the soft light from the lamp. When he turned and tossed the shirt aside, she saw the vividly colored bruises marring his back. They reminded her of how much he had done for her. He was her hero. He had saved her life the first time they met, rescued little Joshua from certain drowning, and whisked her to the doctor when she might have bled to death.

She began to unfasten her nightdress, beginning at the top button of the high, ruffled neckline.

"That is the primmest nightdress I have ever seen," he said. "It makes me want to uncover every hidden part of you."

"Oh." She didn't know what else to say. His unwavering gaze made her fingers fumble the buttons.

He gently pulled her hands away. "Let me." The deep timbre of his voice set butterflies free in her stomach. Their wings beat more swiftly with each button that came undone. The backs of his knuckles skimmed her breasts as he worked.

She drew quick, shallow breaths, and her back arched involuntarily.

He smiled at her, a smile so open and easy and knowing that it took away what was left of her breath.

Her nightdress soon fell to the floor with a whispered rustle, pooling around her ankles. The air was cool on her body, the bandage around her middle the only covering. She felt no shame. This was what she wanted, what they both wanted—the real beginning of their life as a married couple.

Alex's gaze roved over her. Julia felt herself warm. Her breasts swelled, and her nipples tightened to small peaks. When he offered her his hand, she took it and stepped clear of the garment at her feet, holding onto him with a trust she had never given to anyone before.

* * *

Pulse galloping, Alex stood in front of his wife. He recognized the trusting look in her eyes, and he vowed to control his passion. Though he was more than ready to make love to her—long-overdue ready—he didn't want to frighten or hurt her. He would take great care with her wound. He would also take his time, following through on his promise that their first time together would be slow and sensual, every moment worth savoring. Their postponed wedding night would be as wonderful for her as it would be for him, if not more so.

He let go of her hand and stroked her glorious hair. The ash-blond strands shimmered in the light from the lamp, draping her neck and back and shoulders. He lifted what felt like a thousand silken threads.

"Your hair is as beautiful as the rest of you."

"Will you be touching the rest of me, too?" she asked, tempting him, a wanton yearning filling the innocent, brilliant blue of her eyes. Her scent of sweet and tangy orange blossoms floated on the air, drawing him to her.

"Oh, yes. I will be touching every inch. Starting now."

Her breasts were high, with dusky-rose nipples beaded tight. Softly rounded hips led to legs that were longer than he had imagined. Dark blond curls seemed to glisten between her thighs. With excruciating slowness, Alex stroked his callused hand from her shoulder, down her arm, over her hip, and along her leg.

She moaned softly and swayed under his touch. Her body trembled.

"You all right?"

"Yes," she croaked.

"Shall I continue?"

"Oh, yes."

He smiled and placed his hands on her hips, careful not to dislodge the gauze holding the dressing at her waist. "Lean back a little. Trust me. I won't let you fall."

She did as he said, her chest lifting like an offering to his palate.

He lowered his head and took the bud of one breast into his mouth, gently nibbling at the hardened nipple, laving his tongue over it.

She released another moan. When he switched to her other breast, nipping and sucking, she gripped his arms, arched, and gasped her pleasure, a boundless longing in the stirring sound.

His body lurched, every part of him burning for her. He lowered her onto the bed, then stepped back and shucked his canvas pants and cotton drawers, kicking them across the floor.

She watched, and her potent gaze made him painfully harder than he already was. His heart beat like a steam engine at full throttle.

"Are you afraid?" he asked.

"No. Not with you." She shimmied into the middle of the bed as her gaze roamed over him again. "Besides, you're beautiful. I never thought a man's body could be so captivating."

He wasn't beautiful, not with his scarred face, but he liked hearing that his wife admired his body.

"You're the one who's beautiful." He knelt on the edge of the bed, captured her hand, and lifted it to his lips, kissing the palm and each fingertip, sucking on her littlest finger. When he lay down beside her, he slowly swept his hand down the length of her arm to the soft curve of her hip and thigh.

Tonight, Julia Fairbanks MacLean would be his wife in every respect. He had never wanted any woman as much as he wanted her. He was a lucky man.

* * *

She waited, nearly breathless from the lingering feel of Alex's hand on her body. She'd had no idea a man's touch could elicit this many sensations or that just looking at his naked body could arouse her. Seeing the proud jut of his manhood had started a throbbing deep in her womb and the private place between her legs.

Waves of desire as relentless as the surf buffeted her. When she recalled her innocence of a week ago, when she had first seen Alex without his shirt, she could hardly believe she was now seeing all of him, and feeling no shyness or shame. Everything in her hummed with a craving she had never known. She wanted nothing more than to open herself to him, welcome him into her body—and do her marital duty. She smiled.

He leaned over her. "What are you smiling about?"

"I was just thinking how enjoyable a wife's marital duty can be with the right man, 'a man of experience,' as Kate would say."

"Hmm. How about a man who wants to please his wife more than himself?" he murmured between kisses.

She suppressed a frisson of anticipation. "I think I'd prefer an equal give and take between us," she managed to whisper, "though I apologize in advance for my limited experience."

"I'm not sorry at all." His kisses moved lower, trailing across the hollow below her ear. "I like knowing I'll be your first and only lover."

Julia loved that he intended to be the only man ever to lie with her. He was her future. Even if she lost the hotel, she would still have Alex. She would never regret marrying him.

His kisses dropped to her chest. His lips tantalized and tormented one breast while his fingers teased the other. A powerful need grew inside her. She didn't even try to stifle the moan building in her throat.

"Please, Alex," she begged, barely recognizing her own voice, not even sure what she wanted.

"Don't rush me, sweetheart. Try to relax."

"How can I relax when you're doing what you're doing?"

He chuckled hoarsely. "I suppose I could stop what I'm doing."

"No! Don't you dare!"

"Your wish is my command." His hand slid up the inside of her leg, his fingers grazing her private place and moving against her.

"Oh, my." She threw her head back. Her legs seemed to open of their own accord.

His finger slowly slid inside her, stretching her, finding sensitive places she hadn't known existed.

"Does that hurt?" he asked.

"No," she moaned, writhing beneath his expert touch.

Dazed, her breathing shallow, he continued his exquisite torture until time lost all meaning. Every nerve ending felt on fire.

Finally, her husband poised himself above her. She gripped his arms, digging her fingertips into them.

"Open wider, sweetheart. I don't want to hurt you." Despite the tension visible in his jaw, neck, and shoulders, he smiled down at her reassuringly.

She smiled back, trusting him completely, wanting this and him more than anything. She gave herself up to him, her body quivering as he lowered himself between her thighs.

He pressed into her, pushing so slowly she gasped. A sharp pain quickly followed, but the ache receded amidst the greater awareness of Alex filling her, making them husband and wife.

"Is this what you wanted?" he asked, moving inside her, his voice rough, his breathing fast.

"Yes," she answered through her own helplessly quick breaths. A feverish sensation flared throughout her body. She raised her hips, and her pounding heart seemed full to bursting with the sensations and emotions overwhelming her. His claims were true. Now she knew what he meant. A rushing noise as loud as the sea on a stormy night flowed inside her ears. "Oh, Alex."

He paused.

Their gazes met, and Julia nearly blurted out her feelings for him. She loved Alex MacLean and couldn't imagine life without him.

She started to tell him, but he began to move again, and she lost the ability to think let alone speak.

Lamplight bathed his sweat-slicked muscles in a shimmering gold. Each of Alex's thrusts built within her an indescribable tension, one that grew and grew until she thought she could no longer bear it.

Senses overloading, she wedged her eyes shut and gave herself up to it.

In sudden, astonished release, she cried out, "Alex!" Behind her eyes, the world exploded in a wash of white sea foam.

* * *

Beneath the blanket and quilted bedcover, Julia lay in Alex's arms. Sometime during the night, he must have switched off the lamp. Pale light from a rosy dawn filtered into the room. She felt as if they were in a world of their own, just the two of them. The back of her body was melded to the front of his, and she had never felt such contentment and belonging. They belonged to each other.

Her husband sighed, his warm breath tickling her nape. "Are you awake?" he murmured.

"Yes." Taking care with her wound, she rolled to her other side and smiled at him. "Is there something you wanted?" she asked.

"I can think of several things, but right this minute, I just want to look at you." He gave her a smile filled with pleasure. "How do you feel?"

"I think you know the answer to that."

"A man still likes to hear he has pleased a lady."

"Your previous claims were not empty boasts. You pleased this lady indescribably, incredibly, inordinately, in—"

He pressed his index finger to her lips. "That'll do. Too much flattery isn't good for a fellow."

She laughed and lay back, her head on his arm.

"My stepmother led me to believe lovemaking was an act to endure, not enjoy. I feel sorry for her now."

"Me, too. What was her name?" he asked, twirling a lock of her hair around his finger.

"Harriet Lincoln. She was from New York City, and she told us she had come west in search of a quieter place to live. I'm embarrassed to say I wasn't very welcoming. She was nice, but I'd just turned eighteen and was still devastated by my mother's and Lily's deaths."

Alex tucked her hair behind her ear. "I'm sure she understood."

"She did, and eventually we became friends. Father, however, became dissatisfied with her. She miscarried two years into their marriage and did not conceive again. She ... died when I was twenty-three. It was a cancer in her female organs."

"I'm sorry." He brush a tear from her cheek.

She curled herself closer to him. "I'm not sure she ever loved my father. She always seemed wary around men. I remember her telling me, 'Be very careful when choosing who you smile at or speak to, Julia. You never know what that man is really thinking.' She felt I was being too friendly with the hotel's male guests and employees. She was quite adamant about it."

"Maybe she'd had a bad experience herself and was trying to protect you." He kissed her shoulder.

"I don't know. She never said. I miss her at times, but, fortunately for me, I have you." She leaned up on one elbow and kissed him, feathering her tongue across his lips until they opened to her.

"Oh, Julia, what have I unleashed?"

"You haven't 'unleashed' anything. You've shown me why our two Bridal Chambers are popular not only with couples on their honeymoon, but also with couples who've been married for many years."

"Maybe we should try one out ourselves." He gently pulled her on top of him.

"They are both occupied for three more days," she said, her stomach clenching against the sensations swirling within her.

"I guess we'll just have to continue christening our own personal bridal chamber."

He cradled her face in his hands, bringing it down to his, where he laid siege to her mouth, his kiss hot, deep, and full of promise.

Chapter Fifteen

Late Saturday morning, Julia pushed back from the breakfast table, ready to return to work. She felt guilty for neglecting the hotel, but she did not regret the reason for her neglect. After a night filled with passion, she had awoken late with a lasting sense of contentment, happiness, and love.

The man of her dreams was still in her bed, catching up on the sleep they had lost.

Glancing around the apartment, she decided to move the Reid brothers' plans from the coffee table. She set them in a corner of the sitting room, where Alex could bring them out whenever he was ready.

Her bedroom door opened, and he padded into the room wearing nothing but his pants from the night before. They were partially undone.

Her appreciative gaze slid over him. When her eyes eventually met his, he was smiling with one dark brow quirked upward.

"Morning," he said, his voice deeper than usual. "I woke up and you were gone. I missed you."

She shrugged, feigning indifference, but his words made her feel as if a cozy quilt had been wrapped around her. "I still have a hotel to run." She waved toward her recently vacated chair. "Breakfast is on the table, if you're hungry."

"I'm starved. For you." He reached for her.

She playfully dodged his grasp, feeling only a slight twinge from her wound. "Mr. MacLean, if you don't keep your hands to yourself, I'll never get any work done."

"That's the idea."

She laughed. "I'm not going back to bed with you, no matter how tempted I may be. It's already late, and I need to find out if there are any telephone messages or telegrams from the banks I contacted. If none of them are willing to loan me the money, you and I won't have a bed."

He sighed. "Well, if you put it that way …"

"I do."

"All right, but you could at least take some of the sting away by giving me a morning kiss." He tapped his finger against his bottom lip.

She chewed hers, trying to decide whether to accommodate him. "I don't think I dare. You'll take advantage of me."

"Damn. How did you get to know me so well so quickly?" He grabbed for her again, this time succeeding.

Laughing, she tried to wriggle out of his hold, but then his mouth came down on hers, and Julia forgot that she had wanted to get away.

Sixty seconds later, breathless and nearly boneless,

she leaned back in his arms. "You don't play fair."

"Not always, no."

"But I do have to go to work."

"Not without me. In case you've forgotten, there's a sniper on the loose. I failed you yesterday. I won't let it happen again."

"An army couldn't have protected me yesterday. Whoever shot at me tricked us both and hid himself well enough to elude your observation. You mustn't blame yourself, Alex."

He looked away. "Let me get dressed and eat something, then we'll go."

She hesitated, wishing she knew how to free him of his penchant for feeling guilty about events beyond his control. No bright ideas came to mind, though. "All right, but don't take too long."

As he disappeared into his room, someone knocked at the apartment's door.

She walked over and called out, "Who is it?"

"Your brother. Tyler Wolff."

Julia curled her hands into fists, struggling between her normally hospitable nature, her dislike for the man who had set her loan problem in motion, and her desire to have her questions about him answered. Ultimately, she cracked the door open a few inches. "What do you want?"

"To see how my sister is faring after her ordeal yesterday," he said with perfect seriousness.

"I'm fine, as you can see. If that's all, good day." She started to close the door.

"No, it's not all. Julia, I want to talk to you, and not through a sliver of doorway."

Alex, dressed in his work clothes, entered the sitting room. "Who is it?" he asked, frowning, probably unhappy she had opened the door at all.

"Wolff. He wants to come in and talk."

"Maybe you should let him. I'd like to hear what he has to say."

She closed the door and huffed out her breath. "But he willfully tried to take my home from me."

"He's still your brother."

She lifted her chin. "Half-brother."

"Right. A half-brother you must have questions about. Don't you want to know why he was kept a secret from your father? I know I'm curious."

She was curious, about that and other matters. "Fine." She swung the door open. "Come in, Mr. Wolff."

"Thank you." He inclined his head to her and stepped inside. "Do you think you could call me Tyler? We are brother and sister."

She didn't answer, taking a moment to study his perfectly tailored, iron gray cutaway suit. She didn't want to give in to him, but no matter what Wolff had tried to do to her, there was no disputing they were family.

"As you wish, ... Tyler. Even though you don't deserve to be heard, I admit there are a few things I'd like to know." And once she had her answers, she would send him back where he came from.

"I will answer them to the best of my ability."

"I hope you'll answer them truthfully," she dared to say.

His eyes—her father's eyes—narrowed, and his lips

thinned. "You'll get the truth."

"Good." She waved him toward the sofas and chair. "Please sit down."

He unbuttoned his jacket and took the chair.

Mindful of her wound, Julia eased herself onto the sofa. Alex joined her, a united front against the man who had acted more like a predator than a brother.

"What is it you want to know?" Tyler asked.

She took a moment to arrange her skirts. "To start with, when did you find out Lloyd Fairbanks was your father?"

"Eight months ago, when my mother was on her deathbed."

She laced her fingers together and twisted her hands in her lap. "My condolences."

"Thank you." He peered toward the window and the sunny day outside. His throat flexed, but then he turned back to her. "Next question."

She nodded. "Why is owning the Hotel Grand Victoria so important to you?"

"That answer is more complicated. According to my mother, when she met Lloyd Fairbanks, he was still a single man, and there was a mutual attraction. More importantly, he wanted female companionship and she needed money. Her husband, an able-bodied seaman, was rarely home and never left her with enough to live on. She arranged with Mr. Fairbanks to be his paid mistress whenever her husband was away."

Mistress? Julia had never imagined her father, even unmarried, would have a mistress, especially a married one. She did not approve of Tyler's mother committing adultery or her father being part of it. And

249

yet, who was she to judge? If Alex hadn't married her, she could have ended up penniless and homeless. What might she have had to do to survive? And what more would she have done if a child were depending on her?

"Shall I go on?" Tyler asked.

Alex stretched his arm behind her head, along the back of the sofa. His very nearness soothed her, calming her nerves and giving her the courage to learn more about her father and his past.

"Yes. I want to hear it all."

Tyler crossed one leg over the other. "The arrangement between Mr. Fairbanks and my mother ended when he met the woman who became his wife—your mother. My mother's husband returned soon after, and two months later she realized she was pregnant. She had always wanted children and was thrilled, believing her husband was the father. After my birth, however, she saw the truth, which frightened her. On many occasions, Mr. Fairbanks had mentioned how badly he wanted a son. My mother believed if he knew I existed, he would try to take me from her. So she never said anything."

"What about her husband?" Julia asked, caught up in the story despite her uncharitable feelings toward Tyler. "Did he realize it, too?"

"Not at first. He was at sea most of the time, including during my birth. When I was about three, he figured it out, but Mama told him nothing about Mr. Fairbanks. She was afraid if she did that he might tell him, or even attempt to sell me to him. When I was five, the three of us moved to Boston, where the man

I'd always thought was my father could get more work and be gone more often. Eventually, he abandoned us."

She felt a wave of sympathy rise in her heart. Alex's hand came down to rest on her shoulder, and she touched her fingers to his.

"How did you and your mother survive?" she asked.

"She took on two jobs so I could stay in school. When I was twelve, I started working in a ship chandlery. My real education began there. It has served me well."

"Apparently so," she said, impressed in spite of herself. He had worked his way up from nothing, and now he had enough money to buy the Hotel Grand Victoria. Yes, very impressive.

Alex stretched out his legs, crossing them at the ankles. "I would guess you have that innate talent for business that some call 'the Midas touch.'"

Tyler shrugged. "I've been very fortunate."

Julia studied him. He could be very humble when he wished, but she couldn't forget the arrogance he had exhibited during his recent visit to her office. "When you learned about ... your real father, did you want to meet him?"

"Yes, but there were burial arrangements to make and my mother's affairs to put in order and my own business affairs to take care of because I'd neglected them to be with her when she was ill. When I was finally ready to meet Mr. Fairbanks, I discovered he was not in Philadelphia, as my mother had believed, that he had come here and built a remarkable resort hotel on the shores of Coronado Island. I got excited. I'd never had anything in common with my mother's husband, so when I realized I took after my real father, I was elated. And since she'd been so afraid he would take me away from her, I imagined he would open his arms to me once I introduced myself." He looked away and sighed deeply. "Obviously, I was too late."

She dropped her hand back to her lap and struggled with her conflicting feelings. Through no fault of his own, Tyler had been born into a difficult situation that, in his eyes, would never be resolved. Even so, she couldn't help but resent him. He was everything her father would have wanted in a son.

"I don't know that he would have physically embraced you," she said. "Lloyd Fairbanks wasn't a warm man. But he would have welcomed you. Like your mother told you, he always wanted a son."

"When did you learn of his death?" Alex asked.

"The same week I'd planned to travel west. It was a bigger blow than I'd expected. Until that moment, I hadn't known how much I wanted to be part of his life. Right then and there I decided I had to have the Hotel Grand Victoria. It was his creation, a part of him, just as I was."

Julia smoothed a wrinkle in her skirt. "I can understand why you were so persistent in your attempts to buy the hotel, but those reasons don't excuse your actions. You had no right to involve the bank or use my employees to gather information."

She hadn't yet decided what to do about her two traitors. Perhaps nothing. What would be the point? After next Thursday, if the Hotel Grand Victoria belonged to First California Bank, she would have no say in the matter anyway.

"I used what was at my disposal," he said, making no apology.

Alex pulled his legs in, removed his hand from her shoulder, and leaned forward. "Are you still bent on owning the hotel?"

She didn't move, barely even breathed, as she waited for Tyler's answer.

"Since yesterday, I've thought a lot about what it is I really want. I don't have the father I'd hoped for, but I do have a sister." His gaze swung between her and Alex. "And a brother-in-law. Someday, I may even have nieces and nephews. In the long run, I think having family will be more important than having a hotel."

Julia glanced at Alex. As of this morning, she knew exactly how Tyler felt. She could imagine living her girlhood dreams of having children and a husband who loved her, a man who she loved in return. Her love for the hotel paled in comparison.

Tyler scooted to the edge of the chair. "Julia, I came today, not only to see how you were, but to put several business propositions before you."

"Let me guess," she said, stifling the urge to roll her eyes. "You're offering to buy the hotel."

"That would be one option, yes. After the sale, you'd be a very wealthy woman who could go anywhere and do anything. Neither you nor your husband would ever have to work again."

"I prefer to stay here," she answered, "and I enjoy managing the Hotel Grand Victoria."

"Then that brings us to option number two, in which we form a partnership. I will pay off the balance of your loan, and we can go into business together."

Once again, he was trying to get his hands on her home, but without him, she might very well lose it. "I don't particularly like that option either."

He placed his forearms on his thighs and clasped his hands. "It's a good option. You'd be free to continue in your role as manager for as long as you wished. In the months I've been watching you, despite your sex and society's general opinion of what a woman can and cannot do, I have learned you are an efficient and effective manager. I believe you take after our father as well."

Our father. That would take some getting used to. She appreciated Tyler's compliment, though, and felt warmed by his belief in her. He recognized her abilities, seeing what her father never could.

Alex covered her hand with his. "Julia, with the second option, you'd be losing nothing."

"But I'd be gaining a partner I barely know." Tyler was a man accustomed to being in control, and he'd probably question her decisions or interfere with her way of doing things. She wasn't ready to give in to him yet. "Is there a third option?"

"There is." Tyler straightened. "I have persuaded the board of directors at First California to give you an additional month to pay them. You can, therefore, continue your attempts to get a new loan from another institution."

She opened her mouth, but no words came out.

"That was generous of you," Alex said, his hand

squeezing hers.

"Yes," she finally managed, wondering what kind of persuasion he had used on the bank's directors. She decided she would rather not know. "Thank you, Tyler. I'll take the third option."

He chuckled. "I thought you might. If, however, you change your mind at any time, let me know. The other offers will stand."

"I'll keep them in mind and, if necessary, contact you in Boston. You've been away from your business interests so long I'm sure they must be in need of your personal attention."

He laughed, stood up, and fastened his jacket. "My dear Julia, you're not going to get rid of me that easy. You have an older brother now, and older brothers are supposed to look out for their younger siblings, especially their sisters." His expression turned serious. "I'm not going anywhere until whoever shot you is captured."

She swallowed a moan.

Alex got up and held his hand out to Tyler. "Welcome aboard, Wolff." They shook hands. "Any help you can give would be appreciated."

"I'll move into the Hotel Grand Victoria this afternoon," he said.

Julia sank deeper into the sofa. Her new-found brother was here to stay.

* * *

"Alex, I really ought to do my evening rounds," she said, getting up from the table and placing her dinner dishes on the waiter's tray for collection. "As you well know, I need to check on things. I only left my office once this afternoon."

He added his dishes to the tray. "No, you are not going anywhere." He wasn't about to let her put herself in danger again. "You're safe here."

"But whoever is doing this won't know that I'm going now. I'm not responding to any notes."

"Doesn't matter. You're a target." And Julia was his wife. Alex wanted her around for a long time. Last night's blissful hours of lovemaking were only the beginning. "Someone is still watching, and we have to take every precaution."

A knock on the door made them exchange wary looks. Their visitor couldn't be the waiter. They hadn't pressed the annunciator calling for him yet. And Alex knew Tyler had returned to San Diego for a dinner engagement.

"I'll get it." He strode across the sitting room and leaned against the door. "Who's there?"

"Harold Dolan," came the doctor's familiar voice.

Alex slowly opened the door, careful to check the hallway for anyone else. No one leaped out from around the corner, and he let the doctor pass. "Come in."

"Dr. Dolan," Julia said, stepping forward as Alex locked the door, "I didn't expect to see you this evening."

"I know, but I wanted to save you another trip to my office." He carried his medical bag. "I'm sorry I wasn't able to accommodate you this afternoon. Mary told me you and Alex came by."

"That's all right," she said. "You were busy with guests, and they come first."

"Yes, there was quite a line of them waiting to see me." His cheeks puffed as he blew out a breath. "Sunburn, scraped knees, and stomach ailments from overindulging in the dining room. Vacation complaints do add up." He yawned. "All is well now, though, and I'm here to inspect your wound. I'll change the dressing if necessary."

"I appreciate your concern and diligence, Doctor, but you must be exhausted. Can it wait until tomorrow?"

"It could, but I'd feel more at ease once I've determined there's no infection setting in."

Alex put his arm around her shoulders. "By all means, Doc, take a look at it and do whatever you have to."

She sighed. "I'll go loosen my clothes in the bedroom and call you when I'm ready." She turned to Alex, peering up at him with a beseeching look. "Would you please check on things downstairs for me?"

"I'd rather stay here and keep an eye on you."

"I will be perfectly safe with Dr. Dolan, and I promise to keep the door locked. If you take the dishes down yourself, I won't even have to open the door to a waiter."

He rubbed his jaw. The woman certainly knew how to appeal to his rational side.

"I'll sleep better knowing the hotel is running smoothly," she added, though the sparkle in her eyes told him she had more than sleeping on her mind, which instantly made up his mind. The sooner he checked on the hotel, the sooner he could get back to her.

"All right. I'll go, but, Doc, I'm counting on you to stay with Julia until I return."

"I won't leave her," he promised.

Alex left the apartment a few minutes later and made his way downstairs. Though he balanced the tray with both hands, china and silver clinked with each step he took.

Inside the Crown Room, he handed off the tray to a waiter and quickly returned to the Rotunda. Everything seemed to be in order. Guests dressed in evening clothes milled about, some standing, some promenading on the gallery above, and some sitting on the red velvet banquettes conversing or spectating.

The clack of billiard balls drew his attention to the Ladies' Billiard Room, which opened onto the Rotunda. Two women were playing, both of them laughing at each other's shots. From the hallway leading to the Grand Ballroom came the sounds of the orchestra tuning their instruments.

Alex wandered up to Reginald O'Fallon, the night clerk on the registration desk. "Evening, Reg. Anything I need to report to Mrs. MacLean?"

The clerk gave him a little salute. "You can tell her it's been a typical Saturday night. A lot of people came from San Diego for dinner and dancing. We've also had some walk-ins registering for rooms. She'll be pleased with the evening's receipts."

"Yes, she will." Not that it would matter if she couldn't get another loan, though. Alex wished he had the money she needed. Tyler Wolff was the answer to her dilemma, but so far, she was stubbornly opposed to doing business with him. Alex couldn't blame her.

When a man and woman stepped up to the desk, O'Fallon excused himself and went to assist them. Alex walked away and took one more look around the lively lobby. In the last few minutes, the noise level had risen as more people entered from the Crown Room.

He examined the smiling faces, then grunted when Alberta Hensley came out alone, spotted him, and waved. She wore a light purple dress with puffed sleeves the size of the huge vases on the sideboards. The diamond bracelet around her thick wrist glimmered brightly.

Alex waved back and scanned the room for the quickest way out.

But she moved too fast.

"Mr. MacLean," she said, smelling, as usual, of too much lilac water, "please put my mind at rest. I heard a troubling rumor that your beautiful wife was injured yesterday in some sort of accident. Tell me it isn't so."

He purposely kept the scarred side of his face closest to her. "You don't need to worry, Mrs. Hensley," he said, hoping to forestall any further questions. "It was nothing serious. She was back in her office today."

"Goodness, she is such a hard worker. So dedicated. I admire—"

Boisterous laughter rang out near the front entrance, and Alex turned, inadvertently showing Alberta the good side of his face. When the laughter died down, he looked back at her and knew he'd made a huge mistake.

She was staring up at him, mouth agape. Whatever color hadn't been rouged into her cheeks was draining away.

Alex froze.

"You!" she spewed. Her color quickly returned and heightened. "I do know you! Alexander MacLean. Of course! How could I have forgotten?" She made no effort to keep her voice down and heads were turning their way. "You were married to Elizabeth Ellingson. You killed her."

He flinched. "I did not kill Elizabeth," he said through his teeth, keeping his voice low.

"That's not what her parents said. Or the police or newspapers. You were jailed for it." She fanned herself with her hands. "Does your current wife know what you did? No. Of course she doesn't. I can see it in your eyes. A guilty man doesn't advertise what he's done." She pressed her palm against her cheek. "I can't believe I didn't recognize you before now. Gerald and Amanda Ellingson are dear friends of mine. They were absolutely devastated by the deaths of their daughter and grandson. They wanted to see you hang."

As if he didn't know that. They had tried their best. In a sense, they had hanged him anyway.

"I wonder if they know where you are," she said. "You're very far from home."

"This is my home now."

Despite his being a foot taller than she, the woman managed to look down her nose at him. "And what a nice home it is. You married well. Again."

Alex felt his blood surging through his veins. He

forgot about the crowded lobby and stepped closer, looming over her. "Mrs. Hensley," he growled, "you'd be wise to stay out of my business."

She tilted her head way back and glared up at him, not giving an inch. "Your wife has a right to know the kind of man she married. Once she knows the truth, and it is my duty to tell her, she can have the marriage annulled."

Alex felt a rising sense of panic. His life finally had purpose again. He had a beautiful, warm, intelligent, and passionate wife. His ability to design had returned, and he had a home. He couldn't allow Alberta Hensley to ruin it all.

He clenched his fists. "Our marriage is none of your concern. You will say nothing."

She crossed her arms over her ample chest. "Are you threatening me?"

He bent his head lower, crowding her so closely she finally took a step back. "Think whatever you want. Just don't go near my wife."

She raised her chin, harrumphed, and stalked off toward the elevator.

Alex scowled at the matronly busybody's retreating backside. He may have won this skirmish, but not the battle. Mrs. Hensley would, if given the chance, tell Julia what he'd been trying so hard to put behind him.

He spun away from the noisy Rotunda, feeling as though he were back in his small, reeking prison cell. He had to get out of here and think.

He strode through the Garden Patio and ended up on the Paseo del Mar. The salt air entered his lungs. The ocean's smell was potent as waves pounded the beach. He inhaled deeply. A beam from the lighthouse on Point Loma shone every few seconds across the water.

Eventually, the sea and shore calmed him. When he came to terms with what he knew he must do, he started for the hotel.

Chapter Sixteen

"There. All done." Dr. Dolan snapped his medical bag shut. "You are healing nicely, Julia, and there's no sign of infection. Just a bit of the oozing I mentioned before. The new dressing will help with that."

"Thank you, Doctor."

"No trouble at all. I'm very pleased with your progress."

"Alex will be relieved. He's been worried about infection." She got up from the bed. "If you'll excuse me, I'll straighten myself up in the bathroom."

"Take your time."

She crossed the room and closed the bathroom door behind her. As she refastened her corset, she wondered what was taking Alex so long. If some hotel-related issue had detained him, she should have been the one dealing with it.

While tucking her shirtwaist into her skirt and petticoat, she heard male voices—the doctor and someone who wasn't Alex—coming from the sitting room.

Easing open the door, she listened. Alex wouldn't be pleased when he found out Dr. Dolan had let someone into the apartment.

"Doctor, please, you must come," the man said, sounding short of breath. "You're needed immediately."

Julia recognized the voice of Brian Pearson, one of her younger bellboys. Someone must be hurt.

"Calm yourself, man," the doctor said. "Tell me what this is all about."

She padded across the bedroom and peeked into the sitting room. Brian's normally tanned face was flushed. He appeared distraught and disconcerted. He did not appear to be a cold, calculating murderer.

"What's wrong, Brian?" she asked, entering the room.

"Mrs. MacLean." He dragged his pillbox hat off his blond head. "I'm sorry to intrude, but the night clerk sent me after Dr. Dolan. I'm also to tell you about it."

"About what?" She started to worry. "Has something happened to my husband?"

The bellboy's sun-bleached eyebrows lifted high into his forehead. "No. Leastways, not that I know of. It's the guest in room two twenty-eight. She's dead."

Julia clapped a hand to her mouth. "Mrs. Hensley?"

"That's her. That's the name Reg, uh, the clerk, gave me. He said she was old and it was probably just her time, but, following protocol, he telephoned Marshal Landis. He should be here soon."

She had trouble believing that the woman who had demanded to see the manager the day she arrived, who had chased after Muffie in the park, could be dead.

Despite her white hair, Mrs. Hensley hadn't seemed all that old, but then, Julia knew her father hadn't been terribly old when his heart stopped beating.

"Who found the body?" Dr. Dolan asked.

Brian pulled at the gold braid circling the cuff of his uniform's sleeve. "Another guest from this floor. He told us Mrs. Hensley's little dog was making such a ruckus he couldn't sleep. He went to her door, found it ajar, and looked in." Brian swallowed so hard his Adam's apple twitched. "Apparently she's on the floor in her sitting room. I haven't been there myself."

"And the dog?" Julia asked.

"Still yapping. I heard her all the way over here."

"Poor Muffie. And poor Mrs. Hensley." She grabbed her key off the parlor table. "I'll come right away. Hopefully I can quiet the dog before too many guests complain."

Dr. Dolan held up his hand. "Julia, there's no need for you to leave the safety of this apartment. Marshal Landis and I will take care of the dog and situation. This isn't the first death we've had here, and it won't be the last."

"I know, but I'm still the manager. I should be there." She knew Alex wouldn't want her to go, but she would be safe with the doctor and Tom. "Besides, you told Alex you would stay with me until he got back. Either you stay here with me, or I go with you."

Dr. Dolan muttered something unintelligible. "Where is that husband of yours anyway? Shouldn't he be back by now?"

"Brian," she said, "did you see Mr. MacLean downstairs?"

"No, ma'am, but I've been pretty busy, it being a Saturday night."

"Never mind. I'm sure he's fine." She prayed he was fine. Her assailant wouldn't go after Alex, would he? She forced her fears from her mind. "I'll leave a note so he'll know where we are."

While Dr. Dolan retrieved his medical bag, she went to the desk in her bedroom. She quickly wrote on a tablet of paper. *We've gone to room 228. J.*

Brian and the doctor preceded her out of the apartment. She laid the note on the parlor table and locked the door. "Brian, you may return to your duties downstairs."

"Yes, Mrs. MacLean." He hurried away.

She and Dr. Dolan, halfway to their destination, met up with Tom Landis. They exchanged stilted greetings amidst the yapping barks and occasional whines drifting through the corridor.

"I telephoned the coroner," Tom said, "but it'll be a few hours before he can get here. Doctor, if you could do a cursory examination of the body, I'd appreciate it. I don't expect anything out of the ordinary."

"Glad to oblige, Marshal."

As they turned the corner, Julia cringed at the worsening noise of Muffie's barking. Outside Mrs. Hensley's room, at least ten guests dressed in evening clothes, nightshirts, and wrappers stood together at the open doorway, some with their hands over their ears.

"Everybody back!" Tom marched toward them. "Clear the way!"

They turned en masse, saw the gold star pinned to his blue uniform, and allowed him, herself, and the doctor to enter the room. Julia almost wished she hadn't.

Mrs. Hensley, not yet retired for the night, wore a lavender evening dress and lay deathly still on the floral-patterned carpet. Though her hair was bound with pins on top of her head, many strands had come loose, some partially covering her grayish face. The room smelled of lilac water and death.

Julia felt her stomach twist. Perhaps even worse than seeing Mrs. Hensley's body, though, was the sight of Muffie sitting vigil beside the older woman. The dog's constant yapping was like the chanting of nonstop prayers.

Julia crouched a few feet away and reached her hand toward the tiny dog. "Come here, Muffie. It's all right, girl. I'll take care of you."

Muffie stopped barking. A collective sigh from the hallway broke the sudden silence. The little dog would not leave her post, though.

Julia tried again, but Muffie stood her ground. When Dr. Dolan approached Mrs. Hensley's body, the dog bared her sharp little teeth and growled.

He scuttled backwards.

"I'll get a blanket and catch her," Tom said. "She won't hurt anyone that way."

"Tom, no," she said. "That would just upset her more. Let me try again."

"Well, make it fast."

Julia scooted close enough to touch the dog. "I know you're upset, sweetheart. It's okay." She tentatively reached out her hand again.

The terrier whined.

"You're a good girl. There's no reason to bite the good doctor. He'll be gentle with your 'mother.'"

While Tom wandered around the room, she succeeded at rubbing between Muffie's ears, then stroking the soft fur of her back, and finally picking her up. The poor thing's body quivered. She huddled against Julia's chest.

"Bravo, Julia," Dr. Dolan said. As she stood and moved back to give him room, he knelt beside Mrs. Hensley, brushed her hair away from her face, and frowned.

"What is it?" Tom asked.

"Just a moment." Dr. Dolan drew Mrs. Hensley's high lace neckline lower and whistled under his breath. "Marshal, this woman did not die of natural causes. She was strangled."

A gasp rose from the hallway.

Julia gasped as well, then cringed, wishing Tom had closed the door. She'd been too intent on Muffie to think about privacy, and now it was too late.

"See the slight bruising on her throat?" He pointed it out to the marshal, who leaned over the body and nodded.

She didn't want to look. This was a nightmare. Who could have done such a thing? The same man who shot her? But if it was, why go after Mrs. Hensley?

The doctor hoisted himself up. "Someone deliberately put his hands around this poor woman's neck and killed her."

"Someone strong." Tom paced the length of the room. "Strong enough to immobilize a lady her size."

His gaze alighted on a sheet of hotel stationery lying on the desk. From where she stood, Julia could see that something was written on the paper, the beginnings of a letter. Tom picked it up and started reading. He smiled.

"Marshal?" A man dressed in evening clothes stood on the room's threshold, his arm around a woman's shoulders. "I'm George Farley. My wife and I are new arrivals at this hotel, and we saw a man arguing with that lady some thirty minutes or so ago in the lobby. We didn't hear what was said, but the argument appeared to be heated. He stood over her in a threatening manner."

"George!" His wife poked him in the stomach, her head swiveling between him and one end of the hall. "George, it's him. The man from the lobby."

George looked for himself and quickly turned back to Marshal Landis. "It is him."

The crowd backed away from the doorway, out of someone's way.

Julia stared, holding her breath and waiting. Had Mrs. Hensley's killer dared to come back?

Alex filled the doorway.

Her breath escaped in a shocked rush. She whipped her gaze toward Tom.

Beneath his full mustache, the marshal smiled broadly, a satisfied glint in his eyes. "I've got you now, MacLean." He chuckled, and the paper in his hand rustled, "You are hereby under arrest for the murder of Mrs. Alberta Hensley."

* * *

Alex felt his mouth drop open. He forced it shut

again and looked from Landis's gloating expression to Julia's blanched face to the lifeless body lying on the floor—Alberta Hensley's. He could hardly take it in. Just a short time ago, she'd been full of righteous spit and vinegar. This was wrong. How could she be dead?

He held up his hands, palms out. "Whoa. Murder? Alberta's been murdered?"

"As if you didn't know," the marshal said. "You were seen arguing with her. Do you deny it?"

He glanced at the faces around him, already seeing where the marshal was going. He dropped his arms and stepped across the threshold. "No, I do not deny quarreling with her, but I wouldn't hurt her. I did not do this." He gestured toward her.

"Several witnesses say otherwise. In the lobby, you appeared to be threatening her."

Alex looked at Julia, needing to know that she believed him, believed in him, but she seemed to be in shock as she cradled Muffie in her arms. Or was she unsure what to think? Did she doubt him? He didn't think he could bear it if she did.

Dr. Dolan disappeared into the bedroom, then returned with a blanket and covered Mrs. Hensley.

"How was she killed?" Alex demanded.

The doctor looked up. "Strangulation."

"But you already knew that," Landis sneered, "didn't you, MacLean?"

Alex narrowed his eyes on the closed-minded marshal. "I didn't touch her, and I have never been in this room before."

"Prove it. Where were you at the time of her death, shortly after you were with her in the lobby?"

Alex suppressed a groan. Dammit. He should have never left the hotel, just as he should have never left his home the night of his last argument with Elizabeth. "I was on the Paseo del Mar."

"With anyone?"

"No." He had passed several couples strolling the walkway above the beach, but they had paid him even less heed than he had paid them.

"Exactly as I thought. Let me tell you what happened here. You argued with the victim, then you followed her here and killed her."

"Tom, please," Julia finally said. "I don't—"

The marshal held up his hand. "Julia, I have it on good authority that this man you married arrived on the ferry barely twenty-four hours before your wedding. How much do you really know about him?"

She opened her mouth, and Alex thought she was going to defend him, but then she looked into his eyes. She closed her mouth, as if she'd seen the truth, that he had not shared a crucial and damaging part of his past with her. Her shoulders drooped, and she seemed to wilt in front of him.

Alex felt his legs weaken. He was losing her.

Landis smiled smugly. "Just as I thought."

"Julia," Alex said, "I'm sorry I didn't tell you everything, but I swear to you I did not hurt Alberta."

"Of course you did," the marshal said. "She knew something about you, MacLean. Something you didn't want anyone in San Diego to know, especially Julia. But now everyone will know." He waved the sheet of stationery in his hand. "Your victim put it in writing."

Alex felt his stomach plummet to the floor. How

much had Alberta written?

Muffie yapped, and Julia quieted her. "What does it say, Tom?" she asked, her voice no more than a whisper.

"It's a letter addressed to a Mr. and Mrs. Gerald Ellingson, Baltimore, Maryland. MacLean's former in-laws, if I read this right."

Rivulets of sweat trickled down Alex's spine, but he felt chilled all over. "Yes, their daughter was my first wife."

"Dearest Gerald and Amanda," the marshal read. "You will never guess who I have discovered out here on the shores of Coronado Island—your dreadful son-in-law! It's absolutely scandalous. A travesty. He should never have been released from prison. I am shocked to say that, before I knew his true identity, I attended his outdoor wedding to the heiress of the Hotel Grand Victoria. She is a beautiful and accomplished young woman who has no idea of his criminal past. It's not right! He is taking advantage of her just as he did your poor Elizabeth. Well, before he can set fire to this lovely hotel in the same manner he did to the home you so generously provided to him, I intend to notify the local police and Mrs. MacLean, the former Miss Fairbanks, before she is killed, too. Someone has to protect her, and I …" Landis looked up. "It ends there."

Alex gritted his teeth. This looked bad. Really bad. "I did not set the fire. I wasn't even in the house at the time."

Landis laughed. "I bet you were close by, though. Most arsonists like to watch their handiwork."

He didn't answer. What was the point? He had been close by, and the marshal would use that against him. Landis didn't care about the truth.

"May I assume you were arrested for the murder of your wife?" the marshal asked, though the question sounded more like a statement.

Alex winced. "Yes. And my son and a servant girl. I was put in jail."

Julia stared at him, her disillusionment as clear as the moisture glistening in her eyes.

"Julia, I told you what happened." His heart drummed with his desperation. "I didn't kill them."

"You left out a lot of the story, though." Her voice shook. "I trusted you, Alex, but you didn't trust me."

He felt as if a knife were being plunged into his chest. He loved Julia. Had known it for days now, but until this moment, he hadn't realized how much, nor how important she had become to him in the short time they'd been together. He needed her in his life.

"I'm sorry, Julia. I didn't want to remember. You know I would not have hurt Alberta any more than I would have intentionally hurt Elizabeth or Danny."

"But you were arrested for their deaths," she said.

"My in-laws blamed me. They convinced the police I was guilty and had me thrown in jail. Two weeks later I was released for lack of evidence."

Landis folded the letter and stowed it in his breast pocket. "Released for lack of evidence doesn't prove you were innocent. I don't know what your motive might've been back then, MacLean, but your motive for this crime is clear. You killed this lady to keep her quiet."

Every muscle in Alex's body tensed. "You're wrong. I was falsely accused in Baltimore, and I'm being falsely accused now."

"I disagree." The marshal pulled out a pair of handcuffs.

Alex sidestepped away. "Don't do this, Landis. Somebody wants you to think it was me, someone who must've witnessed my disagreement with Alberta." Realization struck him like a fist to his face. Whoever wanted Julia dead had killed Alberta to get him out of the way. If he hadn't argued with her in the lobby, she would still be alive. His knees nearly buckled as he added the weight of another death to his burdened conscience.

"MacLean, you're a no-account drifting murderer, and you're under arrest. Turn around and put your hands behind your back."

He ignored the order. "It wasn't me. If I had killed her, I would not have left that letter lying around for anyone to read."

Tom Landis swung the handcuffs. "Turn around. Now."

Alex stayed where he was. "Julia, please. You're in terrible danger." He couldn't lose her. They had only just found each other. "This is what the killer wants."

She hugged Muffie closer. "I'll hire a lawyer for you."

"I don't want a lawyer. I want you to be safe."

Landis edged around him and yanked his arms behind his back. "MacLean, you duped a good woman into marrying you, but you won't be taking advantage of her anymore." He clamped the cuffs around Alex's wrists. The metal clicked shut, the sound seeming to echo in the room. The marshal spun him toward the doorway.

He winced at the pain in his ribs and lurched forward.

Muffie whined.

The marshal gave Alex a shove into the hallway. The crowd scattered, opening a path.

Alex twisted around to face Julia. "Promise me you'll be careful. With me gone, your assailant will have a better chance at getting to you. Let Tyler watch over you. And Theo and the doctor. Don't go out alone."

She didn't respond.

"Promise me! I can't protect you from jail."

She swiped at a tear and finally nodded. "I promise."

Alex stared at her hard, afraid to look away. In spite of her promise, there was no guarantee she'd be safe. And if anything happened to her … well, he wasn't sure what he'd do.

Chapter Seventeen

From her desk chair, Julia peered down at Muffie. Daylight from the Garden Patio filtered in through the window and lit the tiny dog who lay on a pillow in the corner of the office. Muffie stared back at her with big, sad eyes.

"It's all right, girl," she said, trying to reassure herself and the dog. "Everything will be all right." But how could anything ever be all right again? Her husband, the man she loved, was in jail, charged with murder, and not for the first time.

What a fool she'd been, dreaming that her marriage of convenience could be a marriage of forever. She had allowed herself to fall in love with a man who had abused her trust by willfully keeping an allegedly criminal portion of his past from her while letting her think there was nothing more to tell.

Obviously, there'd been plenty more.

She slowly swung her head from side to side. How could she have lost her heart so completely to Alex MacLean? She had considered him a hero—her hero.

Now it had all come crashing down.

And yet, even with the evidence against him, now that she'd had time to absorb everything, Julia could not bring herself to believe that Alex was a murderer. How could the man who had made such sweet love to her, who had risked his life for her and again for a little boy, be a cold-blooded killer?

On the leather blotter, she laid her head on her arms. All night these same questions and more had spun through her brain, leaving her exhausted and without answers, feeling an emptiness that swept outward like rings from a stone tossed into the bay. She didn't know if Alex loved her, but as Tom Landis had dragged him away, he had been consumed with worry for her safety rather than concern for himself. The desperation in his voice reverberated in her mind and heart. He was afraid for her. She remembered what he'd said to her before they climbed the gazebo steps and spoke their vows. "I promise I will always do my best to help you. I hope you'll remember that."

"Julia?" Tyler's voice came through the door.

She sat up and dashed a hand across her eyes.

He knocked, then the doorknob shook.

Muffie lifted her head and yapped.

"I know you're in there. I've heard all about what happened. Let me in."

Sniffling, she plodded to the door, smoothed her hands over her pale blue shirtwaist and gray walking skirt, and let her brother in.

He wore a solid black coat over charcoal, pin-striped pants. "I am not happy." He threw his fedora onto her desk. "I returned to the hotel late last night and was told nothing until this morning. You should have sent word to me, or at least left a message for me at the desk."

"I'm sorry, but it was all such a shock. I could barely think straight. It's still a shock. I have to do something to help him, but, other than hire a lawyer, I don't know what I can do. The evidence is against him."

He studied her face. "You love him, don't you?"

She briefly shut her eyes, then nodded. "Yes."

"Do you think he could have killed her?"

"No," she answered firmly, "but what I think doesn't matter."

"Not to the courts, but I'm sure it does to him. Does Alex know how you feel?"

Swallowing hard, she shook her head, remembering the way he had looked at her while proclaiming his innocence, both past and present. He had needed to know she believed in him, and she had disappointed him.

A pang of guilt quaked within her. Julia grasped the edge of her desk and leaned heavily against it.

"Are you all right?" Tyler took her arm. "Do you need the doctor?"

"I'm tired and emotionally drained, but I'll be all right."

Muffie trotted over and laid one paw on her shoe.

"Is this the victim's dog?"

"Yes. Muffie. She was Mrs. Hensley's closest companion." Julia lifted Muffie from the floor, shuffled around the desk, and sank into her chair with the dog on her lap. "Tyler, what am I going to do?"

"First, you're going to let Alex know you haven't abandoned him. After that, you'll hire the best defense attorney in San Diego."

His decisive manner gave her the burst of energy and determination she needed. She straightened. "I've already gathered several names, but will the jail let me in to see Alex?"

"If not, we'll figure out a way to make it happen. I'm coming with you." He fitted his black fedora to his head.

"Thank you." She stood with Muffie in her arms. "I never thought I'd say this, but I'm glad you're here."

"We're family, and we'll sort this out." He led the way into the lobby.

Trying to decide what to do with Muffie while they were out, Julia glanced around. Mr. Chalmers was a possibility, but he was currently occupied with several guests who were most likely checking out. Since Mrs. Hensley's death, some of the registered guests had chosen to leave before the scheduled end of their stay. The majority, however, felt they were safe, the supposed killer having been caught and removed to the San Diego County Jail.

If they only knew. Certain that Alex hadn't killed Mrs. Hensley, Julia knew the real murderer was still at large, and very likely somewhere inside her hotel.

She shivered and held Muffie closer. Though she felt reasonably safe with Tyler watching after her, she would have been more at ease if Alex were with her.

Across the Rotunda, Theo and Tilden stood beside the bell desk's podium. Nearby, a cartload of cases and hatboxes waited to be wheeled outside.

She crossed to the bellboys, Tyler following on her heels. "Theo, I have a huge favor to ask of you."

"Anything, Mrs. MacLean. You know that."

She did know. He had already confided to her how sorry he was about Alex's arrest. He had taken off his spectacles, wiped them with his handkerchief, and said, "I just can't believe it. I don't want to believe it."

She nodded down at the dog. "I need you to watch after Muffie while I'm in San Diego with Mr. Wolff."

"Happy to do it. If you'll be seeing Mr. MacLean, please give him my best."

"I will." She held Muffie out to him.

The dog growled, sniffed the air, and growled again. Her little head turned this way and that as she continued sniffing. She began wriggling like a freshly caught fish.

"Muffie, what's wrong?" Julia struggled to keep from dropping her.

The Yorkshire terrier let out an ear-piercing yap and jumped to the floor. She landed on all fours, bared her teeth, and pounced at, of all people, Tilden.

"Muffie, stop," she ordered.

The dog sank her teeth into the cuff of his uniform pants.

Hissing at the dog, the bellboy shook his leg, but Muffie didn't let go.

"I'm sorry, Tilden. I don't know what's gotten into her." Julia started to bend down to grab Muffie, but Tyler stayed her with a hand to her shoulder. She glanced up at him.

"Wait," he said, his voice nearly lost amidst the growling. "Let's see what this is about."

Muffie released Tilden's pants, backpedaled, and leaped nearly as high as his left pocket. Again and again.

Tilden inched backwards. "Shoo! Get away! Down!"

Muffie kept jumping.

Julia exchanged glances with Theo and her brother. "Tilden," she said, cocking her head, "what's in your pocket?" She imagined him carrying some food that he might have pilfered from the kitchen.

His gaze flicked around the hallway. "Nothing." He backed up even more.

Muffie jumped again.

Julia followed, with Tyler and Theo beside her. "There must be something that's attracting her. Show us what's in your pocket, and the matter will be settled."

His expression hardened. "I'll settle it all right." He leaped at her, grabbing Julia by the throat.

* * *

Alex paced the dank, stinking confines of his cell. Every so often he slammed the heel of his hand against the bars, the noise reverberating along the second-floor tier of cells. The other inmates grumbled.

A guard shouted, "Keep it down!"

He had spent most of the night pacing the concrete floor, worried sick about Julia, but also reliving the doubt he had seen in her eyes when he most needed her trust.

Could she truly believe he had killed Alberta?

He dropped onto the narrow, creaky, moldy-smelling cot and buried his face in his hands. He loved

Julia, but she obviously didn't love him. If she did, she never could have doubted his innocence. She hadn't even come to check on him.

When he'd been out on the road, drifting from town to town, he had been lonely, searching for a place to belong, but that loneliness was nothing compared to what he felt now. He had found where he belonged, found the woman he wanted to spend the rest of his life with, but in a matter of minutes, it had all been snatched away from him.

He was utterly alone again, worse off than ever.

"Hey, you, new guy next door," came a deep, gravelly voice. "What are you in for?"

Alex straightened, pulled at the striped cotton prison-issue shirt abrading his neck, and pushed to his feet.

"Who's asking?" He pressed the side of his face to the bars.

"Marvin Sisko, occasional pickpocket enjoyin' the county's hospitality for a few days. I got food, a bed, and no worries about gettin' sent up to Folsom or San Quentin." He belched contentedly. "You going to be here long?"

"I ... don't know." Before last night, Alex had had a future to look forward to. Now he had nothing and no idea what the future held. If he was convicted of Alberta's murder, his life would end on a gallows. He would never see Julia again, never make love to her again, and never have a family again.

Alex started to shake. He didn't want to die. Married to Julia, he had just begun to live.

"What did you do?" Marvin asked.

"Nothing."

"You must've done something."

"Somebody else did it. I got blamed for it. Murder."

The man cackled and slapped what sounded like his thigh. "I've heard that before."

"I expect you have, but it's true. My wife, however, doesn't believe me any more than you do." Alex dropped back onto the cot and leaned against the rough, whitewashed wall.

"I've got me a wife, too," Marvin said. "And in my experience, wives are usually more interested in what we can do for them than what they can do for us."

Alex nodded to himself. Julia had married him to obtain ownership of the Hotel Grand Victoria. In the beginning, she had wanted him to disappear after the ceremony, leaving her alone with her hotel. Maybe she would be happy to have him gone.

Even as he thought it, Alex didn't believe it. They'd been content together. He hadn't imagined that. She even wanted to have children with him.

"They're all the same," Marvin added. "O' course, there are times when they do earn their keep." He laughed, a bawdy, you-know-what-I-mean laugh.

Alex refused to let himself think about the night he and Julia had made love. Those memories didn't belong in this filthy place. None of his memories of her belonged in this place. But like a series of moving photographs playing across his mind, he once again saw her approaching him that first day on the carriage drive. She had shown no revulsion at the sight of his scarred face. Next, a fascinated Julia brazenly, yet naively, watched him taking off his shirt in the doctor's office. Then his mind showed her walking toward him in her wedding gown under the twilight sky. Lastly, she stood unselfconsciously before him in her prim nightdress as he unfastened the buttons.

The images tortured him, and he pounded his fist into the hard, lumpy mattress.

* * *

Rendered helpless by Tilden's unexpected attack, Julia could do nothing. His powerful hands gripped her throat. His fingers dug ever more deeply into her flesh.

Face to face, she clawed uselessly at his hands. Time slowed to a crawl. The vicious determination in his eyes mesmerized her. Unable to breathe, she mouthed, Why?

He didn't answer.

She struggled harder for air, trying to gulp it in, but there was nothing. Her head didn't feel right. She heard things as if from a distance—the ring of the telephone, Muffie's yapping, a woman's scream, and Theo yelling something. Tyler was trying to pull Tilden's arms away from her, but the bellboy was too strong.

Darkness fringed the corners of her mind, and she felt like sobbing. Her regrets rolled through like a winter storm. She desperately wanted to see Alex again, tell him how much she loved him and apologize for not standing by him. Tilden had obviously killed Mrs. Hensley, strangling the matronly woman the same way he was now strangling her.

The bellboy's mouth curved into a smile of absolute pleasure. He laughed, a hideous sound that jerked her out of her stupor.

Fury surged through her, giving her more strength than Julia knew she had. She would not allow Tilden to end her life, separating her forever from Alex and the life she had dreamed of living since she was a girl.

She raked her fingernails down both sides of his face, scoring it deeply.

He shrieked, and the pressure on her throat lessened.

A trickle of sweet-tasting air entered her lungs. The blackness crowding her mind receded. She heard the thud of a fist slamming into soft flesh.

Tilden grunted. His body arched back. His fingers went slack, and she was free.

She swayed, unable to catch her balance.

"I've got you," Theo said, his arm coming around her waist.

She grabbed him in return, steadying herself as Tyler yanked Tilden's hands behind his back.

Chalmers ran up with a length of twine. When he tied Tilden's wrists with an excess number of wraps and knots, Julia decided her clerk had earned a little leniency. Once everything settled down, she would confront him about his betrayal and give him the choice of shaping up or leaving. Feeling generous, she would do the same for Jacques.

Tilden swore, struggling against the bonds and causing himself more pain.

She looked away from the eight trails of blood that inscribed his face. Injuring another human being sickened her, but she was not sorry about it. He had forced her to do what was necessary to save herself.

"Mrs. MacLean," Chalmers said, "I telephoned Marshal Landis and sent for the doctor."

"Thank—" She cleared her sore throat. "Thank you, Mr. Chalmers," she said, speaking softly.

"You'd best sit down." Theo gently led her to the red velvet banquette. "You'll get your strength back quicker."

She gratefully accepted his suggestion and let him lower her to the seat. Muffie jumped up beside her, laying her little body against her thigh.

Dr. Dolan arrived moments later, examined her throat, and sent Theo to the kitchen for a linen towel filled with chipped ice. "You're lucky, Julia. There's some swelling and redness, but no permanent damage. However, you will have bruises almost as colorful as your husband's back."

She tentatively touched her raw skin. "I can hide them with my high-necked shirtwaists. No one will see them."

"Alex will, once he's set free," the doctor said. "He won't be pleased that you've been hurt."

"He can't see this. Not yet. I have to change. But I must go to him. Last night I let him down." She started to get up, glancing toward the front entrance, then the stairs to her apartment, then the entrance again.

Dr. Dolan pushed her back down. "Julia, take a breath. You're flustered. I don't want you putting yourself in the same state of hysteria that you did in my office."

"I'm fine."

"You're not fine. A man just tried to kill you with his bare hands. Breathe."

A barrage of tremors struck her like aftershocks from an earthquake. She wished the doctor hadn't spoken so plainly. She breathed.

"That's better. Alex isn't going anywhere for the moment. Let's hear what Tilden has to say for himself. Marshal Landis is coming in now."

Tom Landis raced into the lobby, his booted footsteps pounding the floor. His gaze darted from Tyler holding Tilden captive to her and the doctor.

Tom came to an abrupt halt before her. "Thank the Lord," he said, panting. "From the way Chalmers sounded on the telephone, I was afraid you might be … well, never mind what I thought. I'm very glad you're all right, Julia."

"So am I." She had too much to do before dying, namely, getting her husband out of jail and telling him how much she loved him.

Tyler steered his captive closer, but not close enough that the bellboy could reach her in any way.

Calmer, she smiled at Tyler, obliged to him for his well-placed punch.

Marshal Landis grimaced as he took in Tilden's face. "Looks like he's wearing Indian war paint. Are you responsible for that, Julia?"

She bit her lip. "Yes. I had no choice."

Tilden shot her a venomous look, but she refused to let him frighten her, or at least see that he frightened her.

Muffie growled at him.

Tom chuckled. "Looks to me like he deserved it. Nice going."

She did not thank him for the compliment.

"Marshal," the doctor said, "after I've seen to Julia, I'll clean and dress his facial wounds."

"Good," Tom said. "Not that he deserves your ministration."

Theo arrived with the ice-filled linen towel, and Dr. Dolan arranged it around her neck. "Hold that in place," he told her.

She did as ordered. The cold felt wonderful against her sore flesh.

"Now tell me what happened here," the marshal said. "How did it start?"

Tyler explained how she had been asking Theo to watch after Muffie. "The dog attacked Tilden."

Julia said in a soft voice, "Muffie seemed intent on something in his pocket, but Tilden refused to show it to us. Suddenly his hands were around my throat."

The marshal patted the bellboy's pockets, slid his fingers into one, and brought out a glittering diamond bracelet. "Very pretty."

Muffie stood up and yipped.

"Why, that's Mrs. Hensley's bracelet," Julia said. "She wore it all the time. It proves Tilden was the one who killed her, not Alex."

Tom rubbed at his mustache with one hand while admiring the bracelet in the other. He didn't seem ready to concede Alex's innocence quite yet. Julia considered strangling some sense into him, then chose a more sensible course. She fastened her gaze on the bellboy. If he confessed, there would be no question.

"Did you kill her for the bracelet, Tilden?"

"Hell no!" he exploded. "You stupid woman, that was a bonus."

She ignored his insult as Tom deposited the bracelet into his uniform's shirt pocket and took out a small notepad and pencil. "Then why?"

His lips curled back into a snarl. "To make you suffer and get MacLean out of the way. I saw him arguing with the old hag, and it was perfect. He'd botched my plans once too often. I wasn't going to let it happen again." He struggled against Tyler's hold, bending toward her. "You needed to die. You should've died when I threw the flowerpot." Hatred poured out of him.

She leaned back, but there was no getting away from it. Muffie whined, and Julia stroked her little body, trying to soothe them both.

Tyler gave the bellboy a shake. "What did she ever do to you?"

"Not just her. Her father, too. Lloyd Fairbanks."

Tyler exchanged a puzzled look with her.

"What are you talking about?" Tyler demanded.

Tilden spat onto the floor. "He stole my woman!"

"Tilden, you're not making sense," she said. "What woman?"

"Harriet! Harriet Lincoln! She was mine. He had no right to take her from me."

She stared at him in disbelief. "Harriet? How could you have possibly known my stepmother? She died more than a year before you started working here."

"She was my girl back in New York. She knew I loved her. I showed her how much after I caught her talking to another man." Tilden smiled like a feral cat. "That fellow had to find himself some new teeth." His smile turned brittle. "But I landed in prison for it."

Julia now understood the reason for Harriet's warnings about being too friendly with a man. "She came all the way to San Diego to get away from you, didn't she?"

He twisted his shoulders, rocking his bound hands from side to side. "We loved each other. I had to have her back. But after I got out, I couldn't find her. I spent months searching." He growled out his words. "Her trail finally led me here, but by then she was dead and I could never have her back." He spat at her.

Julia threw up her arm. His phlegm fell short, splattering at her feet.

Tyler yanked him back a step. "Stop it."

Tilden's malevolent gaze never wavered from her face. "You and your father stole her from me, and you both had to pay. Once he hired me, I had access to the both of you. I patiently planned your deaths, laughing the whole time. No one suspected a thing. I could do away with you whenever I wanted, even making it look like an accident. Nobody'd ever be the wiser."

"But my father ruined your plans by dying ahead of schedule, didn't he?"

Tilden howled with laughter.

She looked to Tyler, but he shrugged his shoulders, as puzzled as she.

Tom Landis grabbed the front of the bellboy's uniform. "What's so funny?"

Tilden grinned. "She thinks her father died of natural causes."

"He did," she said, her stomach tightening. "Of a heart attack."

Tilden laughed again. "His heart stopped all right.

Some poisons cause that, you know."

She clapped a hand over her mouth and fell back against the banquette. He had murdered her father, and she had never once questioned his death. In fact, she had blamed herself for aggravating him with her desire to help run the hotel. She should have questioned his death, should have done something.

Tilden's continued laughter echoed throughout the Rotunda until Tyler punched him in the back again, cutting the bellboy's laughter short.

"That's for killing my father before I could meet him," Tyler said.

Tilden grimaced and coughed several times.

Julia couldn't blame Tyler for his feelings. "Tilden, why did you wait so long after my father's death to make your first attempt on my life? Or was there an attempt before the flowerpot?" Had he tried to poison her, too?

He smiled. "I did wait. I liked the anticipation. I especially liked imagining all the scenarios that would lead to your death. In the meantime, I hoped to witness your downfall. No woman has the right to operate a hotel. I wanted to witness your embarrassment and humiliation as you brought the Hotel Grand Victoria to ruin. When it didn't happen, I knew it was time to take matters back into my own hands." He started laughing again.

A shudder rippled through Julia's body as she remembered the feel of his hands around her throat. She longed for Alex and his enfolding arms to wrap her in his embrace, the one place she felt truly safe, protected from evil.

291

Chapter Eighteen

Alex lay on his cot, breathing through his mouth to avoid the reeking odors of unwashed men and dried urine. He supposed he should try to get used to the smells, but that would mean giving up, and he couldn't do that. He had too much to live for, if Julia could forgive him.

Loud, booted footsteps hammered the iron balcony outside the row of cells. Keys jangled.

"MacLean!"

He sat up, his pulse suddenly racing.

A uniformed guard holding a ring of keys strode into view and stopped in front of his cell door. "Stand up, turn around, and hands behind your back."

He didn't move. "What's going on?"

The guard pinned him with a fierce look. "Shut your mouth and do as you're told."

Out of self-preservation, he followed orders. In Baltimore's jail, he had seen firsthand how much some guards enjoyed their position of power.

"That's better," the guard said. Metal clanked

against metal as he unlocked and opened the door, then fitted a pair of handcuffs around Alex's wrists. "Now turn around and start walking. Slowly."

Alex walked. Slowly. Behind him, the door clanged shut. The guard followed and poked him in the shoulder, prompting him down the flight of stairs. A slight shove turned him down a bare hallway.

"In there." The man motioned toward an open door with a small window in it.

Alex hesitated. Was he about to be interrogated? If they expected him to confess, they had another think coming. He would not admit to a crime he didn't commit.

The guard gave him a shove, and Alex stumbled, grimacing, into a simply furnished room. A scarred wooden table and four equally scarred chairs marked the center of it. A single gas lamp hung from the ceiling, casting a light that didn't even reach the corners of the small room.

"Wait in here." The guard locked him in.

Several minutes later the door opened. The warden stood on its threshold, studied him, and stepped back out of sight.

Julia took his place, framed by the doorway.

Alex wanted to run to her. The urge to throw his arms around her nearly overwhelmed him, but the shackles biting into his wrists stopped him, giving him time to remember their last painful moments together. She had not believed in his claim of innocence. She had not believed in him.

Though his feet remained rooted to the floor, he swept his gaze over her from top to bottom, reassuring himself that she was unharmed and he had been worrying needlessly.

She wore a gray skirt, matching jacket, and high-necked pink shirtwaist. Her ash-blond hair was piled stylishly atop her head. Blue eyes shone in the flawless perfection of her creamy skin. She took a step toward him. Her scent, orange blossoms in the spring, drifted across the room, cleansing Alex of all the rank smells that had assailed him since his arrival. She was spring itself, and her beauty in this dreary place brightened everything around her.

He could have looked at her indefinitely.

"I'm sorry it took me so long to get here." Her voice was almost a whisper as she took in their surroundings and his striped prison garb.

"I hope you didn't come alone."

"No. Tyler is waiting for me in the warden's office."

"Good." He was glad, but it should have been him watching over her. She was his wife, the woman he loved.

The warden, a short man whose frock coat strained over his belly, edged around her. He swung a ring of jingling keys like the one the guard carried.

"I'll take off those handcuffs for you, MacLean," he said. "Just don't try anything stupid."

Alex wasn't sure he wanted them off now. Julia was so beautiful, and he felt as if he hadn't seen her in weeks instead of hours. He wanted to touch her, hold her, confess everything to her, and make love to her, but he was still a prisoner accused of murder.

With several clicks, the warden removed the

handcuffs. "Mrs. MacLean, if you need anything, a guard will be posted outside the door."

Alex heard what the man left unspoken, that if she felt threatened, she need only scream and help would come running.

"Thank you, Warden," she said. "I have nothing to fear from my husband. All I ask is some privacy with him."

Alex felt his heart give a hopeful leap. She wasn't afraid to be alone with him.

"As you wish." The warden retreated and locked the door behind him.

Alex stayed on the far side of the small room.

Julia barely glanced at him. She seemed to be studying the ravaged tabletop while playing with a fold in her skirt. The high, ruffled collar around her neck must have been scratching her because she readjusted it. "Have they treated you all right?" she finally asked.

"Well enough."

She took a step closer and looked up. Their eyes locked. "Alex, I owe you an apology. When you needed me last night, I failed you. Deep down, I knew you could never have harmed Mrs. Hensley. Despite being caught off guard, I should have spoken up for you right away."

His heart lifted. Maybe there was hope for them, if he could somehow get out of here. "Thank you, but it's my fault for keeping secrets I wanted to forget about my previous arrest." He dragged out one of the chairs, scraping the legs over the concrete floor. "Last night," he said, "dropping onto the chair and clasping his hands on the table, "after Alberta recognized me, I knew I couldn't keep the truth from you anymore. I was planning to tell you when I got back to the apartment, but you weren't there. And by then, Alberta had suffered the consequences of knowing me. I feel responsible."

She joined him at the table, lowering herself onto the chair opposite him. "You're not responsible, and you're not staying here. You're coming home with me."

"I wish that were true, but I know better. Marshal Landis has made up his mind about my part in Alberta's death. I didn't think I could be held for the deaths of Elizabeth, Danny, and Sarah, the servant girl, either, but I was. For a while, anyway."

"How did that happen?" she asked, again fiddling with the ruffles at her neck.

He briefly closed his eyes. Sharing with her those terrible weeks after the fire would bring the pain of it roaring back. But he had to do it, putting it once and for all behind him.

Unable to sit still, he jumped up and paced the length of the room's rough back wall. "You already know I fell from a tree that ripped open my face. Two days after my fall, I regained consciousness and found myself locked in a dimly lit jail cell. The only medical attention I received was from my cellmate. He'd wrapped a dirty rag around my head to hold my cheek together."

A visible shudder moved through her, but she didn't interrupt.

"My in-laws used their influence to have me

arrested. It was days before the guards treated me with any kind of decency. My business partner had to bribe his way in, and when James saw my face"—Alex jabbed his hand toward his scarred cheek—"he vomited more food than I'd been given to eat in the three days I'd been awake. Then he demanded a doctor be sent for. By then, though, it was too late to do anything that would minimize the scar."

"I'm sorry," she said on a shaky breath. "When Dr. Dolan commented about a delay in treatment, I assumed you'd been out in the country, away from any doctors."

He laughed, not a trace of humor in the sound. "No." He leaned back against the cold wall, feeling again the anger and despair, frustration and defeat, that had haunted him since then. "After that, James got me a lawyer, a very good one, but even he had trouble fighting the pressure my in-laws brought to bear on the courts. I was kept in that rancid jail for two weeks. They wouldn't release me for even a few hours to attend the burial services of my family."

The gas lamp flickered above them, casting parts of Julia's face in shadow, but revealing tears in her eyes. "I wondered how your in-laws could have kept you from the services," she whispered. "I never imagined you were incarcerated."

"The Ellingsons were furious when I got off for lack of evidence. I was surprised they hadn't manufactured some, but they'd been too busy ruining me instead. They spread damaging rumors about my architectural work. Claims were made that I stole my designs from other people's work, or I designed buildings with inadequate structural foundations." He smacked the heel of his hand against the wall. "With cold calculation, they cast doubt on every one of my projects."

"What despicable people!"

At her outrage, Alex felt the beginnings of a smile. "Over the years, I've come up with some choice descriptions of them myself. Gerald and Amanda Ellingson smeared my professional reputation and my character the length and breadth of the Eastern seaboard. Instead of grieving like normal people, they did everything they could to punish, humiliate, and ruin me. When I was released, I had nothing."

"No money at all?"

"None. What Elizabeth hadn't spent before the fire was used to pay the burial expenses. Ownership of the property had strangely reverted to my in-laws. The only clothes I had were what I'd been wearing the night of the fire and what my partner gave me before we severed our connections. It was the only way I could protect him. He could not afford to be seen with me."

"So you left Baltimore," she said softly, "and took to the road like a drifter."

"I was a drifter, but I didn't leave Baltimore until I'd touched the headstones standing over my wife and child."

Alex blinked hard against the stinging in his eyes. That had been another life. On Coronado Island with Julia, he had forged a new life, but now that was in jeopardy as well.

He pushed away from the wall and spread his arms

wide. "Now it's happened again. I've been arrested for a crime I didn't commit, and I may lose you, too."

"No. Never." She came to him, pressing her palms to the rough cotton covering his chest. "I love you, Alex MacLean, and I always will."

He slipped his arms around her narrow waist and planted a kiss on each cheek of her upturned face. "I love you, too. I think I've loved you since the first moment we met, when you saw my scar and didn't flinch." He smiled down at her. "You brought me back to life when I thought my life was over."

"Oh, Alex, I didn't know how you felt. Growing up with my father, I haven't had much experience with love from a man. Now I realize you've shown me your love in countless ways." Her hands slid up to his shoulders, and her arms wound around his neck. "Can you forgive me?"

Alex mourned the family he would never have, the years that he could have spent with Julia. "There's nothing to forgive. I brought this on myself. I was wrong to keep my past from you."

"Thank you for saying that." She stood on tiptoe and tantalized him with a light kiss on his lips.

He felt an immediate stirring in his lower body and tried to quash it by pushing her away. "You should go now. This place is not for you."

"Nor is it for you. I tried to tell you before. Mrs. Hensley's killer—my assailant—has been arrested."

He held her at arm's length. "What? How? Who?"

"Tilden. Muffie alerted us to him this morning in the lobby. I believe she must have smelled Mrs. Hensley's lilac scent on him. He was carrying her diamond bracelet in his pocket. You were right about him wanting you out of the way so he could get to me. I would have been his third victim."

"Third?"

"He also killed my father."

Alex shook his head, trying to grasp it all. "But I thought …"

"I know. I did, too. Nobody knew, and I never questioned his death, never even suspected." Tears glistened in her eyes. "I should have."

Alex recognized her feelings of guilt. He reached out and stroked her arm. "Why did Tilden do it?"

"He was obsessed with my stepmother. They met back in New York, and he ended up in prison for beating a man she'd only conversed with. He thought of her as his property with no rights of her own. She escaped him, moving as far from New York as she could, but even so, after he was released from prison, he tracked her here. He was too late, though. When he discovered she was dead, he blamed my father and me and decided we had to die, too."

"Thank heaven he didn't finish what he started."

She glanced away, a troubled look on her face.

"What? Did something else happen?"

She shivered and touched her ruffled collar. "He attempted to strangle me, too."

Alex felt his blood boil. With shaking hands, he pushed her hand away, undid the top two buttons of her shirtwaist, and gently drew the collar away from her neck. Her perfect skin was an angry red blotched with darkening bruises.

He had trouble speaking. Had to clear his throat

several times. Judging by the marks, he had come very close to losing her. When he dropped his hands, she quickly refastened the buttons.

"Tilden made sure you wouldn't be there. Even if you had, he acted so quickly he would have surprised even you. Tyler and Theo were only inches from me when he attacked. They tried to pull his hands away from me, but he was too strong. I scratched his face. Even that wasn't enough. Not until Tyler dealt him a crippling blow near his kidneys did Tilden let go. "I'm all right now. Just a little sore. There's no permanent damage."

"I could kill him." Alex wanted to punch the bellboy himself, and keep on punching him. He wanted to mash Tilden's face in and make him suffer for the damage he'd done and the lives he had taken.

"Don't say that. The law will take care of him. He will hang for what he did to Father and Mrs. Hensley."

"Where is he now?"

"On his way here with the marshal. He admitted to everything. Not even Tom can question your innocence. You're coming home with me once the warden has spoken with Tom."

Alex could hardly think beyond what he wanted to do to Tilden. The bellboy had nearly killed Julia three times, and he dared to put his hands on her.

"Alex, are you listening? I'm taking you home, but you are not leaving here in those clothes. I won't have people seeing my husband in prison garb." She strode to the door and rapped on the window.

The guard's face appeared. He unlocked and opened the door.

"Please bring my husband's clothes to him. He will be leaving momentarily."

The guard's deep-set eyes widened with amusement. "Oh, yeah? That's news to me."

"Well, I assure you it's true. The real killer has been apprehended and will be here shortly, if he isn't already. He is in Marshal Landis's custody."

"I haven't seen him, ma'am, so as far as I know, your husband here is still a guest of the county."

Her back stiffened, and her chin came up. "The warden knows," she said. "I told him the situation when I arrived."

"Ma'am, he didn't tell me nothin'."

"Why do you think he removed the handcuffs from my husband's wrists?"

He shrugged.

"Please go and speak to the warden. He'll clear up everything."

"Can't leave my post."

"Then I'll go." She huffed. "I don't want my husband staying in those clothes any longer than is absolutely necessary. He is an innocent man." She started through the doorway. "Oh, there they are now."

Alex surged up behind her and through the doorway. Tilden shuffled toward them along the corridor with Tom Landis. He wore his innocuous bellboy's uniform, minus the pillbox hat. Bandages covered his cheeks. When the bellboy spied Julia, the blue of his eyes seemed to flare like the hottest part of a flame. Alex ducked around her and lunged at him.

"Alex!" she cried. "Stop!"

He kept going, but something was slowing him

down. He glanced around to find his wife hanging onto the back of his shirt. He was towing her, her feet sliding over the concrete floor.

The guard raised his arm, a wooden club gripped in his hand.

Fearing he might hit Julia by mistake, Alex stopped short and threw up his hands. "I won't do anything." His consolation was in knowing Julia had fought the bellboy and left her mark on his face. She had bested him, and Tilden would go to his grave knowing that.

Arm still raised, the guard glared at him, looking as if he'd like nothing better than to knock him to the floor.

Julia faced the guard. "Don't you dare strike my husband."

Alex liked having her defend him, but not when it put her in harm's way. He grasped her shoulders and shifted her to one side.

"What is all the commotion?" The warden had stepped out of his office, pudgy hands propped on his hips. "Laramie, put down that club."

"Yes, sir." The guard tossed Alex a narrowed glance and slowly lowered his arm.

Tyler came out of the office as well and nodded to Alex.

He nodded back, grateful for what Tyler had done to save Julia from Tilden.

Marshal Landis shoved his prisoner forward. "Warden, this man is charged with two murders and the attempted murder of Julia Fairbanks MacLean. Her … husband"—he sounded as if he might choke on the word—"was set up to take the blame for one of those murders. As much as it pains me to say it, he's innocent."

Alex cocked his head at the marshal. "Landis, I appreciate your statement, as begrudging as it was."

Tom gave him a minuscule nod.

Julia took Alex's hand and smiled up at him. "You see, it's all straightened out now." She turned to the warden. "Warden, may I please have the clothes my husband arrived in? I'd like to take him home now."

"Yes, ma'am. Laramie, get the man's clothes. I'll process our new arrival."

The guard returned shortly and handed her the clothes.

"Thank you," she said, though not as sweetly as she could have, Alex noticed. "Come with me, Alex."

He would follow her anywhere. They reentered the interrogation room, and he closed the door. Nobody locked it, and when he peered back out the window, no one was guarding him. He truly was a free man. Soon he'd be going home with his wife, to the future he had hardly dared to dream of.

She laid his clothes on the table and watched him as he removed his prison-issue shirt and tossed it into the farthest corner. "When we get home," she said, "you are going to get a thorough scrubbing in the bathtub. This place has a distinctly unpleasant smell."

His fingers paused in the act of buttoning his shirt. "Will you do the scrubbing?"

Her eyes sparkled. "I believe I could be persuaded to perform that task."

As his breathing turned shallow, Alex decided he had better postpone any thoughts about their immediate future until they were alone in their apartment.

He quickly changed his pants, noticing that Julia averted her gaze and withdrew a folded paper from her skirt pocket. "What's that?"

"A telegram. It was delivered as I was leaving the hotel." She unfolded the paper and held it out to him.

Alex fastened his pants, took the paper, and read aloud. "The Bank of New York would be pleased to loan you the amount specified in your correspondence regarding the Hotel Grand Victoria, Coronado Island, California."

She smiled at him.

He picked her up, careful not to hurt her wounded side, and spun them in a circle. "You did it." She laughed and held tight. When he set her down, Alex brushed her lips with a kiss. "I knew someone would recognize a good investment when it was offered to them."

"You were right, but I'm not sure I'm going to take it."

"What are you talking about?" He gripped her shoulders. "Julia, you love the hotel, you belong to it." How could she think of letting it go? She'd married him to get it.

"I'm thinking about accepting Tyler's offer instead, the one in which he and I would become partners."

"Oh," he said, drawing the word out.

"I know my relationship with him didn't start out on the best of terms, but I think he has redeemed himself. With his financial help, the hotel would be paid off, and, for the most part, he'd be a silent partner. What do you think?"

"It's your hotel, Julia. Your decision."

"No, it's our hotel and our decision." She clasped his hands in hers. "I love you, Alexander Devlin MacLean, and I want to spend the rest of my life with you. I want your children, and I want to raise them on Coronado. Hopefully they'll love the Hotel Grand Victoria as much as I do, but if their interests lie elsewhere, I will support their choices."

"They'll love it. They'll race through the hallways, climb into the towers, and tell each other stories about their fairy-tale castle and a princess named Julia. Most of all, though"—he raised her hands to his lips and kissed each one—"they will have us and their uncle."

"Does that mean you approve of a partnership with Tyler?"

"I do. And I think he'll be especially pleased that you chose him over the Bank of New York." He slid his arm around her shoulders and steered her toward the door. "Shall we tell him the good news?"

"Yes." She slipped her arm around his waist and smiled up at him. "We'll tell him on the way home."

Epilogue

On a blanket spread over the warm sand, Julia struggled to keep six-month-old Lily from yanking off her little sunbonnet. Her daughter had a mind of her own, and her determination had no limits.

Muffie watched from a corner of the blanket, safe from the wriggling Lily. Though the summer sun beat down, the breeze off the ocean cooled the air.

Julia smiled under her straw hat, more content than she had ever thought possible. She had a brother, a husband she loved and who loved her, a growing family, and a position as manager of the Hotel Grand Victoria. The hotel was thriving under her direction and the occasional suggestion from Tyler. Theo, promoted to assistant manager when she discovered she was pregnant with Lily, kept the employees happy and hardworking. Mr. Chalmers managed the reception desk, his attitude much improved since receiving her ultimatum. Jacques Levesque had chosen to seek employment elsewhere.

She smiled and studied a line of pelicans gliding

above the waves. The surf was gentle today, and many of the guests frolicked in the water. Two boys and a girl shrieked with laughter as they splashed each other.

She laughed, too. "See that, Lily? Someday that'll be you and your brothers or sisters." She looked forward to adding more little ones to her family. Lily's birth had been easier than she expected. Alex had insisted on staying with her the entire time, holding her hand and calming her fears. Dr. Dolan, upon Lily's delivery, had stated Julia was one of those women who seemed destined for a large family.

Lily wasn't looking toward the ocean. She gurgled and held out her arms.

Julia turned to see Alex plodding toward them through the sand. He smiled broadly, as he frequently did these days, so different from the first day they had met.

"How are my two best girls this afternoon?" He reached down for his daughter and swung her up through the air.

Lily laughed and kicked her feet.

"We're very well," Julia answered.

He lifted Lily once more, then plopped down onto the blanket. He settled his daughter against his shoulder and kissed Julia on the mouth.

She responded in turn, not caring who saw them. He often kissed her or hugged her no matter where they were or who might be watching. She'd become accustomed to it, though she had to admit she was looking forward to the privacy and space their new home would afford them. Under construction on a nearby lot was a house designed especially by Alex to hold a big family.

"You're home early," she said. "What's the occasion?"

"I'm celebrating. Alonzo Horton himself was so taken with my design for the building he wants to put up on Broadway that he hired me on the spot."

"Oh, Alex, that's wonderful. Does Liam know?"

"He was with me, smoothing the way with a proper introduction followed by praise for the designs I've done for his projects."

"He knew a good thing when he saw you scribbling on that stationery in the bar, just as I knew a good thing when I asked you to marry me."

"Hmm. That's funny," he said as Lily patted his jaw. "Dr. Dolan told me our marriage was his idea."

"The good doctor has a short memory." She adjusted a ruffle on Lily's dress. "I get credit for the original idea, although I didn't seriously consider it an option when I said it out loud. Mary helped me see the light, and the doctor quickly agreed that you were just what I was looking for, a down-on-his-luck drifter who would take the money and go."

He laughed. "My luck changed that day." He leaned into her and kissed her with all the love, tenderness, and passion she had never expected to experience in her life.

Julia responded in turn, loving him with her heart, soul, and body. She had been very fortunate the day Alex MacLean arrived in search of a job.

The End

Author's Note

I hope you've enjoyed visiting the shores of Southern California's Coronado Island with Alex and Julia. In real life, the Hotel Grand Victoria is the Hotel del Coronado, a storybook Victorian resort hotel designed by the Reid brothers and originally owned by Elisha Babcock, Jr., and partners. Construction began in 1887, and the hotel opened its doors to guests in 1888. Still operating today, it has hosted United States presidents and been the setting for books, television shows, and such films as *Some Like It Hot* with Marilyn Monroe, Tony Curtis, and Jack Lemmon. The Hotel del, also known as The Del, is a National Historic Landmark and a beautiful place to spend the day or stay overnight.

About the Author

Ann Collins is a native San Diegan who enjoys bringing her hometown's history to life for readers. She is a writer and photographer. Her first historical romance novel, *Protecting Jennie*, was published by Harlequin Enterprises, won the romance category of the San Diego Book Awards, and received four stars from *Romantic Times Book Reviews*. *Protecting Jennie* is available as an e-book. Ann loves the ocean in all its moods and never tires of photographing it. She enjoys traveling for her photography and books research, her eyes and ears attuned to the next scene and story to capture her attention.

To see a sampling of Ann's photography, please visit *www.ImagesByAnnCollins.com.*

To read an interview with Ann about *A Matter of Marriage*, please go to *www.CompassPointPress.com.*

Made in the USA
San Bernardino, CA
30 November 2013